BETTER THAN MOM'S

Where You Don't Have to Be
Told to Clean Your Plate

Barbara Angermeier Malcolm

Barbara Writes

Barbara Writes
Barbara Angermeier Malcolm

eBook: ISBN 978-1-970552-17-1
Paperback: ISBN 978-1-970552-18-8

Cover design by: GetCovers

Published by Barbara Writes.
Printed in the United States of America

This book is dedicated to my aunt, Barbara Rehder. I was named for her and she has always been my biggest cheerleader. Thanks for believing in me, Aunt B.

CONTENTS

PREFACE

Brady Gallagher swore as he parked his dark blue Ford pickup behind his Better Than Mom's Diner. It was just past four-thirty A.M., and usually when he rounded the Dumpster Dicky Lenz would be huddled there, cigarette cupped in his shaky hand, John Deere gimme cap pulled low over his slitted eyes. Dicky was Brady's new assistant cook, dishwasher, and busboy, a nineteen-year-old misanthrope with a bad complexion and worse companions, but he had been reliably there for the last week. "Today he's late," Brady fumed as he jiggled the balky lock and let himself into the diner. He flicked the switches next to the back door, and a row of fluorescent lights lit like a string of Black Cat firecrackers, flooding the room with flickering greenish light.

Casting a baleful eye over the gleaming stainless-steel pots sitting cold on the burners, Brady hung his jacket on the peg just inside the office door and got the coffee started. He had learned in his twenty-three years as a navy cook that nothing got done without a generous amount of coffee. Brady's coffee could put hair on your chest in the morning and strip paint by closing time. Once the tarry liquid was gurgling into several pots, Brady got busy making soup. He prided himself on having three different homemade soups on the menu every day. No copping out by always having chili and chicken noodle with one new one. Brady made three separate recipes each and every day. One was always creamy, one hearty, and one vegetarian. He missed Naomi. Brady was chopping a mountain of onions when he heard a tapping on the back door. "It's open," he said, not wanting to stop.

"Excuse me, sir?" A soft voice drifted in like a wisp of smoke.

Brady turned to see a slender man leaning into the narrow opening, his hands worrying the brim of the cowboy hat he held like a shield in front of his chest. "Sorry, buddy," Brady said, "no handouts today. I'm too busy here."

The man took a hesitant step into the kitchen. "I'm not looking for a handout. I need work."

Thinking of the recent rash of Immigration and Naturalization Service raids in small restaurants and businesses in town, he said, "Got some ID?" certain that when he turned again the doorway would be empty.

"Yes, I have identification."

Brady looked down to see a tanned hand holding a driver's license next to the pile of onions. He squinted at it. "You're John?"

"Yes."

"Not John's brother or cousin or nephew?"

"No, I am John Petrona."

"And you're from Texas?"

"Yes, El Paso, Texas."

Brady looked at the man. He saw clean and pressed jeans, well-worn but not worn out, a long-sleeved cotton shirt of similar vintage and showing similar care, and topping it, a face trying not to show too much desperation or need. Proud, Brady thought, this is a proud man. I respect that. "When can you start, John? I'm short a man as of this morning."

"I can start right now if you will show me where to hang my hat and give me an apron."

Within ten minutes, there were two knives flashing silver through the morning quiet. "You mind if I turn on the radio, John?"

His new employee turned a sweaty face up to answer with a smile. "You're the boss, Mr. Brady, you do whatever you want."

Brady watched as John's knife kept up its rhythm. "Keep your eyes on that blade, John. I can't afford a trip to the emergency room and don't want any extra meat in the soup, if you get my meaning."

John dropped his eyes to his hands as he pushed a mound of diced onions away with the blade and pulled another whole one toward him. "My mama, she taught me to cook. I know what I'm doing. But I'll be careful."

Brady reached over their heads and turned on the radio to his favorite jazz station. He pointed at the rest of the onions. "You finish these. I'll get to work on the carrots. We've got three kinds of soup to get simmering before we open at six."

By the time the Ike's Potato Soup (that day's creamy offering), the Scotch Broth (the hearty soup of the day), and the Chunky Vegetable (the vegetarian choice) were all bubbling merrily away, Brady found himself glad that Dicky had decided not to show up, and he thanked his lucky stars that John wanted to work in a restaurant rather than in a garage or a factory.

The men took a break once the soups were simmering to have cups of coffee and work through the hiring paperwork. John confessed he had a bit of trouble reading, especially the convoluted wording of the insurance and tax forms.

"Don't worry," Brady told him, "most people can barely figure out this stuff."

By then it was ten minutes before six o'clock, and Fay, the breakfast waitress, made her entrance. "Rest easy, kind sirs, salvation is at hand." She flung her hands up into the air and struck a pose like a stripper at the end of a runway.

Brady whistled and applauded; John gaped.

It might have been the not peach, not orange, not henna, definitely not natural, red hair. Or maybe it was the almost one pound of jangling bracelets that weighted both slender wrists. Or it could have been the frosted green eye shadow, purple eyeliner, and caterpillar black eyelashes topping Dagger Red lip gloss that stopped him in his tracks. Fay dropped her hands and turned to hang up her jacket. "Who's the new guy?" She reached over and tickled John's lower jaw. "Close your mouth, honey, haven't you ever seen a real woman?"

Brady shook his head. "Leave him alone, Fay. His name is John, and I hired him to replace Dicky, who didn't show up this morning. He didn't give notice yesterday. Do you know where he is?"

Fay finished tying her apron, rooted in the pockets, and pulled out a pencil that she sharpened before answering. "I don't know where he might be. It's not my day to watch him." She held up a finger to stop Brady's retort. "And yesterday wasn't either. Call his mother if you're worried."

"I'm not worried. I'm pissed. The little creep slouches around here with a bad attitude, and he feeds all of his lazy friends my food, which I could charge him for, but I don't, and then he leaves me in the lurch. And on Friday, when we're always busiest."

Just then, there was a thump from the front of the building. "That'll be Raymond," she said. "I'd better go open the door before he kicks it in."

Brady watched the sway of her hips as she bumped open the swinging doors. He saw her pause to get the key out of the can under the till, then paste a smile on her face as she went to unlock the door to let in the trickle of customers that began every day in the diner.

First through the door were what Fay called "the coffee codgers." The codgers were a group of retired men--some executives, others blue-collar workers, whose wives had passed on or who just plain kicked them out of the house early--that gathered in Better Than Mom's every morning to drink endless cups of Brady's corrosive coffee and debate. Fay told Brady that if even half of what the codgers said they had done was true, America would be in much better shape. She regularly tried to coax the more vocal of the codgers to run for office and put his reputation where his mouth was.

Every once in a while, the idea took flight and one or another of the men took a half-embarrassed, half-proud shuffle down to the City Clerk's office for nomination papers. Once one of them, Elmer Bump, had gone so far as to goad the other codgers into helping him collect the required number of signatures to get on the ballot. But once the campaign had begun, the enormous financial resources needed to mount a run for city alderman in their small city of eighty-five thousand took the wind out of Elmer's sails and quieted all the codgers' opinions for a time. But they rallied and lately had taken up the gauntlet of illegal immigration.

"Send them all back where they came from," Raymond said.

Fay hurried over and refilled his mug. "For God's sake, Raymond, keep it down. You can't be talking like that. It's offensive. Be nice." She laid a finger softly over his lips. "Dicky didn't show up, and John did. He's working hard and seems like a nice man." Raymond opened his mouth, but she was faster. "Ah! I don't want to hear it. You clean up your attitude, young man, or you'll be making your own coffee from now on. And I happen to know it is even worse tasting than Brady's."

A ripple of laughter that spread down the counter greeted that last remark. "She's got you there, Raymond," the man seated around the corner said.

"Shut up, Leo," said Raymond. "You wouldn't have had the balls to talk to me like that ten years ago."

Leo grinned at him. "No, you're right. I wouldn't have, but then you aren't my boss anymore, so you can't fire me for speaking my mind."

The men on either side of Leo clapped him on the back while Raymond grumbled into his coffee mug.

"A man of my age having to put up with smart asses like that. And for a woman to talk to me and tell me to change my ways, well, times sure have changed. And not for the better is all I have to say."

Fay walked by with heavy white china plates stacked down her arm, and said, "I doubt that this is the last time we'll hear you say something like that, Raymond. Your opinion knows no bounds." She breezed around the end of the counter and served the heaping plates to four construction workers at a table, gracefully maneuvering between the chairs, never losing an American fried potato, or dislodging a piece of toast. "Eat up, boys," she said. "Got to keep your strength up to finish the high school before the middle of August. I'll get the pot and refill your mugs."

For the next four hours until nearly ten-thirty, Fay was never still. She handed out menus, took orders, poured coffee, served and cleared, and still flirted with the men and joked with the women.

Brady stayed behind the grill, frying eggs every which way, keeping ham, bacon, and homemade sausage from burning, giving it just the right crispness before whisking it onto the plates, and directing John to start the meatloaf and chicken and dumplings for lunch. John was a natural. He followed Brady's cooking directions to the letter and also kept the bus tubs empty and a supply of clean dishes ready when Fay needed them.

As she reached under the warming lights to pick up an order, she said, "Brady, I don't know what guardian angel sent John today, but I sure am grateful. He's the best."

Brady, sweat running down his face and dripping off to sizzle on the griddle, said, "I think he might work out okay." But he couldn't hide the grin of satisfaction, as if he had specially ordered John.

John thought he was in heaven. His cousin, who had come to Stinson before him, worked in a slaughterhouse where it was hot and smelled of fear and death. The owners didn't treat a man like a man there either. John had decided to find work in another place. He was staying with his cousin just one block from Better Than Mom's and had gone in for coffee once. He thought the man behind the grill looked honest, and he liked the homey air of the place. Last night when he couldn't sleep because his cousin was fighting with his wife, John resolved to get up before dawn and come to the diner asking for a job. He knew he could do the work, knowing that what would be offered him would be menial jobs, dishwashing or busboy, because he had not gone to school to learn a job, and people wanted to see a certificate saying a man could do the job they were applying for. No one that John had met understood that some men just knew how to do things, knew without going to school how to fix a car or build a house or season meat to make the cheapest cuts taste like choice. But John had a gift in the kitchen; his mama had taught him to cook for the family when she worked late at the resort. John was the oldest, his sisters were all babies in his eyes, six, seven, and eight, and not trusted with knives and fire, so he cooked. While the rest of his friends swaggered down the streets, he sweated and chopped, making the evening meal for his family.

That morning, he watched the boss man, Brady, closely and took his cue from what he saw. From his station behind the counter, he could see when Brady's massive shoulders would begin to rise and tighten, that meant it was time for John to step from behind the sink and retrieve the bus tubs that were filling with dirty plates and coffee mugs. Between times, John assembled meatloaves and put them in to bake and followed Brady's instructions for making chicken with vegetables and dumplings. By the time the breakfast rush had slowed and the three of them had a moment to rest, the kitchen was redolent with the scents of baking meat and savory vegetables.

Brady motioned John away from the sink, handed him a frosty bottle of water, and led him out the back door to stand for a few minutes in the shade of an old maple tree, enjoying the cooling breeze. "Man, we're lucky it's cool today," Brady said.

"Yup," said John, willing to let the older man lead the conversation.

"When it's humid, like it was last week, no amount of air conditioning keeps that kitchen cool."

"No."

Brady was silent for a time, and the two men drank their water, drops sliding down their necks and dampening the necks of their shirts. "Tomorrow you might want to leave your nice shirt in the office and just work in a t-shirt." Brady tugged his own white Hanes. "You'd be cooler."

"Okay."

They finished their break and turned back toward the steamy heat of the diner.

"You like it so far?" Brady asked, carefully masking his hope that the younger man would say he did.

"I like it fine, Mr. Brady, so far you're not working me too hard." John turned to smile at him. "But I think that won't last too long, huh?"

Brady laughed, and John joined in. "No, you're right. As soon as it gets really busy one night, maybe tonight, or the waitress doesn't show up, you can be sure I'll be yelling at you just because you're standing there in the target area. But I won't mean anything by it; I just holler when things get busy, or I see people wait too long for their food."

John pulled a tray of clean dishes out of the dishwasher and began sorting them. "I understand, Mr. Brady, sometimes yelling is the easiest way to blow off steam." He clattered a handful of spoons into a crock. "I don't mean nothing when I yell too. Most of the time." He wiped his hands on his apron. "What do you want me to do next?"

After stirring and seasoning the simmering soups on the back burners, Brady had John chop lettuce for salads and assemble pasta salads to slot into the buffet that got set up for supper.

Brady did not believe in shopping at a big box store, buying vats of pre-made salads and sides. He wanted his customers to know that someone had cooked a meal just for them at least once a day.

Brady was not what he appeared. A hardened veteran of the navy, he had spent his career in the service feeding sailors on each of the seven seas. He had served soup to men on decks and in submarines, and carried coffee to the captains of destroyers, aircraft carriers, and just about every other kind of vessel the navy floated. His years in the service had taught the softhearted Brady to build a hard shell around his emotions and bottle up his heart. Too many of his buddies had fallen for a soft pair of eyes in some foreign port and lived to regret it. Oh, there were a few happy marriages that grew out of those chance encounters, but most of the women took their new husband's money and PX card, outfitted their family hovel at the sailor's expense and then disappeared.

CHAPTER 1

Fay was a single woman. She had run through or worn out a couple of husbands and a significant other or two in her skid toward her fortieth birthday. Her hair had started out white-blond, aged to dishwater in junior high, and never been a natural color again. These days it was red, Knock 'Em Dead Red according to the box. She favored the old-style party curls that were popular with waitresses in the seventies, and Fay considered herself a waitress rather than a server, damn political correctness.

She got the job at Better Than Mom's over a year ago when her ninety-seven Honda Civic decided to throw a tie-rod on the interstate that formed the northern border of the city. She rode in with the tow truck driver, took a room at the Super Snooze Motel right next door to Better Than Mom's, and ate her first meal in Stinson there. A visit to the mechanic down the block had convinced her that the great, vast, undefined middle of the country was where she was meant to stop—at least for the time being.

She left her last husband as he ran down the back steps of their doublewide in semi-rural New York as she pulled away with all her worldly goods and the proceeds of the sale of his prized custom-made pool cue to some sucker on eBay. She figured that over the year and seven weeks of their marriage he had spent a lot more time fondling that damned cherry wood stick than he did her. She considered it "the other woman" in her marriage and once she had decided to cut her losses and move on to the west coast, she had no qualms about taking fetching photos of the offending stick, posting them on the online auction site with an enticing description mentioning the famous maker and the fact that it had been instrumental in the winning of more than one state tournament. She put a reasonable reserve on it and watched the bids climb. The only way she got away with it was her husband was only interested in Internet porn and sites that analyzed the strategy of pro pool players he might meet across a table. She kept her fingers crossed that none of his pool-playing buddies would see it on the site and give her away. No one did.

The bidding topped out at six hundred eighty-seven dollars, so she gleefully packaged it up and sent it off to the happy winner with a note inside telling him how she hoped he would win a lot with the cue. That the stick went to a buyer in North Carolina was a bonus. Players from that area of the country regularly came to New York for tournaments or workshops, so there was every possibility that her soon to be ex-husband would face his own cue one day.

Two days after her ignominious entrance into town, she counted her remaining money, knew there was no way short of prostitution she would have the money to ransom her car in the near future, and resigned herself to spending some time in Stinson, Wisconsin. She left the Super Snooze and stood on the sidewalk surveying her options. To her right stretched a string of tire shops, bedraggled strip malls, and mechanics' garages that catered to people who had taken the Stinson exit by accident or ignorance. The neon glimmer of a couple of no-tell motels across the street did not attract her interest. She was too old and too selfish even to consider earning her living on her back and too proud to embark on a new and exciting career as a chambermaid in such places. To her left was the Better Than Mom's diner where she had eaten at least one meal a day, a used car lot that offered vehicles that looked like they had barely made it to the patch of asphalt on which they stood, a cluster of what were obviously low-rent welfare class apartment buildings, one end of the group scorched from what must have been a grease fire. Maybe she could get a job at the diner and an apartment without even leaving the sidewalk. She patted her hair to make certain it was in place even though she always used enough hair spray that any renegade hairs that escaped would have cut a less careful hand.

This was a stupid idea, Fay thought as she pushed through the door of the diner. It was midafternoon, and the place was deserted of customers. But it was not empty, not by a long shot. Every corner of the converted gas station was filled with the crashing of crockery and angry voices, both male. A lovers' spat? she thought. Do I want to work for an unhappy gay couple? It's hard enough working for a straight couple that's having a fight; how would I know which one to side with if it's two men fighting? She was predisposed to side with the woman in any fight she witnessed, her experience with men not being reliably positive.

But then she heard, "This is the last time you try to sneak lumpy gravy past me, sonny boy. You're fired."

Well, guess that solves the problem of a lover's quarrel. Fay walked up to the counter and sat down, dropping her purse on top with a clatter.

"Be right out," said the voice that had just fired somebody.

Tempted to crane her neck and try to see into the kitchen through the pass-through, instead she swiveled around on her stool and checked out the place. She couldn't hold back her grin. The place was a testament to bad taste. The walls of the area around the cash register were covered, no, paved with every imaginable shape of faux copper gelatin mold—pineapples and fish and Christmas trees and roses and train engines and hearts jostled plain squares and three-tier ones that reminded her of lunches at her aunt's house when she was a kid. Tucked in a corner was a fake Franklin stove with a flickering fake fire inside, surrounded by a huge bower of garish fake flowers, hundreds of them by the looks of it. I wonder who has to dust all of those so the Health Department doesn't close them down, she thought. She turned to look down the length of the dining room and saw a small buffet gondola with room for about four hot courses, six four-top tables, two two-tops, and six, no, seven booths under the windows.

The windowsills made her giggle. They were crammed with the most amazing assortment of old-fashioned kitchen utensils, wooden cheese boxes and scary-eyed dolls dressed in brightly colored clothes. While she was surveying the place, deciding if she wanted to ask for a job or not, she was also keeping an ear out for what was going on in the kitchen. She could hear the older man's voice urging someone to "get your things and I'll get your pay." Fay knew the hard footsteps she heard stomp across the floor had to belong to the owner. The scuffing steps had to belong to whoever had made the lumpy gravy. They moved much slower and were accompanied by a sniffling that Fay could not tell if it came from stifling tears or chronic sinus problems. Judging by the mix of exhaust from the nearby interstate and what had to be factory effluent she had noticed that passed for air when she left her motel room that morning, she hazarded a guess that anyone who lived in Stinson for any length of time ended up with sinus problems or allergies. But the diner was clean, and if the owner didn't turn out to be too much of an asshole, she might actually like working there.

"Help yourself to some coffee," the voice from the back yelled. "I'll be a few minutes yet."

"Okay," she said back, and slid off her stool.

Around the corner behind the counter was just as clean and tidy, if not more so, than the public side of the place. This was a good sign. She had worked in too many places where the kitchen and work areas were just barely clean enough to pass health inspections. She noticed that her shoes didn't stick to the floor either. All good. But the coffeepot was empty. Damn. She shrugged, rinsed out the pot, rummaged around under the counter until she found the filters and coffee, dumped out the used grounds, and pushed the button to make a fresh pot. While she waited for the coffee to brew, she wandered over to the buffet table to investigate what looked like three kinds of soup. According to the little sign above each one, what she would find under the lids was Vegetable Beef, Cream of Asparagus, and Vegetarian Vegetable. She lifted each lid and gave the soup a stir with the ladle leaning in the pot. Looks like the vegetarians were hungry today. The Cream of Asparagus was getting a little pasty, so she looked in the cooler and found a quart jar of chicken broth. She uncapped the jar and poured a ladleful into the soup and stirred it in. Better, she thought.

"Can I help you?"

Fay whirled around, the ladle in one hand, the jar of broth in the other. "Oh, you startled me." She replaced the ladle in the soup pot, settled the lid on to keep it warm, recapped the jar of broth, and returned it to the cooler. "I got up to get coffee, but it was out, so I made some. Then I smelled the soup, so I came over to see what kind and noticed that the Cream of Asparagus was getting a little thick." As Fay was talking, she waved her hands around as if she were leading a cheer. "I've worked in a few restaurants and figured you might have a jar of broth handy to thin it out, looked in the cooler, and there it was." She threw her hands up as if she were a magician's assistant. "I hope you don't mind."

The man stared at her for a beat. "No, I don't mind." Just then, the last of the water gurgled through the coffee. "I'm Brady Gallagher; I'm the owner here. Can I pour you a cup, ma'am?" Brady stepped forward out of the doorway and uncrossed his arms. "I believe I'll have one with you."

"That would be nice, Brady. I'm Fay Taylor."

He nodded toward the nearest two-top, poured some fresh coffee into a carafe, grabbed a pair of mugs, and walked around the end of the counter.

Fay got her purse from the counter and followed him across the room. She sat with her back to the empty end of the restaurant and out of the direct sunlight, so she looked her best. She figured that one day she would stop worrying about how she looked when she met a new man, but today would not be that day.

Brady poured each of them a mug of coffee and sat down

opposite Fay. He took a long sip of the scalding brew, never taking his eyes off her. "You new in town?" he asked.

Original, she thought. "Yeah, my piece of shit Honda threw a tie-rod just outside of town a couple of days ago, and I found out this morning that it'll cost more than all the cash I have to fix it." She shook her head as if she couldn't believe how untrustworthy cars were. "Guess that means I get a job and a place to live until I can afford to ransom it." She sipped her own coffee, put it down and looked at Brady as if to say, your turn.

He looked around the diner, sipped a bit more coffee, and then he said, "I guess you heard me fire that kid, huh?"

"Yes, I did."

"Do you know how to make gravy with no lumps?"

"No, I don't. I can nuke a TV dinner or frozen burrito. That's about the extent of my cooking abilities. I'm a pretty good waitress though."

Silence fell between them as each of them wondered what would happen next.

Brady cracked first. "I suppose I could do all the cooking myself until I find someone who is not too stupid. That would free me up from waiting tables."

"I suppose you could," Fay said with a smile, knowing what was coming next.

"When can you start?"

She pretended she had to think about it for a minute. "Tomorrow, do you?"

He nodded.

"What time do you open?"

"At six." He stretched a ham-sized hand across the table toward her. "Welcome aboard, Fay."

She watched her not-small hand disappear in his. I had better stay out of his way if he gets friendly, she thought. "Thank you, Brady. I think it will be a pleasure to work for you."

She spent the next couple of hours after eating a bowl of Brady's delicious Cream of Asparagus soup, "on the house," going over the apartment rental ads in that day's paper, hoping to find one within walking distance. She checked with him as to the location and climate of each neighborhood. One apartment for rent was in the cluster of buildings right behind the diner.

"You don't want to live back there," Brady said, even before she finished reading the ad.

"Why not?"

"Because it's full of low-life creeps, drug dealers, and welfare mothers whose boyfriends play that loud thumping music in their cars and smack them around for entertainment. There's a pack of kids on bikes that amuses itself by riding down the middle of the street; the little shits won't move over no matter how close you get to them. And they keep trying to scam me out of sodas." He looked as angry as if a gang of gun-wielding robbers had invaded the diner.

She had to cover her mouth with her hand to hide her grin. "You say a gang of nine-year-olds is trying to hold you up?"

"They keep coming in here, ordering Cokes, drinking them, and then running off without paying. I followed them one day last week, and they ran into the building at the end. When I talked to the manager, he told me he didn't know anything about anything. Typical."

The picture of Brady bulling his way into an apartment manager's office complaining about nine-year-olds ripping him off finally proved more than she could take. Her laugh bounced off the tiles and echoed from the frying pans hanging from the rack. "Maybe you should try making friends with them instead."

"What do you mean?"

"Well, maybe you could hire them to clean the parking lot or take out the trash after school. You could pay them in Cokes, no need to involve the IRS."

He looked unconvinced. "What good would that do? They'd probably figure me for a chump and make even more trouble."

She shook her head at him. "Weren't you in the army or something?"

"Navy."

"Well, didn't you learn anything about yelling at kids? If you're tough with them but fair, somehow they end up respecting you. Try it. Can't hurt and one of them might just turn out to be able to make gravy without lumps one of these days."

"Humph." He turned his back on her and stomped into the office off the kitchen to get the hiring paperwork for her to fill out.

She smiled and circled the ad for the apartment behind the diner, anyway. She would go over there and get herself a place to live that very afternoon.

CHAPTER 2

The first few weeks Fay worked for Brady were like those magical first months in a relationship. They were careful of each other's feelings, never yelling, stopping short of snappy remarks, painfully polite to each other.

By the end of the first month, Brady was sick of doing all the cooking and missed talking to his customers. He had made a habit of walking around the tables, especially during suppertime, gathering compliments and complaints in nearly equal measure, and picking up hints of things he could add to the menu. When he heard Fay could not, or more likely would not, cook, his heart sank. That meant he would be back trapped in the kitchen, or galley as he kept calling it from his navy days, drenched in sweat and grease and seeing his world through the pass-through.

He imagined himself as a genial host, in the manner of the fat but friendly pub owners in old black and white movies, serving hearty fare to weary travelers. That's why he didn't hesitate when he learned that the old Home Towne Diner in Stinson was closed and for sale. He plunked his pension down on the realtor's desk the very next day. When US Highway 58 was the main road across the country and cut straight through town becoming Mason Street, the diner did a thriving business, as did the muffler and tire shops and the motels which began as nice places owned by locals, but once the interstate had been completed and bypassed Stinson, the area had just plain declined. The tire and muffler shops did all right fixing cars that broke down nearby, but most of the motels had degraded into hot-sheet motels run by hard men with broken noses and Italian last names.

Brady hated the way the neighborhood had declined over the years, but he kept his place up, kept planting red geraniums in the window boxes out front and white petunias in the planters next to the door no matter how many times the plants got stolen and the planters got overturned. He believed you had to keep doing what you believed in, no matter the odds, even if the odds were roving bands of nine-year-old vandals on bicycles and rollerblades. He was sure the planters' nemesis was driving a car. One morning he had arrived to find the planters overturned, a broken chain still attached to one, and twin skid marks across the parking lot, over the curb, and down the street. But he kept righting the heavy concrete planters with the help of a few friends, scooping the dirt back into them, taking out all the cigarette butts and bottle caps and other trash inconsiderate people threw in them, and replacing any broken plants. He would give the reborn planter a nice long drink of water, pat the scratched cement side, and go back to his kitchen.

In the last week of the first month Fay worked for him, he hired a woman to be his assistant. She was one of the single mothers from the apartment complex behind the diner. Fay had encouraged him to hire her; her name was Naomi. She worked out pretty well; her gravy was like silk, and she had the habit of singing along with the songs on Brady's favorite jazz station, so the place was filled with music. Even the customers commented on how much they enjoyed Naomi's singing, especially the Sunday lunch crowd. Naomi had herself just come from church services, where she was a leading light in the choir, and she would belt out the songs as if she could soar to heaven on the notes. More than one person was observed patting away a tear.

Peace reigned at Better Than Mom's now. Brady was happily back to wandering through the dining room of an evening, clapping people on the back, and pouring coffee. Fay and Naomi laughed to see him.

"He acts like he's a king greeting his loyal subjects," said Naomi.

"He does, doesn't he?" Fay said.

The women had become friends the day after Fay, with the help of the tow truck driver and his pickup truck, moved her two suitcases and seven boxes from the broken-down Honda into the one-bedroom apartment she had rented in the complex behind Better Than Mom's. That had taken about fifteen minutes, and then it took her half an hour to convince the driver she didn't need more personal help. She closed and locked the door behind the grumbling man, slid down the door to sit on the floor, broke down, and cried.

She gave herself the rest of that hour to feel sorry for herself, then she unpacked her belongings, and shoved around the sticks of furniture that made up "furnished" at this level of housing—a bed she had no intention of sleeping in until she fumigated it or replaced it, a beautiful maple dresser that looked like an antique, a Formica and chrome kitchen table with three chairs in gray and pink, and a brown and orange plaid loveseat, that looked like it had done time in a kennel, leaning toward an end table made of two cinder blocks with a scrap of plywood on them and a lamp without a shade. All in all, not quite ready for a spread in House Beautiful, but it wasn't the worst place she had ever lived in and frighteningly close to the best.

"I have got to figure out a way to attract better luck," she said to the smoke-stained and peeling walls.

She walked down the block to the Safeway, bought a giant economy size box of baking soda to clean with, coffee, and a cheap pot to brew it in, some skim milk, a box of no-brand cereal, bread, generic oleo, house brand jam, real mayonnaise and a jar of Extra Crunchy Jif (a girl had to have standards, after all), cheap lunchmeat, two bananas, three different flavors of ramen noodles, three for a dollar boxes of macaroni & cheese, a four pack of toilet paper, a six-pack of sponges and a toilet brush, a roll of paper towel, a dishrag and kitchen towel set, a bath towel, hand towel and washcloth, a three pack of bar soap, two bowls, two plates, two each of knife, fork, and spoon, two mugs, two glasses, a fry pan and a saucepan. She asked the bagger to get it in as few bags as possible so she could carry it all and went back to her new place to get started making it livable.

Her first task was to scrub out the refrigerator with the hottest water she could stand and plenty of baking soda to sweeten it. That took her an hour, but when she sat back on her heels and surveyed the gleaming interior, she was proud of herself and her ability to make mighty tasty lemonade out of the lemons life kept handing her.

Her supper that night consisted of a half of a peanut butter and jelly sandwich and a bowl of pork flavored ramen noodle soup, which was not nearly as good as Brady's soup she had eaten for lunch, but she was not going back there again until tomorrow morning when she clocked in for her first day of work.

She didn't have a television or a radio so she opened her windows and listened to the music of her new neighbors while she moved around her tiny apartment wiping down everything she could reach with one of her new sponges and her new saucepan filled with hot soapy water. Fay used colorful sarongs from her suitcase as temporary curtains and resolved to get acquainted with someone in the building who might own a vacuum cleaner. She also wanted to walk down to the mall past the garage after she got off the next day. Surely there would be a dollar store or maybe a Kmart where she could buy a mattress pad and some inexpensive sheets so she could sleep in the bed like a human. Fay had turned the mattress over hoping to find the cleanest side but, no matter how she turned it, it still looked like someone's dog had lost its dinner on it. That is what she told herself, that the stains were the fault of an accident-prone dog with an upset stomach. If she let herself imagine what humans would have had to do to make those stains on the mattress, she would never get to sleep on that bed no matter how many layers of plastic and fabric were between her and it, just like The Princess and the Pea, her all-time favorite fairy tale.

She had always thought she was a princess who had

accidentally been born into a commoner's family. How else to explain her desire for pretty dresses and sparkly jewelry? Fay was good at walking in high-heeled shoes the first time she tried on her mom's red ones when she was six. Even though the shoes were way too big for her and scuffed across the floor, Fay didn't lose her balance or have to hold on to chairs and tables like her cousin Mildred did. But it stood to reason that someone named Mildred would not be good at walking in high heels, even if she told everyone to call her Millie. I mean, really.

Fay slept well in her new place. She locked the door, slid the chain in the slot and closed the deadbolt; there was no reason to be careless in a new place. She also closed and latched all the windows, even though she was on the second floor and couldn't see how anyone could climb up since there was no balcony. The lack of a balcony almost made her refuse to rent the apartment. Everyone knows a princess has to have a balcony, but she had come to her senses and realized that no balcony and a one-minute walk to work every morning beat a balcony and having to walk for a half hour after spending the day on her feet.

She saw her neighbor in the hall as she left for the diner the next morning. The woman was frog marching a young man Fay assumed was her son down the stairs, all the time lecturing him on how important it was to get an education. When they got outside, Fay saw that the woman was carrying a backpack and did not let go of the boy's arm. She propelled him to a rattletrap sedan, shoved him into the passenger seat, got behind the wheel, and drove away, giving Fay a terse "good morning" as she went past.

"Good morning to you, too," Fay said to the one working brake light as the sedan slid past the stop sign on the corner.

Fay kept an eye out for the woman's car in the lot, and when she saw it, she sat on the bench outside that evening to try to meet her. "Hi," she said when the woman she had seen that morning came out into the twilight with a book and a can of soda. "Come sit by me."

The woman looked at her suspiciously, took one step toward Fay and said, "Why?"

Deciding that honesty would get her farther with this lady than some fantastic story, she said, "Because I'm new in town, my car is in the shop until I can make enough at the diner to ransom it, and I need a ride to the mall to get some things. I see you have a car. I'll pay for gas if you'll take me." She stopped talking. "Oh, my name is Fay. What's yours?" She held out a hand.

"I'm Naomi." The woman slightly raised her full hands. "Sorry, let me sit down and we can shake if you want."

"Whatever." Fay moved over to make room.

"Hell, I'm not that wide. You don't have to perch on the edge to give the fat woman room."

Fay's hands flew to her face. "Oh, I didn't mean anything. It's just a reflex to slide over when I invite someone to share my bench. At least you have some padding; my ass is so bony I get bruises if I sit too long. No offense meant."

Naomi sat down and put her book and soda can down between them, then folded her arms across her chest. "Now, you need a ride to the mall?"

"Uh-huh."

"And you chose me why?"

"Well, at first, because you have a car that runs." She looked at Naomi, who was staring off into space with a slight frown on her face. Fay got the distinct impression that the other woman's bullshit meter was switched on and working overtime, so she kept on with the truth. "Then I realized that the way you were talking to your...son?"

The other woman nodded.

"Your son, that you're just the kind of woman I need to meet. Someone who values honesty and does not take any crap from anybody." Fay stopped talking and let the silence between them stretch out.

Finally, Naomi turned to face her. "Most people think women who live in a place like this are tramps, whores, and thieves. How come you don't?"

Fay reached over and patted her on the elbow. "Honey, I've lived in places like this my whole life, and I have never once been a tramp, a whore, or a thief. Well, on second thought, I might have had a few tramp-ish times in my life, but not recently and not so you would notice." She saw that Naomi's arms were not folded quite so tightly. "I know all about wanting to live in a better place and not being able to afford it or get to it or find it or, worse still, not being allowed to leave a bad place."

Naomi's head was nodding in agreement.

"So," Fay said, "I thought you and me might have something in common."

"My boy Marcus is fourteen. He thinks he's a man and wants to lie around and do what he thinks men do, which is not work and drink and carouse all night. It's all I can do to keep him in school and out of trouble. I can't find a job that'll let me keep track of him, so I'm still on welfare. And I hate it. I'm glad my mama has passed. She would paddle me good if she knew."

Fay could see tears in the other woman's eyes and felt like she was hearing words Naomi had said to no one else. "It's hard, I'm sure," Fay said, "that's why I am happy I never had any kids. I think I'd be a terrible mother, since I never really grew up myself."

"Oh, you grow up fast when you have that little baby lying in your arms. You realize it needs to be fed and have a safe place to live and stay warm in the winter. It gets you to thinking about how your mama warned you against men who use you and then disappear and how she won't have anything to do with you if you disgrace yourself."

"How old were you when Marcus came?"

Naomi smiled a rueful smile. "I was two weeks before my eighteenth birthday the day he was born, all by myself but for a nice nurse who stayed after her shift to hold my hand."

"Where is Marcus' daddy?"

Naomi flapped her hand. "As soon as that man knew I was in the family way, he took off for parts unknown. I never heard from him again and never saw a dime either."

"Did you try to find him to get some support?"

"Nah, he wasn't the kind of man who filled out job applications or paid into Social Security. He was a slick con artist, I see that now, preying on innocent, well, not so innocent, but angry, young women looking for a little excitement away from their mama's rules. I was stupid. I had a good B average in school and was thinking of going to college to learn to be a nurse when I got pregnant. I finished high school, but I looked like I was ready to pop in my gown. Mama didn't come to the ceremony. She said she was too ashamed, but I was not going to do all that work and not get my diploma." Naomi turned to look at Fay. "Can you imagine how I felt to see all my friends with their families gathered around them, praising them, and know that my own mama was sitting at home, angry at how her daughter had turned out?" She slapped the bench between them. "No, you can't because you didn't do that to your mama, did you? People don't do that to their mamas."

It was Fay's turn to look at the other woman. "Are you nuts? Young women get knocked up and disowned by their parents for being gullible and stupid all the time. At least you graduated high school. I cut out just after Christmas of my senior year to follow a loser to Florida who spun tales of how he was going to make a killing in the post-hurricane roofing game. Huh. He dumped me like a rotten tomato soon after we got to Miami because I wouldn't turn tricks to keep him in drugs while he 'scoped out the competition.' His words, not mine. I was too broke to go home and too chicken to call collect for a bus ticket, so I got a job waitressing in a strip club out by the airport. The manager wanted me to dance, saying I would make a lot more money in tips if I was a dancer, but I could no more face dancing around with my titties flapping in the breeze than I could take off my clothes and have sex with someone for fifty bucks. I mean, I have standards. They might be low in some people's eyes, but they're all I've got."

By that time, Fay and Naomi had turned toward each

other and were leaning closer together as if they could get to know each other better that way. Each of them saw something of themselves in the other, and something to admire. Naomi admired Fay's snappy talk and the way she flaunted her independence; Fay liked Naomi's determination to raise her son the way she wanted him raised despite the squalor and loose morals of their surroundings.

Checking the time and finding it was barely seven o'clock, they went back to their apartments to get their purses and met again at Naomi's car.

"I told Marcus I might be back in twenty minutes, or it might take us an hour, and he damn well better still be at his desk and at his studies when I get back. I think for once I put the fear of God into him."

"Why is this time different?"

Naomi unlocked the car, and the women got in. "The football coach called me yesterday. He said he thinks Marcus might have the makings of a professional class running back, he's that fast and good at avoiding tackles, but unless he applies himself to his studies, he won't play high school ball, much less college or pro."

"Ah."

"Hey, I can hear that you are not too impressed with professional sports, but for a poor kid with no daddy, it's a way out of the ghetto."

Fay sighed. "I suppose where we live is the ghetto in Stinson?"

"Yes, ma'am, it is. There aren't too many worse places to live in this little city. You picked good, Fay."

Fay shook her head. "I keep clawing myself out of one hole in life only to have my temper land me in another."

She spent the rest of the drive and most of their stroll through the K-Mart telling her new friend all about selling her husband's custom-made pool cue on eBay. Naomi thought that was one of the funniest stories she had ever heard.

"At least you had a man to punish. Mine ran off at the first sign of trouble and never came back."

As they pushed their laden cart back toward the car an hour later, Fay said, "I probably would have been better off if I had sworn off men when the first one dumped me. Would have saved me a lot of tears and money."

Naomi was shoving bags into the back seat of her car. "Yeah, but then you wouldn't have broken down outside of this town and been lucky enough to meet me. That would have been a shame."

Fay stood with her hands on her hips, surveying the mountain of bags in the car and remembering the thin state of her wallet. "Seeing as how I let you talk me into buying all this stuff so now I am really and truly broke, I would have to say the jury is still out on how much of a shame that will turn out to be."

Both of them were chuckling as they got into opposite sides of the car.

"Don't feel bad, you poor little thing, how about I buy you a DQ as a treat?" said Naomi.

"Can your budget stretch to chocolate-dipped?"

"It can."

Fay smiled at her new friend. "I'm feeling better about Stinson already."

"And we'll get a cone for Marcus too. That way he won't complain about helping us carry all this upstairs."

"He won't?"

"Well, he is fourteen after all, so he'll feel he has to complain just on principle."

"Ah, so true."

Two much happier women arrived back at the complex half an hour later. Marcus was drafted to help carry Fay's new things inside after he ate his cherry-dipped cone, of course. Naomi helped Fay put the quilted and plastic-backed mattress cover on her bed and admired Fay's sarong-covered box tables. "You've got flair. My style is more church-lady conservative. I've got to get me some bright fabric for my house."

Fay said, "I have a sewing machine in the trunk of my car.

If you'll drive me down there one of these days, I'd be happy to help you run up some curtains. I'll bet we can find some good stuff at the thrift store. Sheets for sale there are cheaper than yard goods."

Naomi was amazed to discover that more than half of the boxes that Fay hadn't unpacked had shoes in them. She held up a dainty silver slipper with a four-inch heel covered with rhinestones. "You've got enough shoes in here to buy two new cars. You should sell them on eBay, make some cash, and get a little ahead. Or at least get your car fixed."

Fay looked at her as if she couldn't believe what she had heard. "I'm not selling my shoes, no matter how desperate I get. A girl is nothing without fabulous shoes."

Under her breath so Fay could not hear, Naomi muttered, "You can't eat shoes."

The new friends would have sat long into the night getting acquainted, but Fay had to be up before dawn to get to her new job on time. "Gives a bad impression if you show up late on your second day," she said as she watched Naomi walk down the hall to her door.

"I'll see you tomorrow." Naomi waved as she put her key into the lock and went inside.

CHAPTER 3

Fay was up bright and early and enjoyed her new job. By the second day, she had learned the names of most of the retired men who came for coffee every day and declared them to be the "coffee codgers."

She convinced Brady that he should have some sort of punch card so that people who came in for a meal, a full meal, mind, not just a sandwich or a drink, would get their card punched and then a free meal after, say, buying ten. Brady was so taken with the idea he sat at his office computer and made up a sample that very day, and also made what he called the "coffee lovers" card, which gave the holder a free piece of pie after twenty punches. The coffee codgers loved that one until they understood refills didn't earn them punches; that they had to buy twenty separate cups of coffee to get free pie.

Raymond Tolliver was especially vocal in his displeasure of the new program. "I'm here every day, and I bring in customers by telling everyone how good the food is here, and you begrudge me a piece of pie?"

Fay patted his hand. "Raymond, my dear, Brady can't afford to give you a piece of pie every day. I am sure you drink at least that many cups holding court each morning. Be happy to get free pie once a month."

He opened his mouth to retort, but she shook her head and walked away. For once, Raymond looked abashed. He had spent his working life as president of one of the biggest paper mills headquartered in Stinson with customers and facilities all over the globe. He was having a hard time getting used to being a regular human with no one fawning over his comfort and no one quaking at his wrath.

A month after his retirement, his long-suffering wife had called Two Men & A Truck, had them pack up her knitting and her porcelain cat collection, and moved to Arizona to live next door to her sister. At first, he had missed her, mostly at mealtimes, but then he started watching a few of the cooking shows on the Food Channel, especially the one hosted by that little Italian girl with the... well, the wardrobe full of V-neck blouses. He enjoyed watching her even if she was cooking something he would never eat. Raymond began to cook. When he made his first lasagna, he called his wife's sister to tell her. He had always liked Rona, thought he should have married her, but couldn't stand to have gone through life as Ray and Ro. That was too pedestrian for him to even imagine, given his exalted opinion of himself. Rona was happily married to a plastic surgeon who kept her in facelifts and liposuction. He supposed Susan had all that done to her too in the year since she left. I wonder if she has perky boobs now, Raymond thought sometimes at night. I like perky boobs. And he would flick the remote to see if that little Italian girl was cooking.

Every day, Fay flirted her way through the day, and by the time two-thirty rolled around and Taffy, the college girl who was the supper waitress, came in, her feet were aching, and her ankles were swollen. But on most days her apron pocket was full of tips. In fact, she usually had to empty her pockets into the tip jar after the lunch rush.

Naomi got into the habit of either inviting Fay down to her place for supper or sending Marcus over with a plate when she learned that Fay really could not cook. That her friend was sitting down to either a peanut butter and jelly or lunchmeat sandwich, or a bowl of ramen noodles was impossible to grasp. She could not believe that someone could have gotten to be close to forty without learning how to cook a proper meal.

Fay just laughed when Naomi asked her about it. "My mom's idea of cooking was prying the lid off a bucket of chicken;

how would I ever learn? I'm pretty good at nuking frozen burritos, and a few times I got food from the deli and reheated it. I think my last husband, Butch, never knew that I didn't cook. He thought I had made the meatloaf and mashed potatoes and gravy that came home in foam containers. I just threw those things away and put the food in pots and heated it up. He never knew the difference. Men are so dumb," she said to Naomi.

"Yeah," Naomi agreed, "most of them can't see past the end of their peckers."

The more the two women spent time together, the more they liked it.

CHAPTER 4

Shortly after being hired at Better Than Mom's, Fay made it a point to learn about the regulars. She figured that the better she knew her customers and the better they knew her, the better her tips would be. She was right.

During that first week, every time Fay walked down the length of the diner, she couldn't help looking at the lone man in the last booth. He sat with his back to the end wall of the building and had pads of paper, pens, and pencils spread all over the top of the table. When she approached his booth to offer him a coffee warm-up, he would either hunch over the paper in front of him or, if he saw her coming nearer, he would flip the page so that all that was visible was a blank page.

The next time she leaned into the pass-through to slide an order onto the carousel, she motioned Brady closer. "Who is the geek in the back booth that's always writing?" she asked.

"Oh, that's Steve. Stevie the scribbler, some regulars call him."

"What's he writing?"

"I don't know, and you shouldn't ask him."

"Why not?"

"Because it's nosy and what he is writing is none of your beeswax, that's why."

"Humph."

Not very happy about the turn of events, Fay went back to making sure all her customers were well-fed and watered, even Stevie the scribbler. Stevie stayed until noon almost every day. Fay watched for him to arrive, and she was surprised to see him come in right on Raymond's heels. Raymond was always waiting in the parking lot in his car if it was cold out, or if the weather was nice, he would stand right outside the door, one hand on the handle, tapping his foot as she walked toward him with the key.

"About time" was his usual first sentence.

"And a good morning to you too, Raymond," was Fay's usual retort.

At the dollar store, Fay bought herself an atomic clock guaranteed to have the correct time to the millionth of a second and set her watch to it every morning so she could remind Raymond that six o'clock meant six o'clock and she was scrupulous about opening the door at six o'clock. Not five-fifty-nine or six-oh-one, but exactly bang on the dot of six o'clock because she was a woman who valued punctuality. She was not all that concerned with being on time, not really, but it got Raymond's goat, so it was worth the blot on her immortal soul for telling the lie.

Once she began watching for Stevie, she realized that on most mornings she had barely turned around from serving Raymond his first mug of coffee before the bell on the door jangled and in Steve walked. It was funny she hadn't really noticed him before. He always wore a plaid cotton long-sleeved shirt buttoned right up to the neck, with the cuffs buttoned too. His pants were old man, pleated wash pants in either khaki or navy, hiked to somewhere between his belly button and his nipples and cinched real tight with what looked like a brown plastic belt. There was a good-sized flash of white from his feet where his socks peeked out between his high-water pants and his low-cut black Converse All-Stars.

In his left hand he carried, clenched much tighter than Fay imagined a courier transporting secrets would carry his bag, an old-fashioned accordion bottom briefcase with the locking flap, you know, like the ones the nerds carried in high school. Stevie's case was worn on the edges to a pale gray color, but the metal corner caps were still on it and Fay was amazed to see him pull a key on a chain from under his shirt to unlock it once he reached his favorite back booth. At first, Fay would hurry over to deliver his glass of ice water, turn over the mug in front of him, and pour his first mug of coffee. But she realized that if she dawdled a bit, he would begin unpacking his papers and pens and then she might see what he was writing. She tried and tried to engage him in conversation, but he always answered her openings either with monosyllables or he ignored her completely. She was getting frustrated.

Even Raymond noticed. "You'll never get a peep out of Steve; he's tighter than Dick's hatband," he said to her after watching her try to get Steve to talk to her for nearly a week.

"Why not? Doesn't he like girls?"

Raymond chuckled.

Fay kept talking. "And who's Dick and what does his hatband have to do with it? What is a hatband anyway?"

Raymond roared with laughter at that. "You know, Fay, I have no idea who Dick is. It's an old saying that usually refers to someone miserly, you know, cheap. But a hatband is the leather or vinyl band inside the crown of a hat that sits on your head."

"Oh. Well, what do you know about Stevie?"

"He used to work for me at the mill. He was in charge of the lab, did quality control tests, and developed uses for the waste products that in reality made more profits for the company than all the paper did. His job was keeping secrets then, and I'm sure he hasn't gotten any more talkative since he retired."

Fay squinted down the length of the building at the solitary figure. "He seems kind of young to be retired."

"He is. He must have gotten an inheritance. He marched into my office about ten years ago and slapped his letter of resignation on my desk. When I asked him why he was leaving, he said he was finished working and didn't need to give me another reason. I reminded him of the agreement he had signed not to go to work for our competition for five years after leaving us. He laughed at me and told me he was done with corporate America. He was going to write."

"What's he writing, do you know?"

Raymond shook his head. "I asked him what he intended to write, and he just shook his head. He said he had always written and now he could afford to stay home and write all the time. Steve worked his last month, cleaned out his desk, and left. He gets a little pension check from the mill, but I know he isn't old enough to collect Social Security yet, so I suppose he had a nice bundle saved or invested to still be at it without working." Raymond looked around to make sure no one overheard. "Let me know if you find out what he writes. I'll, uh, buy you a burger."

Fay flapped her hand at him. "Oh, go on with you. For cripe's sake, Raymond, I work in a diner; I can get a burger whenever I want one." She walked around the end of the counter to wait on the couple who had just come in. "But if I find out, I'll still tell you." She winked at him as if they had a pact, picked up the coffeepot, and crossed the room to the newcomers.

From then on, every time she had the barest excuse to walk toward Stevie, she did. She would wear her quietest shoes and try to creep up on him, but he was too alert. She couldn't get within ten feet of him before he would flip to a blank page and glare at her. After about a month of playing cat and mouse with him, Fay lost patience. One morning she waited until he had all his papers spread out on the table before she carried the coffee pot his way. She picked up an extra mug from the next booth, poured his coffee, slid into the bench seat across from him, poured herself some coffee, and put down the pot. He stared at her without speaking, as if he couldn't believe his eyes.

"Good morning, Steve," she said.

He looked at her.

"Polite people say good morning back," she said after a few moments of silence.

She imagined his bones creaking as his jaw unhinged. "Good morning," he said, and she heard his teeth snap back together.

She sipped her coffee. "Steve, I've been very curious. For all the time I've worked here at Better Than Mom's, you've come in every day, never missed one, and you've written."

He nodded but did not speak.

"Every time I get anywhere close to you, you cover your writing or flip to a blank page."

He nodded, picked up his coffee mug, and took a sip.

"It's hurting my feelings, Steve, that you think I'll steal your words or maybe you think I'll be offended. Are you writing porn, Steve?"

It took all of Steve's self-control not to spit out the mouthful of coffee.

"Porn? Is that what you think?"

Fay shrugged. "Well, a bunch of us were trying to figure out what you were being so careful to hide. I figured that you're married, and you come in here to write so your wife doesn't bother you. And what kind of writing would bother a woman of quality and good breeding? A couple of the guys said they thought you were writing porn, but I said I didn't think you had the look of a porn writer." She noticed Steve was looking over her shoulder at the line of coffee codgers at the counter.

"What have those guys been saying about me? I used to work with a couple of them at the mill. They never understood the stress I was under all the time to keep figuring out new things to do with the waste from the processing plant. And just because I never took part in their silly poker games or went to the golf outings, they thought I was a snob. Well, it just so happens," his voice got louder and louder with every word, "that I am a well-published author, and I don't have time for such pursuits."

The sound of male laughter washed toward the two of them as they sat at the end of the dining area.

Fay nodded back at the lineup at the counter. "Don't mind them; they're assholes. So tell me, Steve, what kind of books do you write?"

Stevie was threading his pen through his fingers and biting his lip. "Do you really want to know?" he asked.

"Yes, I do. I'm dying of curiosity."

"And you won't make fun of me?"

"No, I won't make fun of you. I think anybody who can write even one book is nearly a genius."

He took a few deep breaths and let them out slowly. "Have you ever heard of Layne Wilcox?"

Fay set her mug on the table and sat back. "Of course, I have. Who hasn't heard of her? Her books are everywhere, even in K-Mart. Why?"

Steve looked her straight in the eye. "I'm Layne Wilcox."

"You are not."

Steve turned his notebook around and pushed it across the table to her. Fay leaned over and read the page. She sat back, her jaw slack and her eyes wide. "Holy crap, you are Layne Wilcox! I'd recognize her, I mean your writing anywhere."

CHAPTER 5

Brady was resistant at first when Fay suggested he hire Naomi. "Not on your life. I don't want one of those druggies and sluts back here in my kitchen."

"Brady, I'm surprised at you. You've spent all of your pension and most of your savings to drag this place back from the brink. And you've kept it afloat even after the interstate was built and Mason Street stopped funneling trucks and tourists to your door." She glared at him, her fists on her hips in the universal frustrated woman pose. "This would be a perfect job for Naomi, and I know for a fact that she knows how to make gravy without lumps."

Brady matched her pose with the universal stubborn man's pose of arms crossed across his chest. "And how do you know Naomi makes unlumpy gravy?"

"Because she feeds me nearly every night."

"What?"

Fay dropped her fists from her hips and began picking at a ragged cuticle. "Well, when she found out I either bring something home from here or nuke a frozen burrito or eat a jar of salsa with chips, she hollered at me, said I would get rickets or scurvy or some such one day and she didn't want that on her conscience." Fay plopped down on the end stool at the counter and rested her cheek on her hand. "She sends her son Marcus down the hall about three times a week with a plate. Sometimes she'll call, and I go over there and eat, or she might bring a casserole down and we'll eat at my place. She's a real good cook, Brady, and she really needs a job."

Brady leaned his forearms on the counter next to her. "So

how come she's on welfare if she's such a good cook?"

"She's been trying to find a job that will let her keep closer tabs on Marcus."

"Who's Marcus? Her pimp?"

Fay's hand swung up and slapped Brady's arm. "Man, the way you talk. No, Marcus is Naomi's fourteen-year-old son. She's trying to keep him in school, so he doesn't become like the other slackers. His football coach thinks he might have a future as a, what did she say, oh yeah, a running back, whatever that is. So, she takes him to school of a morning, picks him up in the afternoon after practice, and makes sure he does his homework instead of hanging out under the streetlight with his buddies getting into trouble."

Brady grunted.

Fay kept talking. "I thought that if you gave Naomi a job, she could run home after the early rush, take Marcus to school (it's only about eight blocks), and then be back almost before we knew she was gone. She'd get off an hour before school is out, so the afternoon and evening would be no problem. What do you think, Brady? Are you willing to give her a try?"

Brady got up and poured himself a mug of coffee. He lifted the mug inquiringly at Fay, but she shook her head. "I might," Brady said. "Is she interested in working here or is this one of your harebrained ideas?"

"Those cards weren't a harebrained idea, were they? I thought I'd run the idea by you first. I didn't want to get Naomi's hopes up if you were totally against it."

"So how are you going to handle it? Just tell her flat out I'll give her a job?"

Fay snorted, a very unladylike and un-Fay-like sound. "No. I thought I would float the idea by her like I had just thought of it, tonight at supper. Then suggest she stop in tomorrow after the breakfast rush, but before lunch, and maybe you could offer her a chance to help, just to see how the two of you work together. I mean, it'll still be busy enough that she'll have to kind of leap into action, and you can see how she'd handle the pressure."

"That would be all right, I guess. If her gravy is as good as you say, she'll be hired."

Fay leaped off the stool, kissed his cheek, and swung around him into the kitchen.

The two men sitting at the end of the counter nursing mugs of coffee nudged each other, looked at Brady, and said together, "Oooh, Brady."

He looked at them and turned to go back to his stove. As he shouldered his way through the swinging doors, he said, "Shut up."

That night, Fay stopped at Naomi's door on her way to her apartment and asked her to come eat with her. She didn't want Marcus eavesdropping when she brought up the possibility of Naomi coming to work at Better Than Mom's. Fay took a quick shower and did the few dishes in the sink. She'd stopped at the flower kiosk that set up when it was warm in the motel parking lot next door and bought a bouquet of bronze and pale gold asters that she arranged in an empty mayonnaise jar to put on the table.

Naomi had shown her how to make sun tea in a big glass jar with six tea bags hung in it instead of buying that nasty powdered tea from Safeway. She would get the jar filled and float the tea bags in it before she left for work in the morning, making sure it was sitting on the counter where the sun would hit it for most of the day. By the time she got home around three o'clock in the afternoon, the tea would be mahogany colored and just like she liked it—strong. Fay stirred sugar into it and squeezed half of a lemon in. At first, she just sliced the lemon and dropped the slices in, but that didn't make it lemony enough for her. She liked it really sweet and kind of tart. Naomi was a soda drinker, but Fay was trying to change her mind.

"That stuff in the cans will rot your teeth," she said. "Tea is all natural, and I put in real sugar and real lemon. Soda has a load of chemicals in it, and I heard artificial sweetener kills lab rats.

It's bad for you."

"Do I look like a lab rat to you?" Naomi said, mock anger wrinkling her forehead.

"Not hardly," Fay said back. "But drinking something homemade has got to be better for you. Besides, you taught me how to make it. Why won't you drink it?"

Naomi looked away. "Mama used to drink it all summer long. She and Aunt Tessie drank it by the gallon. I should know how to make it; I made enough growing up to float a boat; I don't have to drink it to know that."

"Okay, I'm just concerned about your health and your teeth, that's all." Fay could tell by the tight set of Naomi's shoulders that the subject was closed. She let it drop.

Fay thought about running down to the bakery next to Safeway to buy a little cake they could have for dessert, but then she thought Naomi would think that Fay had something up her sleeve and be suspicious. Better to let her think Fay had just gotten a cheap bunch of flowers to brighten up the drab apartment and not be on her guard. She heard a door slam in the hall and went to open the door for Naomi. She was embarrassed to see a policeman lead one of the teenagers Marcus hung out with from the end apartment in handcuffs. As they passed Fay's door, the young man hung his head and didn't look at her. The tall, thin policeman nodded at her and said, "Ma'am" before leading his prisoner toward the stairwell.

She pulled her head back into her apartment after the pair went by, feeling like a turtle retreating into its shell. Oh, I hope Marcus isn't in trouble too, she thought, rubbing her suddenly sweaty palms on her slacks. Her next thought took her by surprise; it was the hope that Naomi wouldn't forget to bring her supper.

"Tsk, that's not like me," she said to the empty room. "It's not about supper. I want to tell her about maybe finding her a job; that's why I hope she doesn't forget."

She nodded her head twice as if trying to convince someone. Nervous now from the scene she witnessed in the hallway, she paced from the front door into the kitchen and back a few times until she caught her toe on the edge of the end table. Then she hopped around the living room cursing and swearing.

As she flopped onto the sofa to rub her toe and check if it was bleeding, she heard a soft knock on the door and a cheerful, "Suppertime." She hobbled to open it.

"Oh, thank goodness. I was afraid that Marcus was in trouble too," she said as she swung the door wide to let Naomi in. "Here. Let me help." Fay reached out and took the covered pot balanced precariously on top of the box her friend carried. "Mm, something smells delicious," she said and carried the pot into the kitchen where she set it on the stove.

Naomi gently put the box on the corner of the kitchen table and turned to look at Fay, hands on hips. "What's gotten into you tonight?"

Fay was surprised Naomi didn't know. "Didn't you and Marcus see the police were here? I heard something in the hall and, thinking it was you, opened the door in time to see a cop lead that kid from down at the end away in handcuffs. I've seen him talking to Marcus a few times and was afraid that the boys had gotten into some sort of trouble." She was nearly panting with the rush of words. She sat down at the table and put a hand over her heart. "I guess I was more upset about the idea than I thought."

Naomi looked down at her. "Well, I guess you were. I think it's been a while since you lived in a place quite this far down the food chain." She unloaded the box. "Cops and handcuffs are almost an everyday occurrence in this complex. There's a passel of drug dealers and a pimp or two in those buildings on either side of the entrance. This end is mostly single mothers and welfare families like Marcus and me."

Fay got up and began setting the table while Naomi talked. "Those bad boys down the hall are one reason I keep after Marcus. He sees them with their fancy clothes and jewelry, and the cars. You would not believe their cars; he thinks he should have that sort of thing too. I tell him and tell him that a life lived like that, all bad and lazy and disrespectful, is no life at all." Naomi stopped talking and stared off into space, her hands hanging limply over the edge of the box.

Fay looked at her to see if something was wrong. "You okay?" she said.

Naomi shook her head and said, "Yeah, I'm fine. I sounded like Mama there for a minute. Even though she never talked to me after I got pregnant, sometimes I miss her like crazy."

Fay could see the glimmer of tears in her friend's eyes and busied herself wiping nonexistent water spots off the silverware.

Naomi shook herself like a dog shaking off water after a bath. "Got to stop myself thinking like that or I will sink into the pit and disappear." She lifted a square baking dish from the box and set it on a trivet she had put out earlier.

"That smells terrific," said Fay. "What is it?"

"It's a new lasagna recipe I cut out of the paper. It has sun-dried tomato Alfredo sauce and chopped spinach. Here, let me slide the garlic bread into your oven so it crisps a bit."

Fay grasped the knob on top of the pan to see what was inside, but Naomi slapped her hand away. "No checking out the dessert until you've eaten your supper."

"Hey, I was only going to look."

"Well, don't."

The women sat down across the table from each other, and Naomi served them each a slab of lasagna. Fay hopped up and pulled pieces of garlic bread from the oven and then served them each some, blowing on her fingers after putting them down. Then she thought better of it and licked the garlic butter off them. "I love garlic bread," she said. "I could make a meal of just that."

Naomi nodded. "Amen. There's nothing better than crispy French bread with its soft insides brushed with garlic butter and then the whole thing heated up. But we have to consider our waistlines." She frowned at Fay. "Not so much you; you're as skinny as a toothpick. I even think about eating and I gain weight."

"Oh, pooh. Let's stop talking about eating and eat." Fay planned to wait until they were done eating to tell her about Brady's, well, her plan for Naomi to work at the diner, but she was too excited about it and barely got her first bite swallowed before she started talking. "I have something to tell you."

Naomi's eyes popped up from looking at her food to stare at Fay. "What? Are you moving away already?"

Fay waved her fork. "Not hardly. I barely have enough money to pay my rent and make payments on my car repairs. I'd be a fool to go anywhere. No, I was talking to Brady this morning about what a good mom you are and how good your food is and how you've been looking for a job but can't find one to fit your needs."

"Here it comes," Naomi said. "Miss New York is going to fix the poor woman's problems."

Fay sat back from the table and dropped her fork with a clatter. "Nice. At least hear me out before you pass judgment on my idea, please."

"Fine. Go ahead and have your say."

Fay picked her fork back up and cut a bite of lasagna. "I was planning to no matter what you said, but I was telling Brady how good your food is and he asked me why you're still on welfare if you can cook so well. I told him about you wanting Marcus to stay in school and out of trouble and how you can't find a job that will let you take him to school in the morning and pick him up to keep him on track. How playing football might be his only chance of a life beyond the ghetto. You know how men understand if you relate something to sports, I thought that might get to Brady." She put the bite of food she had been waving around in her mouth and chewed and swallowed before continuing. "Brady is getting real tired of being trapped in the kitchen since he fired that guy the morning he hired me, and I thought you might be just what he's wishing for."

Naomi jumped in when Fay took a breath. "But what about getting Marcus to school and such? What did he say about that?"

"That's the coolest part," Fay said with a grin. "Brady agreed you could slip out when it's time to take Marcus because that's right between the early morning rush and the later breakfast crowd. I told him I thought you'd only need to be gone about half an hour."

Naomi nodded her agreement.

"So, he said you should come over to the diner tomorrow about nine A.M. and you and he could talk."

"Just talk?"

"Well, not just talk; I might have suggested that you would make sausage gravy for him because lumpy gravy is what got the last guy fired, and your gravy is the best I've ever had."

Naomi ate the last bite of her lasagna and used a scrap of garlic bread to sop up the sauce on her plate. "Well, what did you think of it?" she said.

"Of what?"

"Fay! Of the new lasagna recipe?"

"Oh," Fay looked at her empty plate and blushed, "it was delicious." She cleared the table while Naomi got two small bowls from the box and then dished out chocolate pudding from the pot on the stove.

Fay looked at it in amazement. "You made cooked pudding? Wow."

"No. I made homemade chocolate pudding. There's a difference."

Fay took a tentative bite and then dug in. "I never had pudding like this. What brand is it?"

"It's not a brand. It is homemade."

Fay's face was blank with surprise. "You mean you made pudding out of nothing?"

Naomi smiled at the older woman's shock. "No, I started with milk, sugar, vanilla, and cocoa powder and went from there. That's how people made pudding before there was pudding in a box."

Fay was amazed. "I never knew there was a way to make it if you didn't start with a box."

"But then, you're not the world's most experienced cook."

"No, I guess I'm not." Fay scraped up the last of the luscious brown goo in her bowl. "Is there any more?"

Naomi laughed at the success of her surprise for her friend. "Now you sound like Marcus." She got up and refilled Fay's bowl. "I think I might just wander over to the diner tomorrow around nine and make breakfast for Mister Brady. Show him what he's been missing his whole life."

Fay didn't look up from her spoon. "Great."

CHAPTER 6

The next morning, every time the door of the diner opened, Fay's head turned so fast that even Raymond, who was the most self-absorbed of men, noticed.

"Who do you keep looking for, Fay? Your boyfriend?"

She shook her head. "No, you old coot, I am hoping that a friend, a *girlfriend*, stops in soon." She looked at her watch. "Man, the time is sure moving slowly today." She lifted the full bus tub from under the counter with a grunt, carried it back into the kitchen and loaded the dirty dishes into a dishwasher tray.

Brady looked up from the griddle. "Is your friend coming in?"

Fay shrugged her bony shoulders. "She said she would. Maybe she lost her nerve."

"I don't think so," Brady said, looking out the pass-through. He was transfixed by the vision that had just walked into his diner. A tall woman stood just inside the door, regal and proud, dressed in an actual dress and a hat. "I think your friend just walked in. She looks like a queen," he said, wonder in his voice.

"Oh shit," said Fay, wiping her hands on her apron. "I wanted to be out there to greet her." Her hand patted the side of her head. "How does my hair look?"

"Oh, for Christ's sake, Fay, she's the one coming in for an interview, not you."

"I know, Brady, but I want this for her so much I feel like it's me being interviewed."

Brady watched from his safe spot behind the griddle as Fay shouldered her way through the swinging doors. Her practiced waitress eye checked the level of coffee in the mugs along the counter as she sailed by. She was a bit intimidated by the regal appearance of the woman she had only seen wearing sweats or jeans in the past. "Naomi, I'm so glad you came in." She leaned closer. "Are you sure you want to cook in your nice dress?" she said.

Naomi lifted her purse slightly. "I brought my own apron; the dress will be fine."

Fay turned to address the few people in the diner. "Hey, everybody, this here is my friend Naomi. She's going to make you all a little treat." A chorus of grunts and a single "hey" greeted that announcement.

Naomi poked her. "Now, why'd you go and do that? Talk about putting me on the spot."

Fay shrugged. "I just thought that if the customers like what you cook today, Brady is sure to give you the job." She rubbed her arm. "Sorry."

Fay pushed the door to the kitchen open with her hip and motioned for Naomi to go in first. She stepped up behind her friend and said, "Brady, this is my neighbor Naomi Cushing I told you about. Naomi, this is my boss, Brady Gallagher."

She watched as Brady wiped his hand on his apron and extended it toward Naomi. "How do you do? Fay, why don't you see if anyone needs any coffee?"

"Well, I, uh, sure, Brady, I will."

Surprisingly glad to leave the kitchen, Fay went back to her familiar turf and poured everyone coffee, whether they wanted it or not, and straightened the newspapers that the codgers had strewn down the counter. "I swear your wives must go crazy if you all are this messy at home," she scolded them. She didn't realize she was holding her breath until she heard Naomi say something and then Brady's braying laugh float out the pass-through. She felt the air whoosh out between her lips, and her shoulders relaxed back to normal. It was as if sound and movement returned to Fay's perception. She heard the radio as if someone had just turned it on. The rustle of turning pages of newsprint became obvious. The everyday sounds of Raymond pontificating and refuting someone's opinion came back into focus. The final distraction came when a couple of strangers entered and hesitated when they were confronted with the overt hominess of the place.

Fay bustled over to greet them and led them to a booth halfway down the diner. "Coffee?" she asked and received two nods in answer as they had their noses buried in menus. "I'll give you a minute."

She delivered two mugs of coffee to them and then went behind the counter and straightened every napkin holder, salt and pepper shaker, sugar dispenser, fake sweetener holder, and everything she could find to take her mind off what might be happening in the kitchen. She cocked her head so her right ear, her "good" ear, was aimed in that direction, but could only hear murmurs coming from the back. Keeping an eye on the couple with the menus, she went down the counter, refilling mugs again and trading jibes with the regulars.

When the husband (she assumed) of the couple raised his head, she walked over to them, pulling her order pad from her pocket, and retrieving her pencil from behind her ear.

"What can I get you folks?" she said as she stopped at their side.

"I will have sausage biscuits and gravy," said the man, "provided someone in your kitchen knows how to make them. I hate mediocre sausage and canned biscuits."

"Our cook makes fresh biscuits daily," Fay said. She turned to look at the woman. "And for you, ma'am?"

The man spoke up instead. "She will have one scrambled egg with toast and orange juice."

"White, whole wheat, or rye toast?"

He never looked at the woman to check which one she would like. "Wheat."

"Regular or homemade?"

Again, he answered without checking. "Regular."

Man, and I thought Butch was a controlling shit of a

husband, Fay thought.

"Small, regular, or large orange juice?"

"Small."

Fay saw the woman's hands clench the menu at the sound of the man's voice. She made a point of making eye contact with the woman as she took the menu from her and gave the lady a little wink, which earned her the ghost of a smile.

"I'll just put your order in and come back to freshen your coffee."

As she turned away, the "waitress" smile slid from her lips, and she felt a frown start to drag her eyebrows together.

When she leaned up to clip the ticket in the carousel, Brady said, "Anything wrong?"

She shook her head. "Not really, the husband of the couple in number six is a real a-hole. Make sure his biscuits and gravy are exactly right; he's the kind of customer who would find something wrong in the best gourmet place."

Brady and Naomi exchanged smiles that brought a sigh from Fay. They must have hit it off, she thought. I've never seen Brady so relaxed.

In no time at all, the fragrance of baking biscuits wafted out into the diner.

"Hey, Fay," Raymond called, "I think I might be talked into having a biscuit with a little jam over here."

"Me too," said Leo. "They smell too good to pass up."

Fay had to laugh. It was almost as though everyone in the place was on their best behavior all of a sudden, but she couldn't decide if it was because Naomi was cooking for a job or because the guy in the booth was being so rude to his companion.

In a very short time, the bell to tell her she had an order to pick up dinged.

As she retrieved the plates, she said, "Slap a couple of those biscuits on plates for Raymond and Leo too, please. The smell got to them."

She turned and crossed the diner to serve the food. As she laid the plate in front of the woman, she saw the man's head come up and swivel.

Before he opened his mouth, she said to the woman, "I'll get your orange juice now. I like to wait to serve it until the food is ready, so it's not lukewarm when you drink it. I'll be right back."

Foxed you, you old snot, she thought as she poured a glass of juice. She could see that the man was disappointed that she had thwarted his opportunity to point out something negative. She watched him carefully cut into his breakfast, spear a bite on his fork, and slowly raise it to his mouth, scrutinizing it as he did.

Fay could tell by the smell and look of the plate of food that it would be the best sausage gravy and biscuits he had ever eaten. What she didn't know was whether he was man enough to say so. Judging by the way he treated the woman with him, she thought he would rather cut out his tongue than hand out a compliment. When she judged they were about halfway through their meal, she picked up the coffeepot and went over to the booth.

"How is everything?" Her waitress timing was perfect; both of them had just taken a bite, their mouths were full, and speaking would have been rude. He frowned but nodded, so she assumed his food was acceptable.

"And yours, ma'am?"

The woman had swallowed. Fay barely heard her say, "Fine."

"That's great." She held up the pot. "Would anyone like more coffee?" and refilled his when he jerked his head toward his empty mug; the woman held her hand over hers in the universal "no more" gesture.

Fay went back behind the counter and served the codgers their biscuits. They ate them so fast she would have thought they put them in their pockets if she hadn't seen them chewing.

"I guess Naomi makes good biscuits, huh?"

Raymond nodded like a bobblehead doll gone mad. "These are by far the best biscuits I have ever eaten." High praise indeed from a man so hard to please. "Do you think I could get half a dozen to take home?" he asked.

"Me too," Leo said. "These are even better than my mama used to make, and she was from Georgia."

Fay pulled out her order pad, wrote it down, and said, "I'll ask."

She poked her head in the pass-through to find Brady and Naomi, heads together, going over the week's menu plan.

"If you two can tear yourselves away from each other for a minute, I have an order." She waved the scrap of paper at them. "It's not a big one," she said as Brady walked over to the griddle and snatched the order out of her hand. "Naomi's biscuits were a big hit with Raymond and Leo; they each want six to go. Are there enough left?"

Brady smiled. "There are plenty; Naomi made about six dozen."

"Great! Let me hand you a couple of to-go boxes, and you can put six in each for the guys."

She stood leaning on the pass-through's counter watching Brady carefully slide biscuits into the boxes with a spatula when she heard a loud crack behind her. Brady dropped the biscuit he was holding, and his knuckles whitened on the spatula handle. His head came up like a bird dog that has spotted a pheasant.

"What the hell was that?" Brady said.

Fay whirled around to search the diner for the source of the sound. She saw the woman get up from the booth, her hand pressed to her left cheek, and hurry to the ladies' room. The eyes of the remaining codgers and everyone else in the place followed her as she walked the length of the building to the bathroom behind the till.

The man sat in the booth and stared at his empty plate. He was unmoving, his hands clenched in fists, his face and neck blotchy red. She could tell by the tension in everyone's bodies as they stared in his direction that he caused the sound she had heard. There was no doubt in Fay's mind where her next move should be. She took off at a fast walk to the Ladies'. She slowly pushed open the door.

"Honey?"

There was no answer. She entered the brightly lit tiled space and stooped to see if the woman was in a stall. She saw a pair of shoes in the far stall next to the end wall and heard a faint sniff and rustle of cloth.

"Honey, are you okay?"

"I'm fine," came the muffled answer. "Leave me alone."

Fay turned and took one step back toward the door and then stopped. She turned around again. "No, I won't leave you alone."

There was a pause, then the woman in the stall said, "Why not?"

Fay took another step closer. "Because I think too many people have left you alone for too long, and it's time someone did something about it. Looks like I'm that someone."

The next word from the stall came out as a wail. "Why?"

Fay leaned on the cool tile wall and folded her arms across her chest and tried to answer. "I guess because today I am on a roll. I convinced my boss here to give a friend of mine a tryout; she needs a job, and he needs help, but he was too stubborn to consider a woman in her situation. It was hard to convince her to come in too."

Fay kept talking to give the woman in the stall time to collect herself. "Naomi, that's my friend's name, has spent so many years down on herself. She got herself pregnant in high school, and her mama disowned her, and then the father of her son ran off, so she has been on welfare for fourteen years. She tried to get jobs, but she wanted to be home to make sure her son didn't get into trouble or join a gang but could never find the right job. Well, that's her story in a nutshell."

Fay straightened up and put her hand on the locked stall door. "Naomi came into the diner this morning, and it looks like she totally blew him away; those were her biscuits you smelled. It looks like she has a job, and I'm the one who came up with the idea in the first place. So, I'm on a roll." She rapped softly on the locked metal door. "Come on out of there and let me see what I can do to help you."

"Nobody can help me." But the door latch clicked open, and the woman came out, using a wad of toilet paper to dab away the trickle of blood from the corner of her mouth. Her left cheek was all red and swollen; her eyes were puffy from crying.

"What's your name, honey?" Fay said.

"Honey," the woman said, almost smiling.

"No. Really?"

"Yes, really, my pop said I was as sweet as honey when I was born, so that's what they named me." This time she did smile but then winced at the pain in her cheek.

"Just a minute," said Fay, and she went to the door and hollered for someone to hand her an ice pack. She waited, using her body to block the door in case Honey's husband tried to come in. Leo walked to the door with a plastic bucket of ice and a couple of towels.

"Is everything okay in there?"

"Getting there," she said. "How about out there?"

Leo had a bemused smile on his face. "Oh, it's interesting out here too. You take care of that lady in there. We're fine out here."

"Thanks." Fay set the bucket of ice on the counter, scooped a handful into the center of one of the towels, folded it into a nice package, and handed it to Honey. "Here, this should help with the swelling and a bit of the pain."

Honey tossed her wad of toilet paper into the trash and eased the ice pack onto her cheek. "Thanks a lot. It's been a long time since someone took care of me." Tears shimmered in her eyes and her voice got tight.

Fay perched one skinny butt cheek on the edge of the counter and leaned back against the towel dispenser. "So, Honey, how did you get hooked up with Lothar out there?"

Honey adjusted the ice pack and said, "We met in college; Ham was captain of the football team, and I was head cheerleader."

"Natch."

"He was wonderful, not a groper like the rest of the boys I dated. He held doors for me and chairs too. Ham walked on the curb side of sidewalks so I wouldn't get splashed on rainy days. He was everything Mama told me to look for in a man."

Fay shook her head. "Of course, he was. All of them are like that when they are trying to get into your pants. It's only after they get what they want that they turn back into horses…well, you know."

Honey laughed a bit at that. "Yeah, I do know. It was exactly like that. As soon as we were pinned, he started, well, squeezing a bit too hard when we petted. And he would roughly grab my hand and put it you know where, even if I didn't feel like putting it there." She shook her head at the memory. "I have to confess, I kind of liked his roughness. I mean, I come from a very genteel family. Papa was always courtly and polite to Mama and her friends. He wore a tie at dinner. Of course, Mama was a lady and kept a lady's house. We had linens on the table at dinner, cloth napkins, and real silver flatware." Her gaze was far away, as if she were back in her parents' dining room. "They had dinner parties, lots of dinner parties. Mama wore frilly aprons, and no one would ever suspect that she had worked her tail off the whole day. Every hair was in place; everything was perfect. And they had poetry readings and music nights. It was lovely."

Fay listened with amazement. She had read about such lives in novels but thought no one actually lived that way. "Tell me about you and Ham," she said.

"Well, everyone loved him. People went out of their way to tell me how lucky I was to be engaged to him. I couldn't bear to disappoint them by saying I really didn't want to marry Ham, that I wanted to change my mind. So, I let him keep on pushing me around."

Fay reached over and took the sopping towel from Honey. "Let me fix you a new one. This is dripping all down your sweater." She dumped the unmelted ice into the sink, wrung out the towel and hung it over the stall wall next to her. She shook out a fresh towel, loaded it with more ice from the bucket, folded it carefully and handed it back. "When did he start hitting you?"

Honey slowly and carefully eased the fresh ice pack onto her bruised cheek. "Thanks, that feels better. When did Ham start hitting me? Let me see...on our wedding night."

"You're shitting me."

"No, I shit you not." She chuckled at the shocked look on Fay's face. "You're surprised that I said shit, aren't you?"

"Well, yeah."

"Listen, Fay, everyone says shit, even proper ladies."

"I suppose."

"Anyway, after our wedding reception, the biggest, most lavish the country club had seen, we retired to our honeymoon suite in the grandest hotel in the city. Mama and I had shopped for weeks for my negligee and peignoir; it was a vision of white silk chiffon and silk charmeuse. Ham didn't give me a chance to put it on. He pulled me to him after carrying me over the threshold. I thought he was going to kiss me. Instead, he grabbed the two halves of my dress back and ripped it. Tiny pearl buttons flew in all directions. 'Get undressed,' he growled. I was shocked, too shocked to protest. I just stood there, tears streaming down my cheeks, and took off my dress. When I reached up to take off my veil, he said, 'Leave it,' so I did. I stripped down until I was wearing only my veil. 'Put your shoes back on,' Ham said. I did. Then he slapped my breasts, leaving red handprints on the white flesh. After a while, I didn't even feel it. Eventually he pushed me back onto the bed and leaped on me, stabbing his penis into me as if it were a knife."

Fay felt as if she would never breathe again. She watched Honey's face as she told her horror story and not a flicker of emotion moved across her face, perhaps a moment of wonder and regret, but no revulsion, no fear, just blank acceptance, as if it were her due.

"He was very careful not to hit my face. We lived only a few miles from my parents, and he knew my mama had eagle eyes. As the first few years of our marriage passed, Mama would look into my eyes and ask, 'Are you happy? Are you okay?' I think she knew what was going on somehow, but I was never brave enough to say anything. We moved away; she died; I never told her the truth." Fresh tears fell, soaking into the towel to mix with the melted ice.

"So, what set Ham off today?" Fay asked, conscious that time was passing.

"Well, it didn't help that it was obvious you expected me to say something. Ham likes to be masterful, especially when he's in a new place. Then I said I would have preferred homemade toast. That's when he slapped me."

"Oh, Honey, I'm so sorry my behavior made him hit you. I've been hit enough over the years that I know how it feels. And not just the physical pain but the mental and emotional pain too."

Honey reached over and held Fay's hand. "Thank you. You're the first person who has apologized to me since, oh, I don't remember when." She removed the ice pack, stepped to the sink, and opened it, watching the shards of ice tumble into the white porcelain basin. She wrung out the towel as Fay had done and hung it next to the first one. Then she dumped the remains of the ice and water out of the bucket. She dried her hands on a paper towel and used the towel to wipe up any water that had splashed out of the sink. "There, that's cleaned up." She turned to look Fay in the eyes. "I really appreciate you listening to me today, Fay. Don't feel like Ham hitting me was your fault. He would have found another reason before too long. His business isn't doing well, so he's taking it out on me. I can take it." She hugged Fay. "It's okay. Really." Honey looked at herself in the mirror. She ran her fingers through her hair and tucked it behind her ears. "I think Ham needs to see his handiwork in front of everyone, don't you?"

Fay stared transfixed at the transformation in the woman before her. "Uh, sure."

Honey turned toward the door and laid her hand on the handle. "Come on, perk up. I won't die from one little slap."

I'm not so sure, Fay thought, but she stood up, brushed the wrinkles out of her skirt, and stepped forward ready to face that particular demon. An incredible scene greeted the women as they left the sanctuary of the Ladies'. Fay expected to see Ham backed into the corner of the booth by Brady, expecting that the navy veteran and bachelor would have things to say to a man ballsy enough to slap his wife in public. Instead, Brady stood off to the side. Ham was sitting upright in the booth staring in disbelief at Naomi. That formidable woman was leaning over him, her right hand twisted in the front of his shirt, the heel of her hand pressed to the bottom of his chin, keeping his eyes on hers.

Honey stopped abruptly, and Fay heard her rapid intake of breath. Fay hid a smile at the scene. The codgers had turned back to their newspapers and cooling coffee. No one else was in the place.

Fay nearly laughed out loud to hear Naomi telling Ham in no uncertain terms, "No man is ever allowed to hit a woman, ever. And, mister, you had better hope you are far away from me if you ever decide that you are willing to risk it again. Because I'll hear about it, and I will be there to do something about it."

Ham opened his mouth as if to speak, but Naomi forestalled him. "Ah, ah, ah. Don't thank me. I know you're not used to having a woman telling you your business, but, Mister Ham, because I know that is your name, you had better get used to it. Women are going to be running your life from now on. Starting with this lovely lady right here." Naomi turned as Honey walked up to the booth. "Ma'am," Naomi said to her, "I hope you don't mind, but your husband and I have just had a little talk. He will behave himself from now on."

Honey looked down at her husband as he sat rumpled and sweaty in the booth, smoothing his hand down the front of his shirt, trying to press out the wrinkles from Naomi's grip. "Come on, Ham. Let's go home."

He looked at Naomi, who was blocking his way. Naomi smiled at him, with her friendliest smile. "You go on home,

Mister Ham, with your missus. And you just remember, some of my neighbors are familiar with your habits. I think you can be sure I will hear if you do not heed my words." She turned her smile on Honey. "Ma'am, you have my sympathy. And I apologize again for manhandling your husband, but I cannot tolerate a man who strikes a woman. Please come back and visit when you can. We'd love to see you again."

Honey stepped forward to give Naomi a hug. The two clung to each other as if they were lifelong friends parting forever.

Honey stepped back and looked into Naomi's eyes. "I'm sorry our little problem interrupted your job interview. The food was terrific; I trust you got the job."

Naomi nodded yes.

"You can be sure I'll be back to sample more of your good cooking." Honey turned to Fay and hugged her again. "Thanks for listening," she whispered in Fay's ear, "and for caring enough to pry the story out of me. I will be back."

After releasing Fay, she turned to her husband, who still sat in the booth and had not said a word since she came out of the ladies' room. "Are you coming or staying?" She held out her hand. "If you're staying, give me the car keys. I have some errands to run on the way home."

Ham sat for another moment and then slid to the end of the booth seat, cleared his throat, and stood up. Naomi had moved but left him just enough space to stand. He tried to avoid touching her but could not.

"Excuse me, ma'am," he said in a small voice.

"Don't try that on me. I'm immune to your tricks." Naomi put her hand on his shoulder. "Remember what I said. I'll be interested to hear if your behavior improves in the next few weeks. It had better."

Honey winked at her, picked up her jacket and purse, and turned to leave. Ham nodded once to Brady, tugged the lapels of his tweed sport coat, and followed his wife out the door. Brady, Fay, Naomi, and the remaining codgers watched them.

As they left, Fay turned to Naomi. "How did you know that guy's name, anyway?"

Naomi waved her hand. "Oh, Mister Ham is famous with the hookers in the complex. He has very specific tastes and pays very well for the privilege of satisfying those tastes." She gave a little shudder. "Seems like everyone around here knows all about the president of the biggest paper mill in town and his dirty little secret. Business must be bad if he's losing control in public. I understand from a few of the girls that he has a lightning temper that he usually manages to keep under control until the bedroom door closes."

They turned to walk back to the counter. Fay picked up the coffeepot and raised it inquiringly at Raymond and Leo, the two remaining codgers. Leo shook his head.

"None for me," said Raymond. "Now that the excitement is over, I think I'll go on home." He dug into his pocket, pulled out three crumpled dollar bills, and tossed them on the counter. "That should cover my coffee and biscuit, right?"

"Right," Fay said. Leaving an entire quarter for my tip, she thought but did not say.

Leo left a five-dollar bill next to his saucer. "Keep the change, Fay," he said, winking at her.

"Thanks, Leo," she said. "You're a real pal." She knew the wink meant he was leaving extra so she wouldn't be stiffed by Raymond's quarter. Just as the men reached the door, she remembered something.

"Do you two still want the six biscuits Brady was boxing up when all the excitement started?" They both turned right around and came back for the boxes Brady had ready on the pass-through. Raymond had to break a ten-dollar bill to pay for them and actually left her a dollar tip. Fay felt a little lightheaded with surprise at his generosity.

Needless to say, that day Naomi got the job. She and Brady developed a connection that usually only comes after years of working together. Without speaking, one would hand the other the utensil he or she was just about to reach for. Naomi persuaded Brady to add a few of her favorite recipes to the "specials" menu. The fried chicken plate, served with mashed potatoes and gravy, and coleslaw, was so popular with the customers that it quickly made its way onto the permanent everyday menu.

CHAPTER 7

Brady followed Fay's advice and made peace with the quartet of boys from the apartments. The next time they came in and ordered Cokes, he told them they could have them free for a little help around the diner. They emptied the trash and carried bus tubs into the kitchen for Fay. If they worked especially hard, they got ice cream too.

A few days after the work-for-Cokes agreement began, a boy, the smallest one, came late after all the indoor chores were done and the three boys were having Cokes.

Brady looked down at him and said, "The only job left is to sweep around the building and clean the parking lot."

The kid took the push broom and got to work. He swept up all the litter, dropped cigarette butts and small pieces of paper. He picked up all the cans and put them in the recycling bin.

Brady went back to work and forgot about him, but the boy kept working and an hour later came back in for his "pay."

"All done, Mr. Brady," the boy said.

"Let's go check your work," said Brady.

He went out with Brady to show that he'd done the work, and Brady was impressed at the thoroughness of the job.

"What's your name?" he asked the kid.

"Tom," he said to his shoes.

Brady clapped his shoulder and said, "You did a good job, Tom. Come inside."

When Brady offered him ice cream, Tom said, "Can I have a sandwich? Just a little sandwich, please."

"You have ice cream at home?"

"No, sir."

"Things hungry at home?"

Tom kept his eyes on his lap. "Yes, sir, it's hungry at home."

Brady set about making him a ham sandwich. "What kind of bread do you like?"

"There's more than one kind?"

"Never mind." Brady put thick slices of ham and cheese with lettuce on good old white bread. He cut the sandwich in half and put the plate in front of Tom. "Glass of milk?" Brady asked.

Tom nodded his head yes, his mouth full of sandwich.

After that, Tom came by a few days a week asking for the broom. The parking lot had never been cleaner. Brady had his ham sandwich and glass of milk ready when he came in from sweeping.

The next few weeks went by without a hitch. Brady had never been happier. His customers regularly congratulated him on being brilliant enough to hire Naomi, and he came to believe that it was his idea from the get-go. Fay allowed him to believe that; she got a raise and a much easier boss to work for.

Brady hardly minded when, after the early morning rush was over, Naomi hurried across the parking lot to make sure Marcus was up and dressed, that he ate the breakfast she quickly fixed for him or carried over from the diner, then drove him the eight blocks to school. Marcus gave up complaining about the short leash his mother kept on him. He had come to appreciate the time they spent in the car together at the beginning of the day, and to notice how his friends' mothers didn't seem as interested in their sons' lives. At first, he caught a lot of flak about being a "mama's boy" after football practice, but he just smiled and shook his head. He told his best friend James that the reason his mom picked him up was so that he had the best chance she could give him to get through school and get a scholarship for college. James's job was to spread the word among the team members to lay off. It mostly worked, except for one big tackle named Carl. He took exception to James's advice and ramped up his taunting. Marcus finally had to meet Carl under the bleachers for a few minutes of trading punches and shoving, which earned Marcus a bloody lip and a rather romantic-looking black eye but ended up with Carl rolling in the dirt clutching his family jewels. Naomi lectured Marcus about fighting. He nodded and said, "Yes, ma'am" as politely as his swelling mouth allowed, but he knew she understood that a man sometimes had the necessity of establishing boundaries with his fists. Overall, the outcome of that little scuffle was greater team unity. If Coach ever heard of the fight or had an opinion about it, he was smart enough to keep his mouth shut.

As the year progressed, Marcus noticed how few parents were as interested and involved in their children's lives. He came to appreciate the care his mother was taking to make sure he succeeded. Once football season ended (they finished second in the division after a heartbreaking loss in overtime) Marcus asked his mother if she thought he could get a job busing tables at the diner a few evenings a week so he could start saving up for college. After talking it over with Brady, she gave her permission.

"As long as your schoolwork doesn't suffer."

Brady was happy to have the friendly, hard-working young man work for him and, even though it pained him to say, he had to admit Marcus' friends who came in to tease him—and stayed to order fries and a Coke—were a nice group of kids.

Naomi was definitely an asset to the diner. She worked hard and had an angel's touch with biscuits, they nearly floated out of the pan. She thought Brady's insistence on having three homemade soups on the menu every day was right on, and on her afternoons off would scour cookbooks in the small branch library nearby for recipes to add to her repertoire, especially vegetarian ones. On Sundays, customers at the diner were treated to Naomi singing along with the radio. She begged time off to go to church, where she was in the choir, so she would come to work right after the service, uplifted and filled with music. Brady would have the radio tuned to his favorite jazz station, and Naomi would sing along while she cooked to keep the buffet filled.

"You missed your calling, Naomi," Brady said, after fielding compliments both on the food and her singing, which floated out of the kitchen with the enticing smells of simmering onions and peppers.

"What are you talking about?" she said.

"You can really sing. Even the customers say you have a voice like an angel."

"Do you mean the customers can hear me?" She put her hand over her heart.

"Of course, they can. You're singing like you do in church. I am sure the boys down at the muffler shop can hear you too if the wind is blowing right. You're really belting out the tunes."

Naomi turned pale. "I'm so sorry, Brady. I'll stop." She plunged her hands into the huge bowl of meatloaf she was mixing.

"Oh no, you won't," Brady said. "I like your singing, the customers like your singing. I hear you singing, and I think you like working here. Please don't stop."

CHAPTER 8

The roar of a large group of motorcycles going by interrupted the peace of the Sunday morning. In very few minutes, the roar was back, and a number of them turned into the parking lot and stopped. All over the diner, people decided not to linger over coffee. They called for their bills, paid hastily, and left, just as the first leather-clad, bearded man in black pulled open the door.

Those customers not lucky enough to have been served yet or those only on their first trip to the brunch buffet were trapped. People by the windows looked out to see the double row of shiny black and chrome motorcycles neatly parked at the edge of the lot. Cold visions of the Hell's Angels and the havoc they wrought in 1960s California raced through minds that had been chilled by the movie when they had first seen it through the fogged-up windshield of the drive-in. Marlon Brando in black leather, cigarette dangling from his lips, sailing down the highway followed by his gang, though scary in cinematic black and white, was not nearly as frightening as the flesh and blood men who burst into the diner; their rude laughter shattering the Sunday morning calm.

Fay hurried to greet them hoping to steer them to a table in back where she could keep an eye on them and they were far from the buffet, trying to give the regular customers, the normal customers, a chance to eat their food in peace. But she was unsuccessful.

The one she assumed was the leader, a tall, grizzled man with ice-blue eyes, skulls tattooed on his knuckles, and Fearless Leader embroidered on his jacket, said, "That's okay, babe. We'll just sit there." He pointed at the currently empty twelve-seat counter.

"Oh, okay, fine," she stammered, hating that her pulse raced when he winked at her. She hurried around the counter to set coffee mugs at their places as they moved to sit down and was surprised that three of them wanted decaf. She watched their confidence as they walked toward their stools, heavy boots thudding on the linoleum, pulling their leather gloves off, and laughing with high spirits.

"Hey, did you see the name of this place?" the one with Mom's Revenge embroidered on his jacket said, looking proud.

"Yeah, Better Than Mom's," Thunder-pants said with an evil grin. "You are not much of a cook, so they don't have far to go."

"Hey, watch what you are saying," Mom's Revenge said, and he shoved Thunder-pants into the wall, a clatter of gelatin molds fell around him as he staggered upright. The men started laughing at the mess they had made.

From behind the counter, Fay pointed at Thunder-pants. "You pick those up, mister." She turned to point at Mom's Revenge. "And you help."

That wiped the smiles off the men's faces. "Yes, ma'am," they said together, and they bent to pick up the fallen decorations.

The other six bikers chuckled and shoved their way to the counter, leaving spaces for the other two, as if they had assigned seats or a pecking order in the group. Oh, lordy, this is going to be a long day, Fay thought.

The seven men who had followed Fearless Leader into the diner were a motley lot. Most of them had beards wild and tangled from the wind and wore bandanas, mostly black, tied tight above their eyebrows. Fay thought Fearless Leader looked like Sean Connery with his silver hair, neatly trimmed beard, and icy blue eyes. Fay thought Sean Connery was hot. The other seven were a mixture of tall and short, portly and thin, with graying hair worn Oakridge Boys style or bald. She suspected that the bald ones were really balding and had shaved their heads to make it look like they were bald on purpose, instead of by accident. They were all in black leather jackets, all in chaps —some with fringes and studs, some plain and unadorned. The sound of their footsteps in their heavy black boots echoed in the diner. One or two of them wore a single earring in his left earlobe.

Fay could never remember if wearing a flower over her left ear meant she was single or married. She thought, I wonder if there is a similar code for earrings. A quick glance at their hands revealed an even split in the wedding ring department. Dang, Fearless Leader wore a ring. Oh well, you can't win them all.

As with most Sundays when the number of customers was too great for one waitress to handle, Brady was out in the dining room helping to make sure no one was without a full mug for long and answering questions and taking compliments. His expression was grim as he surveyed the lineup of black leather-clad men at his counter.

When he and Fay met at the coffeepot, he quietly said, "Do you want me to wait on them?"

Fay shook her head. "No, I'm fine with them. If I need help, I'll holler."

Brady must have told Naomi about the invasion of the bikers because she poked her head out the door, gave them the once-over and retreated, clicking her tongue over the silliness of the middle-aged man.

Once she had served coffee down the row of them, Fay left them with the menu, hoping that would keep them occupied while she dealt with the sudden line of people at the cash register. The bikers' arrival had signaled the end of brunch for the regulars.

As Fay walked behind the counter stools to get to the cash register, she was surprised to feel a pinch, right on her bottom. She whirled around to look at the eight men but saw only their backs. They seemed to be occupied with discussing what to order; none of them looked as if they knew she was there.

She unconsciously rubbed the spot that had been pinched and continued on, listening for snickers from the bikers, to ring up the customers and punch the Frequent Diners cards of those in the know.

Once everyone had paid, toddled back to leave a tip, or pressed it into her hand with a smile, she made her way past the bikers so she could take their orders. She refilled coffee mugs and went to make a fresh pot because a few of them were still examining the menu.

She was trying to carefully tear open the foil packet of coffee grounds. "Who seals these damned things?" when she heard the scrape of heavy boots on the floor behind her and the sound of breathing very close by.

"Hey, sweetheart, can you take our orders now?"

She jumped when he reached toward her, took the packet of coffee out of her hands, tore it open, and handed it back. It said Mud Face on his jacket.

"There you are, little lady," he said, leaning forward to squint at her nametag, "uh, Fay. Them things are always a pain to open."

From the holster on his belt, he pulled a multi-tool that looked as if it could make repairs on the space shuttle and brandished it in her face. "You need to get one of these little beauties. It has a screwdriver, pliers, three sizes of wrenches and an adjustable one, and a serrated blade that'll cut pretty near anything." He waved it even closer to her as if to emphasize how much she needed one, then slipped it back into the holster.

"Okay," she said, "I'll put that on my list for Santa. And I'll be right over to take your orders as soon as I get this coffee going."

"Thanks, Fay," he said and bopped her bottom as he turned to go back to his stool.

She whirled around ready to give him what for, but his back was to her, his fists were raised, pumping the air as if he had won something, and he was crowing. She reached out and gave him a good shove right between the shoulder blades that made him stumble and made his buddies burst out laughing.

"Asshole," she muttered, pouring out the old coffee before pushing the button to make fresh. "I thought everybody had taken training not to do that sort of thing. I guess Mud Face needs remedial training." She pasted a friendly smile on her face before she straightened up and went to take their orders.

Fay shook her head at their foolishness as she walked over, pulling her order pad from her apron pocket. "What'll you have, boys?" she asked, stopping in the center of the row of them, ready to turn toward whoever ordered first. "Anybody having the buffet brunch can just give me their drink order and then go right ahead and serve themselves."

No one responded. She shrugged and got ready to take eight orders. "Separate checks?" she asked.

Fearless Leader said, "Nah, it is my turn to buy."

That remark kicked off a round of arguing from the ranks.

"You bought last time," Mud Face said.

"No, I didn't, you moron, you did," said Fearless Leader.

"Oh, yeah."

"I thought it was my turn," said Road Rash.

Black Lightning slapped him on the arm. "You paid when we were at Lucky's out on Highway seventeen."

"Oh yeah," Road Rash said, rubbing his arm.

Fay waited while they hashed out who was paying today and whose turn it was next.

Fearless Leader settled the matter. "I'm paying today; Splat pays next time. Everybody say it."

Seven voices mumbled, "Splat pays next time."

Dear God, Fay thought, what a bunch of idiots. I wonder how they manage to ride without killing themselves. Their orders were run of the mill for men their age without wives to disapprove—fried eggs, sausage, bacon, and ham, white toast with real butter.

"Hey, isn't this the place that is supposed to have delicious biscuits?" asked Mom's Revenge.

Eight pairs of eyes looked at Fay with varying degrees of

hope and desire. "Our cook makes pretty good biscuits, yes."

"But did she just start making them here in, oh, say the last month?" asked Mud Face.

"That's about right," Fay agreed.

They all decided to forgo toast in favor of a couple of Naomi's biscuits each. When they were finally finished debating how crisp they wanted their hash browns, Fay went to the pass-through and clipped the crossed out and scribbled over order to the carousel.

"Naomi, your biscuits are getting famous." She turned to find Brady at the other end of the diner schmoozing with a couple of middle-aged women. She yelled, "Order up."

That brought his head around. He excused himself and went into the kitchen to get back to cooking. Despite their disreputable looks, the row of bikers were fairly well behaved, aside from periodic shouts of laughter, which caused a few of the more nervous of their fellow diners to spill their coffee. Fay was kept busy filling the bikers' mugs and mopping up spilled coffee from other tables. She served them their breakfasts, each of them thanking her politely when she set the plate in front of them. By that time, most of the other diners in the place had finished their meals, waved her down for their checks, paid, and left. Fay noticed that no more customers had come in since the invasion of the bikers. She hoped they didn't make a habit of stopping in; she needed the tips that Sunday customers, generally a bit more generous than weekday customers left, and so did Naomi.

Brady had a policy that the waitress shared tips seventy/thirty with the bus person. Naomi argued that the busing was not much work, so she felt like she was stealing Fay's money, but both Fay and Brady insisted. Brady picked up a crock for fifty cents at the thrift store next to Safeway that he put at the end of the pass-through for waitstaff to drop their tips into. He said he did it to save arguments, but Fay figured the afternoon waitress was not as scrupulous about splitting tips with Marcus or James as Fay was with Naomi. Fay used to keep tips in her pocket, but the bills got bulky, and the coins got heavy, especially on Sundays, so she was glad to empty her pockets and put the money into the crock. She wondered what kind of tippers the bikers were as she walked back down past them, a coffee pot in each hand, filling their mugs. She was amazed to hear them discussing T-bills, emerging market funds, and Impressionist art, besides cams and chrome wheels. Fay knew for a fact that most bikers wouldn't know an Impressionist painting if it were tattooed on their arm. But then she wasn't sure she would recognize one if it bit her on the ass either.

By the time the bikers had used the last of their biscuits to sop up the last of the egg yolk and gravy from their plates, they were the only people in the place except for Naomi and Brady in the kitchen and Fay behind the counter.

"Fay, another round of coffee for my men," Fearless Leader said.

She made one more pass down the line of mugs, then she started clearing the booths and tables closest to the counter. One by one, she cleared tables, neatly stacking dirty dishes in a bus tub, and sliding it onto the counter behind the swinging doors for Naomi to put in the dishwasher. Then she wiped each table with a clean, soapy cloth, moving and wiping off the salt and pepper shakers, the sugar jar, the napkin holder, and the seats. She straightened up the menus in the holder, made sure there were not any obvious food spatters on them and the dessert flipper cards, reset the table with clean silverware wrapped in a napkin and fresh placemats, ready for the lunchtime diners. Once she had cleaned her way to the back of the diner, she started on the buffet table. She checked the time to make sure that it was after one o'clock, which was half an hour after the posted end of brunch, and then she began scraping the remaining food into a bucket stored under the counter and stacking the empty steam trays on the pass-through. Once she had the steam trays all emptied, she started unloading the clean dishes from the tubs Brady had lined up on the shelf under the counter so that everything was clean and refilled for later.

Finally, the row of men seemed to be finished. Fay moved down the line with the coffee pots one more time, smiling at each of the men, offering more and removing the soiled dishes. As she reached the end of the row and refilled his mug, Flats thanked her and turned to his friends.

"We should plan our next ride, men." He leaned toward Fay as if imparting a secret. "I'm social director this quarter."

She didn't know what to say except, "Oh."

She stooped to pick up the heavy tub of dirty dishes and looked down the counter to see each biker take out a smartphone.

"What date are you thinking about, Flats?" asked Black Lightning.

"I am looking at either the thirteenth or the twenty-seventh."

Each man poked at the little screen in his hand, some nodding and some shaking their heads.

"The twenty-seventh won't work for me," said Road Rash, "my mother-in-law will be visiting, but the thirteenth is okay."

"I'm free either day," said Splat. "The kids will be at music camp, and Julia is planning two weeks at a spa in Arizona with her sisters."

"We could be free on the thirteenth," said Thunderpants. "Black Lightning and I have a gallery opening on the twelfth, so we should be more than ready to ride the next day. We'll need a few highway miles to blow off that art crowd stink."

Flats leaned back to look down the row. "What about you, Mom's Revenge and Fearless Leader?"

Mom's Revenge was poking at his screen. "Damned technology. I'll have to get back to you. This thing seems to be toast. But I should be able to clear my day unless it's my weekend on call. I'll email you tonight." He turned to the man next to him. "Fearless Leader?"

Fearless Leader was frowning at his screen. "I think I can make the thirteenth. It'll depend on which judge I draw in the case I told you about, but I'll have all my research wrapped up this week, so give me until next Thursday to say with certainty."

Flats shook his head at that. "You put the man in charge, and he loses the ability to make decisions. Okay, men, barring unforeseen circumstances, we ride again on the thirteenth."

Their phones were slid back into inside pockets.

Fearless Leader took a last sip of his coffee, tossed two bills on the counter, said to Fay, "Keep the change, honey," and stood up, pulled his gloves from his pocket, and put them on. "Come, men. We ride."

The seven men pulled on their gloves as they stood and repeated, "We ride."

They followed Fearless Leader out into the parking lot, mounted their motorcycles, and roared off toward the interstate. Fay watched them leave with a mix of relief and regret. Then she saw the money on the counter. She picked up the tab for just over seventy-dollars in one hand and the two hundred-dollar bills in the other. "Hey, mister," she said, lifting the money toward the door, "you forgot your change." She stood looking from one hand to the other, then she called out, "Brady!"

He came out of the kitchen saying, "They stiffed us, didn't they? Dammit, I knew they were going to stiff us." He stopped next to Fay and snatched the tab from her nerveless fingers. "How bad is it?"

She tried to say something. It took her a few tries to get the sounds out. "No, they didn't stiff us." She lifted the bills and waved them under his nose. "They left a one-hundred-thirty-dollar tip on a seventy-dollar tab." She turned to see Naomi peering through the pass-through window. "Naomi, honey, we're rich."

The group of bikers became legend in Better Than Mom's. Fay came to think of them right up there with movie heroes like Indiana Jones, Clark Gable, and her personal favorite, James Bond, or Sean Connery. Her part of the enormous tip allowed her to ransom her Honda and return to feeling like a human being. She hated being without wheels and always thought of a zillion places to go when her car was laid up. Naomi decided they were angels sent from heaven to give solace to her and Fay, and to live as examples to the lowlifes who stiffed them on tips. She used part of the money to buy Marcus new jeans, and the rest she squirreled away into her hidey-hole for a rainy day. Since her adult life had at times seemed like one long rainy day, saving that last thirty-five bucks seemed like the best plan.

Brady grumbled he hoped that they never came back because of all the other business they had scared away. "We need those jokers like we need a hole in our heads," he would say when Fay and Naomi got to fantasizing about where they came from and if they would come back.

Fay never admitted it, even to herself, but that Sunday encounter left her with a lifelong crush on Fearless Leader. She looked for him whenever she saw a line of motorcycles outside a bar or restaurant. Her head would come up and her eyes dart to the window whenever one roared past the diner. And a group of them passing her on the highway would send her swerving to the shoulder to stop and watch them go by, hoping against hope to see Fearless Leader's silver ponytail and beard waving at her from under a midnight blue helmet. They never came back to the diner, and no one ever saw them again.

CHAPTER 9

For a while, the diner chugged along with nothing to mark one day from the next. The employees got into a groove, Fay and Naomi's morning into afternoon work blending seamlessly with Taffy and Marcus or James, who worked late afternoon into evening. There was a reliable supply of clean dishes and set-ups, Fay never came in to start the day to find overflowing bus tubs or sticky tables covered with napkins and straw wrappers. Taffy never came in to find empty silverware racks and plate holders. She appreciated Fay and Naomi's efforts to start her days off well and returned the favor by making sure Marcus and James got everything ready for the morning before they left. It was a happy little family, making good, rib-sticking food for a varied and interesting clientele.

One of both Fay and Taffy's favorite groups of regulars were a foursome of little old ladies who came in on alternate Thursdays to eat cottage cheese and peach half salad plates and then play cut-throat bridge the rest of the afternoon, sucking down amazing quantities of sweet tea while they passed nickels and crowed over every hand. The four ladies: Maralee, Jackie, Connie, and Helen had all worked at the same paper mill as secretaries and played bridge together most days on their lunch break.

Once the youngest of them retired, they realized how much they missed playing with each other and met for lunch a few months ago at Better Than Mom's, talking about old times. Maralee had put a couple of decks of cards in her purse with four tallies and mentioned it to the other three. In a heartbeat, Fay was called over to clear away their lunch dishes, carefully wipe the table, and take the set-ups away so they could play. Brady gave his permission for them to use a table in back for a couple hours in the afternoon, since it was a very slow time anyway, as long as they were finished by three-thirty, which was when Taffy began setting up for the supper crowd. So on alternate Thursdays, except in the dead of winter when it was just too dangerous for four women on the shady side of seventy-five to be walking around on snowy parking lots, the back room buzzed with the snap of playing cards, bids of "three no trump," calls for more tea and maybe a square of Naomi's to-die-for chocolate vinegar cake, and four older ladies reliving the days when they had their fingers on the pulse of the largest business in Stinson.

One Thursday on her way out of the diner, Maralee dropped a deck of cards, and Raymond hopped off his stool to help pick them up.

"I can't believe I was so clumsy as to drop the cards." Maralee said. "That's the way my day has gone. First, I finished last in the game, and now this."

"Let me help," said Raymond. "It's good for my bones to get down here on the floor."

Their hands brush together as they pick up the scattered cards. "Thank you, Mr. Tolliver," she said.

Raymond didn't meet her eyes. "Call me Raymond. How have you been, Maralee?"

"Good... Raymond."

"How long since you retired? Two years?"

Her cheeks turned bright pink. "Yes, two years, well, almost three years now." She reached for the last card. "I think that's got them."

They helped each other to stand and didn't let go immediately. Raymond shuffled his feet. "Maybe one day I could buy you a cup of coffee and some pie?"

She reached into her purse, put the deck away, and pulled out a business card. "That would be nice, Raymond. Call me."

Jackie reached out and took Maralee's arm. "Come on, time to go."

The peace of Better Than Mom's was shattered one morning in late autumn when Fay went through the kitchen, giving her customary greeting to Naomi and Brady as they chopped and stirred to get the day's three soups simmering, into the diner, and turned right around and walked back through the still-swinging doors.

"Brady, you need to come out into the diner." When he did not move, she said, "Right now."

The tone of her voice made him turn pale, drop his knife, wipe his hands on his sparkling clean apron, and follow her into the diner. Naomi was right on his heels. The three of them stood shoulder to shoulder right in front of the door and surveyed the scene through unbelieving eyes.

"How could we have missed this, Brady?" Naomi said.

"We all come in the back, that's how," Brady said, his voice cracking.

What they saw was devastating. The newspaper machine that usually stood beside the door had been thrown through the window in the waiting area, scattering shards of glass all over, some of which stuck out of the upholstered bench under the window like stalagmites from a cave floor. The door was unbroken, but the next window down in the line had been broken by having one of the cement planters tossed through it. All three of them wondered how many people it had taken to lift the heavy planter filled with dirt and heave it through the glass. And it was not just plate glass either; Brady had tempered glass installed because he said if someone rammed their car into the building by accident, he didn't want the customers inside to be cut by flying glass. So, the glass in that booth looked like pretty blue pieces of crushed ice twinkling in the rays of the just-risen sun. At first, Fay thought the vandals had emptied the planter before throwing it, but then she realized that the booth, the table, and the floor next to it all the way to the counter were covered with potting soil and plants.

"Oh, Brady, your pretty geraniums and petunias," she said, focusing on the smallest thing she could comprehend. "Maybe we can save them if we repot them fast."

She started forward, but Brady put his hand on her arm to hold her back.

"Don't touch anything. I have to call the police. Now."

He turned and blindly crashed back through the kitchen doors and staggered into his office, fell into the chair, and stabbed at the number keys on the telephone. 9-1-1. He was grateful to whoever had decided on such a simple number to call for help; he knew he could never have dialed anything more complex.

Back in the diner, Fay and Naomi moved to stand closer together until their shoulders touched. Each of them felt the need for physical closeness in the face of such a shocking invasion of a place they had felt safe in only moments before. Naomi's eyes followed the trail of dirt from the booth to the cash register desk, which stood empty. She craned her neck, reluctant to take even one step into the room for fear of destroying a clue, and saw the cash register itself lying on the floor, its drawer pulled out like it had been gutted. A few coins glittered in a stray shaft of light as if to emphasize what the vandals had been looking for.

Fay's eyes traced the line of dirty footprints the other way down the diner where she saw tables and chairs overturned, salt and pepper shakers strewn about, and napkins grabbed from their holders and stirred into the filthy mess on the tiles. The buffet had been overturned, and all the beverage dispensers had been opened to add a milky, cola-y, orange juiciness to moisten the mix. Fay could smell a nauseating mixture of potting soil, coffee grounds, and sour milk that made her gag until she clapped a hand over her mouth and ran for the back door to heave her bowl of Oatie Ohs and skim milk into the dumpster behind the diner.

Fay wiped her trembling lips on her apron and then stood with her arms folded protectively across her stomach as she listened for the sirens that got closer, eventually screaming into the parking lot. She crept around the side of the building to see what would happen, not wanting to walk through the kitchen, not wanting to smell that awful sour earthy smell that she would identify for the rest of her life with a feeling of exposure, invasion, and not being safe. Three squad cars had stopped willy-nilly in the lot, and from two of them emerged an impossibly young policeman, gun drawn, to crouch behind the open driver's door of the vehicle. From the third squad car unfolded the tallest policeman Fay had ever seen. He looked to be about fifty years old, comfortably paunchy, and graying. He stretched once he was on his feet, his fists digging into his lower back, and his leather gun belt creaked like she was sure his bones did too. He glanced scornfully at his fellow officers.

"Oh, for god's sake, holster your weapons, you two." He shook his head as if he could not believe the stupidity of the young. "The call said the perp was no longer at the diner. That means the bad guy is not here."

When the two younger men did not move, he stepped around the front of his squad car toward them.

"Robinson, Davies, put the guns away, I said. You're making us look like fools." He waved his hand at them as if swatting flies off a cooling pie. "We have enough trouble with credibility in this neighborhood without the two of you gracing us with your Barney Fife impressions. Geez."

He looked to Fay as if he wished he were anyplace else but here, then he tugged a notebook from his shirt pocket, flipped to a blank page, and started toward the front door. Just as he reached toward it, he thought better of it.

"Davies," he said over his shoulder, "get out the digital camera and take shots from every angle of every detail, every piece of broken glass, anything that might give us a hint to who did this. Robinson, you get out the crime scene kit and dust the door handle for prints. I'm going around back to talk to the owner and the help."

He turned toward the corner where Fay stood leaning against the concrete block wall. She squeaked as he got nearer and turned to scurry back into the relative safety of the kitchen and her friends. She knew she was being silly, running from the police, but she was more spooked than she had ever been in her life and suddenly wanted to be standing in Brady's bulky and comforting shadow when she spoke with this Jolly Green Giant of a cop. No, she thought with a stifled giggle, he would more properly be a Jolly *Blue* Giant, or maybe a Jolly *Black* Giant; she really had not paid enough attention to the color of his uniform.

By the time she slipped into the kitchen, her scattered and inappropriate thoughts about what color the policeman's uniform was had struck her as so totally funny, she was having trouble controlling herself. It was all she could do when she saw Brady and Naomi's solemn and scared faces not to burst out laughing.

"What's so funny?" Brady growled as she sidled up to him.

"Nothing really," she said. "I just feel the urge to laugh." She wiped a hand across her lips, as if that would help her keep from smiling. "The cops are here. The tallest one is on his way…"

Just then a loud male voice outside said, "Police!" and the door crashed open, and a policeman appeared in the opening, gun drawn, pointed straight at the three of them. All three raised their hands just like they had seen in the movies. "Who are you and what are you doing here?" the policeman barked at them, holding his gun steady.

To Fay, the barrel of the gun looked as big as a cannon. To Naomi, it looked like her wildest nightmare come true. To Brady, it looked like a tiny piece of hell coming for him. Brady spoke first, hands still in the air.

"I'm Brady Gallagher. I own the diner." He leaned first to one side and then the other. "This lady here on my right is Naomi Cushing; she's my assistant cook. The lady on my right is Fay, um, Fay..."

Fay prodded him with her elbow. "Fay Taylor, you ignoramus," she hissed.

"Fay Taylor, the morning waitress."

The policeman had not relaxed his crouch or lowered his weapon as Brady told them who they were. "Got any identification?"

"If you'll let us put our hands down without shooting us, we can get it," Brady said, beginning to lower his hands slowly. When he was reasonably sure the cop would not shoot him, he turned and leaned into the office and came back carrying his wallet. He flipped it open for the officer, so his driver's license was visible.

"Humph," he grunted. "What about you ladies? Got any ID?"

"Oh," Naomi and Fay said together.

They nearly collided in the office doorway in their haste to get their purses and show him they were who Brady said they were.

After he looked over their identification and called the dispatcher to have them checked out for "wants and warrants," he finally asked, "What happened here?"

Brady shook his head. "I don't really know, Officer...? I'm sorry. I would feel more comfortable if I knew your name."

The cop looked uncomfortable. "Officer Bates."

Fay thought a minute and said, "*Norman* Bates?"

Now the cop turned positively beet red. "Yes, Norman Bates. My ma was a movie buff. Save your breath; I've heard all the jokes."

Naomi turned away to cover her smile, and Fay put her hand over her lips, pressing them into her teeth to keep from laughing out loud.

"What?" Brady asked, looking from one to the other with confusion. "Who is Norman Bates?"

"I'll explain later, Brady," Naomi said. "Tell Officer Bates what happened."

She grabbed Fay by the elbow and dragged her out the door, where the two of them leaned against the back of the building and howled. They stayed outside the diner until one of the young cops came out to say that Officer Bates was looking for them, that it was their turn to tell their story of the morning's events.

"What events?" asked Fay as they followed the officer inside.

Naomi shrugged her shoulders. Since Fay had been the one to see the destruction first, she was asked to sit in Brady's office with Officer Bates and go over and over what she saw when she first went into the diner from the kitchen.

"Did you see a person in the diner when you walked in at," he consulted his notes, "five fifty-seven A.M.?"

Fay answered each question as best she could. "No, I didn't."

"What was the first thing you noticed when you entered the diner?"

"The first thing I noticed was the big shards of glass sparkling in the waiting area bench."

"What did you notice next?"

"The smell." She shuddered at the memory of that sickeningly sweet and sour stench.

"Do you know of anyone who has a grudge against Mister Gallagher or the diner?"

"Well, on the day Brady hired me, I overheard him fire his last assistant because he made lumpy gravy. But I don't think he minded so much. He still comes in for coffee and sometimes for lunch. He and Brady seem to have made their peace."

"And his name is?" She gave it, certain from watching the policeman make a tick beside a line on the previous page that Brady had already told him about the firing. "Anyone else?"

"Well, Brady was complaining a while back about a pack of nine-year-olds who were trying to scam him out of Cokes or ice cream cones without paying. He also suspected they were pulling the plants from the window boxes."

"Nine-year-olds?"

"Yeah. I suggested he offer the boys an opportunity to do little chores around the place. You know, empty the trash, sweep the lot, stuff like that, in exchange for a soda or ice cream."

"And did he do as you suggested?"

She nodded. "Yes, he did."

"And they stopped harassing him?"

"Yeah, if you can call a kid trying to get a free soda harassment, I guess they did."

"Do these boys, all boys?" She nodded agreement. "Do they still come around and help?"

Fay shook her head. "Not so much now that school has started. Mostly in the summer when they're bored, one or two of them will come in looking for a little treat so whoever isn't busy will set them to going around the place emptying the trash or hauling a bus tub or two, then we set them down at the end of the counter and 'pay' them in ice cream or soda, their choice." She smiled. "They have to work more, or do a better job, to get ice cream. They're pretty nice kids. There just isn't much for them to do to stay out of trouble in this neighborhood."

Officer Bates looked up at her. "Ms. Taylor, are you married?"

She smiled her foolproof flirt's smile, guaranteed to make a man weak in the knees. "I'm separated."

From the blank look on Officer Bates' face, Fay understood he was not asking that question out of personal interest. She turned her head and craned around to get a good look at Officer Bates' left hand. No ring. Now, that did not automatically mean he was not married. She had plenty of experience with married men who didn't wear rings. No telltale white marks on their ring fingers, no thinning of the skin to mark where a ring might usually be. Some men just didn't wear rings, and others' jobs wouldn't let them wear them for safety reasons. Yeah, and some men are purely dishonest creeps, she thought, and don't care who they hurt, whether it's the woman they have vowed to love for the rest of their lives or the woman they have just met down at Shorty's Pub on pool league night. She didn't think that Butch had ever been unfaithful. He was too in love with playing pool and his damned custom-made pool cue. Well, she had taken care of that love affair, hadn't she? She thought her idea of selling the cue on eBay right out from under his nose was the most brilliant one of her life. That she got away with it even though some of Butch's pool buddies haunted eBay looking for assorted pool paraphernalia and his prized cue was on there for a full week without them blowing the whistle on it, led her to believe that Butch was not the beloved member of the pool playing community he imagined he was.

"...last night?"

She heard only the last words of Officer Bates' question. "I am sorry; I was distracted," she said. "What was the question?"

The policeman sighed like his day had already been too long, even though it was barely six-thirty in the morning. "I asked where you were last night."

"Oh."

"And...?"

"What?"

"Ms. Taylor, are you purposely trying to be dim?" Officer Bates slammed his pen down on the desk and pushed himself back as if to stand up.

"What? No, I...oh, last night I went to the mall with Naomi, um, Ms. Cushing, and we walked around K-Mart for a while and then went to the Safeway to pick up a few things. That's what I did last night. What did you do last night?" Fay looked at him as if to dare him to answer her. When he said nothing, she dropped her eyes and became very interested in picking at her chipping nail polish.

He sighed and pressed the heel of his left hand to his forehead. "What I did last night has nothing to do with the vandalism of Better Than Mom's. What you did last night might." He paused as if he expected Fay to say something; when she didn't, he picked up his pen, bent back over his notebook, and asked another question.

"I understand you live in the apartment complex behind

here. Did you notice anyone in the parking lot or hanging around when you returned from the mall?"

"No, I didn't, but then I wasn't really looking for anyone. My apartment doesn't overlook this place, you know."

"No, ma'am, I did not know that."

"Besides, you and your buddies out there should have found stuff like footprints to take casts of and fingerprints and stuff, haven't you? On television, they solve even cold cases with a lot less and in only an hour. You'd better speed things up here."

Officer Bates was thinking he would have been happier at a desk job or as a crossing guard. "Yes, ma'am."

Everyone either watched too many cop shows on television or they watched one of the many CSI versions and felt they had all sorts of insights into crime and criminals that the real police had somehow missed learning in their training. He closed his notebook and looked at Fay.

"I think I have all I need for now. Thank you for your cooperation, Ms. Taylor." He stood up and opened the door for her.

Fay walked out into the kitchen, blinking in the bright fluorescent lights as if emerging from a cave.

Behind her, Officer Bates leaned out the door and said, "Mr. Gallagher?"

Even though he knew he would not be opening the diner that day, Brady was still working on making soup. He stood at the counter chopping celery and carrots and onions, just like he did every day.

When Naomi had tried to tell him he did not need to make the soup that day, he said, "Someone will eat it. If I have to drive it over to a homeless shelter or the women's abuse shelter, I will. Someone will have fresh homemade soup today. It won't go to waste."

Officer Bates called his name and said, "I have a few more questions."

Brady wiped his hands on his apron, picked up his coffee mug, and walked across the kitchen.

Naomi looked at Fay and said, "How was it?"

Fay flapped her hand. "No big deal. He asked a bunch of questions that didn't seem to have anything to do with the break-in. Then he got huffy when I suggested that the detectives on *CSI* every night solve crimes with a lot less clues and in a lot shorter time."

Naomi hid a smirk by concentrating on cutting carrots into exactly the same size dice. "I can't understand why he could have gotten irritated at that."

"Me neither." Fay busied herself making signs to put up on the sheets of plywood that Art from the lumberyard had nailed up over the broken windows.

She heard Raymond arguing with one of the policemen that Officer Bates had left outside to keep gawkers away and to keep people from stealing things. "I come here every morning for coffee, young man," Raymond said. "I do not understand why I can't just go around to the back if the front door is locked. I've done it in the past when they were tardy in opening."

It was easy to distinguish Raymond's confident footsteps from the skittering shuffle of the young policeman trying to uphold his superior officer's commands and still not offend this older gentleman with the commanding presence. Fay wasn't surprised to see Raymond appear in the open back door looking mulish and out of sorts.

"Fay, what's going on here?" he said, marching into the kitchen like he must have entered a boardroom when he was running the paper mill. "Why is this child telling me that the diner is closed?"

Fay looked at him as if he were speaking a foreign tongue. "I don't know, Raymond. Do you think it could be because some jackass tossed the planters through the windows and then came into the diner and wrecked everything? Maybe because the whole room is filled with dirt and coffee grounds and sour milk, so there's not a clean place to sit or an unbroken mug or plate? It might be because there's broken glass mixed in with all of that mess and the cash register is sitting behind the counter in about sixteen pieces. What do you think, Raymond? We're closed just to make you angry?"

Raymond looked at Fay as if he could not believe what he had just heard from the woman who had flirted with him and teased him and sometimes chastised him, but never been anything but polite to him.

"Well, there's no cause to be sarcastic, Fay. I just want a cup of coffee." He looked around the kitchen as if expecting someone to walk up to him with a mug on a tray.

Naomi, who had not looked up from her work, kept on chopping. The only other person in the room was the young policeman he had steamrollered past to get in there.

"There is no coffee, Raymond," Fay said. "At the moment, I'm not sure if Better Than Mom's will be open anytime soon. There's a lot of cleaning up to be done. A lot of expensive equipment will need to be replaced. And to be honest with you, I'm not at all sure Brady can afford to start over from scratch. My guess would be that if the place had caught fire, he would have been covered, but I don't know if you can buy insurance against vandalism."

She shook her head.

"Go home, Raymond. Learn to make your own coffee for a day or two. Come back by at the end of the week and maybe we'll know more."

She bent her head back to neatly lettering her sign, dismissing him.

"Well, I guess I'll go on home if you won't even give a man a cup of coffee."

"Try the drive-through at Mickey D's, sir," the young officer tried to help.

"Have you ever tasted that vile brew, young man?" Raymond looked at him as if he had suggested he drink poison.

"Yes, sir, I drink it every morning."

"Then you have never had real coffee. I pity you." Raymond turned away and marched out of the kitchen door.

The young policeman hesitated in the doorway. He

cleared his throat. "Is the coffee you make here really better than at the drive-through?"

Naomi looked at him. "Honey, if that is the only coffee you drink, you are in for a treat." She wiped her hands on her apron, crossed the room, pulled a mug down from the shelf, and poured him a cup from the pot always on. "Cream and sugar?" she asked him.

"No, thank you, ma'am. I drink it black." She handed him the mug. He dipped his nose into the fragrant steam and took a tentative sip. Fay and Naomi watched his face as he swallowed his first taste of real coffee.

Naomi could not stand the suspense. "Well?"

He smiled at her. "You're right. That's not real coffee at the drive-through. Not if this is what coffee is supposed to taste like."

CHAPTER 10

Brady felt awkward sitting in the chair in front of his desk in his office. He was usually the one lolling in the ratty padded desk chair he had gotten on closeout at Big Lots because it was missing a caster. He had bought a replacement caster at the hardware store that was just a teensy bit bigger, so sitting down in his chair was an adventure. Depending on where the just too big wheel ended up, the chair either tried to throw you face down on the desk or toss you over backwards. He smiled when he watched Officer Bates gingerly settle his bony behind in the chair. Ah, Brady thought, he's already learned. This is one smart cop. Officer Bates leafed through his notebook, eyes down, in what Brady interpreted correctly as a ploy to put him off balance.

After about five minutes that Brady spent calmly sipping his coffee watching the policeman play his part, Officer Bates cleared his throat, and squinted at him. "Having financial problems, Mr. Gallagher?"

Brady nearly burst out laughing. How clichéd can you get? "No, I'm not. Are you?"

Officer Bates wondered what made the people in this place think that his interrogation was a two-way conversation. "Did you hire someone to come in and trash the place, Mr. Gallagher?"

"No, Officer Bates, I did not. I love this place and my customers. I have every intention of cleaning up the mess and getting open again as soon as possible. Tomorrow if I can."

Officer Norman Bates scribbled furiously in his notebook. He wished he were like the British police officers he read about in his favorite mysteries. They always had a convenient underling to sit quietly in a corner taking notes, while the Superintendent strode about barking questions and intimidating the suspect. But no, here he sat hunched over this too small desk in the cramped office of a diner in a town the world was passing by, investigating a crime probably done by some illiterate high school dropout with no job, a pregnant girlfriend, and a street name like Metal Head, who he would never find. Or, if he found him, the guy would be too stupid to think of a believable lie but the evidence would be too thin and some slick tongued court-appointed attorney who was not even old enough to shave would get him off on a technicality and Bates would have to look at young Metal Head hanging with his gang as he cruised the neighborhood in his patrol car and know that the little creep was laughing.

God, he hated his job. Even though he had passed the sergeant's test years ago, old Wendell was grimly holding on to the only sergeant position in the small force, and Norman was sure Wendell would die in harness. Wendell sat and snoozed behind the Property Department desk four days a week, bleary-eyed and confused. Every time he tried to organize the crap hole that he had let Property become, things got lost and the mess got bigger. Twice a year, the captain drafted two younger officers to go in on a Saturday to clean up. The following Monday, Wendell would come in, survey his neat and shiny domain, and complain to anyone who would listen that he couldn't find anything since some comedian had messed up his filing system. More like a piling system, Officer Bates thought.

But he had this crime to investigate today, and he was absolutely certain that Robinson and Davies would inadvertently destroy any tiny bits of evidence there might be in that unholy mess out front. He knew beyond any doubt that they would find the fingerprints of every resident of Stinson on the door handle overlaid with the prints of various truckers and vagrants. His vacant gaze fixed on Brady.

Brady sat calmly waiting for Officer Bates' next question. Brady could wait forever. He had spent twenty-three years in the navy. Everyone knew that the real motto of the military, whatever branch you experienced, was hurry up and wait. So, he could wait with the best of them. He was an Olympic-class waiter, patient and happy to be sitting indoors and in a semi-comfortable chair. Not that he was not totally upset that his pride and joy had been invaded, but he wasn't about to let anyone see it. Oh, maybe he would ask Naomi out tonight and bend her ear for an hour or so over a few drinks and a bowl of bar pretzels. He felt so comfortable with Naomi, and he had been so reluctant to hire her. Not only because she was Fay's friend but also because he'd only ever worked with men in galleys, never women.

Brady was patient. He could easily wait while the tall, skinny policeman decided how he wanted to ask the questions Brady knew he would ask. Had he hired the vandalism? Well, he had already asked that one and been told in no uncertain terms that he had not hired some kids to break in. Brady wracked his brain trying to think of other ways the police could think of to accuse him or someone on his staff that the crime was an inside job.

"Are you heavily insured, Mister Gallagher?"

Ah yes, insurance. I should have thought of that, although I would think that had more bearing when a fire was involved. Anyway, burning their way out of debt seemed to be a time-honored way with small businesses; he had never heard of anyone hiring a vandal to get out from under. "Well, I don't know if I would say heavily insured, Officer Bates. I am adequately insured against liability in case a customer is injured on the premises, and of course I pay workman's comp to cover any employee injuries. I have fire insurance on the building and its contents, even though the building is concrete block and few of the contents are flammable. This is a converted gas station, you know. It was built to withstand a lot."

He watched Officer Norman Bates write every word he said. The policeman's knuckles were white as he gripped the pen as if he were taking a test. He also saw that the tiniest tip of the officer's tongue was poking out of the corner of his mouth as he concentrated. I'll bet he doesn't even know that he does that. He wouldn't thank me if I told him either. He kept answering. "I'll have to reread my policy and check with my agent, but I believe that I have coverage for this sort of invasion and vandalism."

Officer Bates raised his head and pointed his Bic at Brady. "I noticed that the plate glass in the window in the waiting area broke into big shards that stuck in the bench below it. You realize that there is a city ordinance requiring businesses to have tempered glass in the windows to prevent people from being injured or killed in the event of an accident. I saw that the glass of the other windows broken was in small pieces, in other words, tempered. What happened there?" He squinted at Brady as if the fact that one window had the wrong glass in it was worthy of great suspicion.

"You know, I noticed that too. I'll have to contact the installer. I paid him a lot of money to install tempered glass in every window in the place. Thank you for bringing it to my attention."

Officer Bates' face crumpled as if he had hoped his question about window glass would elicit a confession from Brady. He looked sadly at his notebook, realizing that nothing he had learned so far got him any closer to solving the case. He sighed. "I guess that's all for now, Mister Gallagher. I'll contact you again if I have any further questions."

Brady stood up, his empty coffee mug dangling from his left hand. "Thank you, Officer Bates. I'm sure you'll do your best." He turned to leave the office and get back to making his soup. He stopped in the doorway. "When do you think we'll be able to get into the diner and start cleaning it up? And I have to call a glass place and get those windows replaced. With the correct type of glass, of course."

Officer Bates scrubbed a hand over his face and looked at Brady framed in the doorway. "Probably later today. I need to spend some time sifting through that mess out there looking for clues, if there are any to find. I'll let you know."

Brady nodded and went back to his chopping. Naomi had

kept working while he was talking to the policeman, figuring she would be next to talk to Officer Bates, and wondering if she would have a job the next day. She hoped she would; she liked her job. She enjoyed standing at the counter, knife in hand, mounds of chopped vegetables heaped before her gleaming like polished gems ready to be turned into delicious things to eat. Most of the recipes she and Brady made were good, old-fashioned home cooking like meatloaf and mashed potatoes, chicken and dumplings, hot beef and gravy, or ham with sweet potatoes. She had convinced him to let her make her personal recipe for fried chicken one weekend about a month ago, and it had been a big hit with the customers. She had made her grandmama's fresh butter beans and Great-aunt Gigi's coleslaw to go with it. Oh, and of course she made biscuits to go on the side. By the time they were done serving, there was not so much as a whiff of it left, and Brady was considering making Naomi's fried chicken a regular menu item. That made her proud. She couldn't stop telling everyone she met about how if they wanted to eat real fried chicken, instead of that fast food kind that came in a bucket, they should come on down to Better Than Mom's on a Saturday and discover what was really meant by their motto. And what was Better Than Mom's motto? Why, it was painted right there on the sign under the name in little bitty letters. It said: Where You Don't Have to be Told to Clean Your Plate. It was printed on the menus too, and she was sure Brady was trying to figure out a way to afford to have it embroidered on the back of the knit polo shirts he had made up for his employees. A couple of the people she told about how good her chicken was had actually come in and tried it. They even called her out of the kitchen to tell her how delicious it was. She had washed her hands and wiped the sweat off her face before she went out to their table to collect her compliments. Her eyes widened when she recognized two of the hookers from the end building with their pimp boyfriends hunkered down in a booth just like regular people, sopping up the last of the gravy with the end of a biscuit. It occurred to her that maybe, just maybe, that foursome was not exactly the clientele Brady hoped to get in his diner, but when she mentioned it to him, he brushed the idea aside.

"I figure everybody has to eat, solid citizens, hookers and pimps, and everyone in between. I would be just as glad if they all came in here. As long as they behave." He winked at her, a very un-Brady-like gesture. "Their money is just as good as the preacher's is," nodding his head at the Lutheran minister and his wife sitting primly at the table just across from the hookers and their pimps, trying very hard not to stare at the women's short skirts, plunging necklines, and the men's flashy jewelry.

Little by little, more of the residents of Fay and Naomi's apartment complex started coming to Better Than Mom's for a cup of coffee or a sandwich. They were on their best behavior, not calling attention to themselves, but quietly enjoying the atmosphere and the reasonably priced food alongside the regulars.

"Money is money, that's my new motto," said Brady, chortling as he totaled up his deposit one Friday afternoon. He noticed that his daily deposits were gradually getting larger since he had hired Naomi. When he walked out into the kitchen past Naomi, he stopped and leaned on his hand next to her at the counter. "You're good for business; did you know that?"

She smiled at him, a small shy smile that peeked out at him, ready to dart back into hiding at the first sign of trouble. "What do you mean?"

He rolled off his hand and rested his back on the counter's edge, arms folded across his chest. "Well, since I hired Fay, the morning business has picked up. Everyone knows you need a sassy waitress working in the morning to perk people up for the day. But since I hired you, our overall business has nearly doubled. I can't decide if it's because of your biscuits, your fried chicken, your peanut butter chocolate cake, or the after-church singing you do when you are fixing brunch." He reached out and patted her on the shoulder. "Whatever it is, just keep doing it, please. Oh, and I'm giving you a fifty cent an hour raise."

Naomi's hands stopped working, and she stared after him.

A raise? "Thank you, Brady," she squeaked out.

That had been last week, and now this. Now the diner was in shambles, and she did not know if Brady had insurance or enough money or even the will to clean up the mess and get back to business. It would be just her luck if he lost heart and locked the place now that she had finally found a job that was exactly what she had been looking to find for nearly ten years. Now that Marcus was doing better in school and working a couple of evenings a week busing here, bringing in a little pocket money, and was an all-around happier young man, now there has to be this catastrophe that has the potential to destroy their little bubble of hope. Tears welled up, and she blinked to keep them from falling, sniffling, and trying without too much success to stop feeling sorry for herself.

"I didn't think chopping onions made you cry," Fay said as she came in the back door from taping a sign on the front of the building saying they were closed. She was grumpy from having to fight with Officer Davies to get close enough to put the danged thing up.

"It's not the onions, Fay; it's that mess out there and me not wanting to lose this job now that I've finally found it."

"You think Brady will just give up?"

Naomi shrugged, unable to say more, unwilling to verbalize her fears in case that would make them come true.

"Not our Brady," said Fay. "He's a tough old bird; he's ex-navy, you know. Those guys just don't know the meaning of the words give up. He won't go down without a fight."

She nodded her head, agreeing with her own words, then she snuck a glance at Officer Bates slowly working his way from one end of the diner to the other, sifting through the mixture of coffee grounds, dirt, and spilled liquids. "You think Officer Bates is married?" she said over her shoulder.

"Don't tell me you think he's cute?" Naomi said with a laugh.

"He's not bad," said Fay with a shrug. "He's kind of scrawny, and I usually go for the beefier type, but he has a good job, and I'll bet he is not addicted to playing pool. He looks to me like a man who would treat a lady with some respect."

Naomi got the giggles. Fay frowned at her. "What are you laughing at?"

"Just the picture of you and Officer Norman Bates, two scarecrows, out on a date." Her giggles turned to chuckles. "Or better still, you and him all tangled up between the sheets looking like a handful of toothpicks wrapped in a napkin." Naomi had to stop chopping; she was laughing so hard she was in danger of cutting off a finger.

"Oh, shut up." Fay tried to look angry, but Naomi's laugh was so contagious, she couldn't help but laugh too. They stood in the kitchen under the glare of the fluorescent light, laughing like a couple of hyenas.

Brady poked his head out of his office, and Officer Bates looked in through the swinging doors. "What's with you two?" Brady asked.

Naomi stopped laughing on a breath and shook her head, wiping the tears streaming down her cheeks.

Fay looked at Brady and said, "Reaction to the shock of the day," which threatened to start them off again.

Both of the women kept straight faces until the men went back to their respective jobs.

Fay leaned on Naomi's shoulder, and they both sighed at the touch. "We need to get lives," she said.

"Amen, sister, amen," was Naomi's reply.

Within an hour all three varieties of daily soups were finished, simmering in their pots, filling the kitchen with their aroma. Brady invited the policemen into the back to have a bowl before they finished their work; then he called the Salvation Army and the women's shelter, and he and Naomi left Fay to keep an eye on things while they delivered the soup to them. They were gone for about an hour, and the Naomi who returned was a different woman from the one who left.

"What's up with you?" Fay asked her.

"Did you ever go to a women's shelter?" Naomi said.

"No."

"Don't go unless you want to be shocked. You should see some of those women—and their children. I've lived in ghettos my whole adult life and I've never seen women beaten down and beaten up like I saw today." Naomi shook her head.

"Did you think men had stopped beating up their women?"

"Oh, not really. I guess I had never seen the damage up close before. The director lady had to make an announcement on the PA before she would let Brady carry in the soup. Some women are so downtrodden that even seeing a man sends them into fits." She shook her head again. "It is a rotten shame that men get away with that sort of behavior."

"Well, not so many of them do anymore," Fay told her. "I think people are paying attention to that sort of thing and trying harder to keep it from happening."

Naomi shook herself like a dog shaking water off its coat. "Hey, guess what Brady told me in the car."

"What?"

"He said as soon as the police are done out front, we're going to start cleaning up and try to be open tomorrow."

"We're going to clean up that mess?"

"Yeah. Who did you think would do it?"

"I don't know. ServiceMaster or somebody like that."

"And who do you think would pay for something like that?"

"Insurance, hopefully?"

Brady's voice came from the office. "Insurance will replace broken things. You and Naomi and I are the cleaning crew. So, you two ought to go home and change into different clothes because this is going to be one hell of a dirty job."

They looked at each other, shrugged, and got their purses to go home and change. Within an hour, the three of them were elbow-deep in the fruits of someone else's labor. Once the police gave the go-ahead, they armed themselves with brooms and mops, rubber gloves and cleaners. They started furthest from the door and cleaned their way toward the worst of it, and they wore masks at Brady's insistence.

"You don't know what's in this mess," he said when they protested. "There's probably mold from the planter dirt, plus the coffee dust, and God knows what else. Put on the masks."

Fay and Naomi had tied bandanas over their hair to try to keep the dirt out of it and keep the sweat from running into their eyes. Later in the afternoon, the guys from the glass company came and started installing all new tempered glass in the windows, removing the plywood that Art from the lumberyard had put up to keep the weather and curiosity seekers out.

Brady had the glass installers neatly stack the wood off to the side.

"Art said he wouldn't charge me for the wood if we took good care of it. He'll pick it up when the last window is in." He turned a stern look on the guys from the glass place. "And all the glass better damned well be tempered, or your asses are grass, and I'm the lawnmower. I won't be cited for having unsafe glass in my diner when I've paid for tempered again."

The foreman of the crew passed the buck. "Hey, it wasn't us, Mister Gallagher, sir. Talk to Mister Hansen; he is the one who ordered the glass, and had it loaded on the truck; we're just the ones who put it in like he told us to. Talk to him."

Brady waved a dismissive hand at his excuse-making. "I can't stand men who are always blaming someone else for their mistakes. I say, admit your screw-up, apologize, and get it over with. The world would be a better place if that happened a little more."

Naomi nodded her agreement.

Fay thought that self-preservation was a part of everybody's makeup; she didn't believe in taking blame you could maybe slide over to the next guy.

They worked all afternoon and into the evening, cleaning and scrubbing, finding more of the restaurant's supplies that the vandals had destroyed. Brady started his cleaning by making sure that the coffee brewer and beverage taps would work. He heaved an enormous sigh when the coffee maker gurgled into action, dribbling a stream of hot water into the pan he put on the hot plate.

"Well, we can serve coffee anyway. I think the milk dispenser is toast; looks like someone kicked the spigot off or stomped on it. It'll never work again; but we can get milk from the Safeway; that'll work fine."

Luckily, he kept a supply of replacement glass pots for coffee because all three of the ones that had been out in the diner were broken. All they found were the metal and plastic handles; the glass had been crushed and ground into the mess on the floor. As they worked their way toward the front of the diner, so did the window installers, so it appeared they were working themselves out of the darkness of despair into the light of hope. They reached the waiting area of the diner at sundown. Brady went and found some thick leather gloves to protect his hands as he carefully pulled the shards of broken glass from the bench under the window. That was the one without tempered glass. He watched carefully and double-checked before the installers lifted the giant pane into place. Brady even got out a flashlight to examine the tiny sticker in the corner that identified the glass as tempered. He ignored the impatient sighs of the glass guys and made certain that this time he got what he paid for.

While Fay and Naomi tackled the job of picking up all the gelatin molds and deciding which ones were too crushed to be hung back on the wall and shook the dirt from all the silk flowers that used to be arranged in the corner, Brady went in back and called to have a couple pizzas delivered. Even though they were in the middle of a restaurant, it had been too long and too upsetting a day to think of cooking a meal.

While they waited for their food to be delivered, Brady sadly picked up the pieces of his brand-new cash register. The vandals had wrenched out the drawer and then, finding no money inside, had flung the entire machine on the floor and stomped on it until parts flew everywhere.

"It's a good thing I saved the old till," he said as he carefully laid the pieces in a garbage bag.

"Do you think it can be fixed?" Naomi asked him.

"No, I don't. It's smashed beyond repair; I'm certain of it. The old one still works. It's just not as fancy." He looked at Fay. "You and Taffy will have to use a calculator to add up tabs. It'll be slower, and you'll have to remember the prices like waitresses did in the old days, but the job will still get done." He shook his head.

Fay couldn't decide if it was because she was notoriously bad at addition or if Brady was mourning the loss of his shiny computerized cash register. She decided it was the latter; she was not that bad at arithmetic.

A car with a pizza sign on its roof pulled in and tooted the horn. Brady motioned for the guy to carry the pizzas around back and went to meet him, pulling his wallet from his pocket as he went. Fay and Naomi were glad to strip off the hot rubber gloves and masks, and to wash up in the ladies' room. They were sorry to see their sweaty, dirty faces in the harsh light of the fluorescent fixtures over the sink.

"We look like hags," Naomi said. "Do you have any lipstick in your pocket?"

Fay patted her pants pockets and her shirt pocket. "Nope, I don't. At least you look semi-human with your dark eyes and olive complexion. I look like a corpse; my eyes are that washed out hazel, and I have sweated off the makeup I put on this morning. I look like hell."

Naomi was squinting at herself in the mirror. "You really think I look alright?"

Fay looked at her. "Why? You got a date stashed in back?"

Naomi shook her head. "No, I just don't want to look like a washerwoman, do you?"

"No, I don't, and I don't even know what a washerwoman is, but I don't want to look like one, whatever it is." She bumped Naomi with her hip. "Shove over. Let me see what I can do with this mess."

Naomi watched in amazement as her friend pinched her

cheeks and bit her lips. Roses bloomed in her pale cheeks, and her lips were suddenly cherry red. "I always knew you pale girls had it easier. Look at you. You look like you've got makeup on."

Fay looked at her friend in the mirror. "You know, Naomi, I would bet that if you tried the same thing, you wouldn't get all the color in your face like I did, but you'd look fresher. Try it."

With a shrug of her shoulders, Naomi leaned closer to the mirror and then pinched her cheeks and bit her lips. Fay was right. She didn't get the flush of color that suffused Fay's pale skin, but her face brightened up. "Thanks, Fay. I'll remember this trick."

A man's voice at the door made them jump. "If you two don't get out here soon, either I'll eat all the pizza or it'll be stone cold."

Naomi and Fay said together. "Coming, Brady."

The three of them sat around the high counter in the kitchen on stools, gobbling down a couple of pizzas and sipping Cokes.

"Mm, there is nothing like a good greasy pizza and Coke after a long hard day," Naomi said.

Brady set his can of soda down. "Are you saying you don't like my cooking, woman?" he said.

Naomi's eyes darted between Brady and Fay as she tried to decide if he was really offended or teasing. The Brady she was familiar with did not tease much. "Um, no, not at all. I love your cooking, Brady. It's just a treat to have good pizza once in a while, that's all."

Fay piped up. "Me too. I love your food, Brady. You are a world-class cook, but every once in a while, a girl has to eat greasy pizza just to remind her stomach who's boss."

He grunted and kept eating.

By the time there were only smears of grease, strings of hardened cheese, and a few stray olives in the pizza boxes, it was fully dark.

"Hey, it's after nine o'clock," Brady said. "Where'd the day go?"

Fay groaned. "My aching bones know where the day went. I don't know when I've worked so hard in one day. I'm ready to go home, take the longest shower on record, and fall into bed." She turned to look at Naomi. "Are you ready? Because I'm fading fast."

Naomi looked at Brady who gave her the smallest flicker of a wink. "No, I'm not ready just yet. You go on. I'll help Brady clean up in here and get ready for tomorrow."

Fay shrugged and looked at the two of them. "Okay, if you all want to wear yourselves to a frazzle, I don't. I'm out of here." And she stood up, slung her purse over her shoulder, and left with a tired wave.

In the silence that followed her leaving, the buzzing of the light over their heads was very loud. Brady reached across the counter and put one of his hands on top of Naomi's hand. "I'm glad you stayed, Naomi."

Naomi looked down at Brady's work-roughened hand covering her chapped one.

"Why are you glad I stayed?" she asked, eager but afraid at the same time.

Brady took a deep breath, and his fingers moved on her hand. "I've been… well, I've been thinking about maybe asking you if you would like to go out for a drink or something to eat some evening. You know, after the supper rush is over." He let out his breath as if he had just run around the block.

To buy time, Naomi said, "You mean you'd eat someone else's cooking? I thought you only ate at Better Than Mom's. Heck, Brady, I thought you lived here." She smiled when she spoke, so he would know that she was teasing him.

He smiled too. "Sometimes I feel like I live here. Before I was smart enough to hire you, I was here so much I thought about putting a cot in the office and just bedding down back there." He scratched the back of his head and stared at the ceiling over her shoulder. "I was thinking, though, now that I have a real reliable staff. Taffy, Marcus, and James do a great job with the supper rush and cleaning up for the morning. I thought that maybe you and me could check out the competition, so to speak."

"Well, a girl does have to eat, and she doesn't always want diner food every day. I think I might be interested in going out for supper with you one day, Brady." She realized he had not looked her in the eyes once during the conversation and she said so. "Are you afraid of me, Brady?"

"What do you mean?"

"Well, I think if a man is asking a woman out on a date, he should maybe look her in the eyes, instead of being fascinated with the light fixture over her head."

He immediately dropped his gaze, and his blue eyes lasered into hers. "I'm sorry, Naomi. I didn't mean to be disrespectful. It's just that it has been years, decades even, since I asked a lady out. I was sure if I looked into your beautiful eyes, I would get lost and forget what I was supposed to say."

The boyish honesty of his words charmed Naomi. "Well, since you put it like that, I guess I understand."

"Are you free on Saturday evening?" he asked. "It's the slowest supper night, and I thought it might be safest to leave Taffy and the boys here alone if it's not too busy. I can have all the food prepared for the steam table, and James is pretty good at grilling burgers and dropping fries, so they should be okay."

"I think I might be free on Saturday. Let me check my calendar to make sure there's nothing going on at school or church. I'll let you know in the morning, okay?"

"Okay."

They sat looking at each other, neither one speaking, their hands warm together on the counter between them for a long time. Eventually the silence became awkward, and they shifted on their stools.

Brady withdrew his hand and stood. "Well, um, can I walk you home?"

Naomi burst out laughing.

Brady looked offended. "What's so funny?"

"For three months I have been walking to the diner all

alone before dawn, and you never offered to pick me up or escort me; I mean it is only a block, so I didn't expect it. And now that we have a date, you offer to make sure I get home safe."

"So?"

"So, Brady," she stood up and walked around the end of the counter and put her hand on his shoulder, "I think it's very considerate, and I thank you. I think I can make it home okay." She picked up her purse from the end of the counter, slung it over her shoulder, and leaned over and kissed his cheek. "I like a chivalrous man." She walked out without looking back.

Brady watched her go, his thumbs hooked over his apron top, feeling that even though his business was in shambles, it had been a pretty good day. He whistled as he disposed of the pizza boxes, finished his soda, and made sure everything was locked up tight before he turned out the lights and left, double-checking the kitchen door lock before he got in his truck and drove home.

Naomi walked home in a fog, not the best idea for someone living in her neighborhood. But it wasn't too late, and the creatures of the night had barely stirred. She let herself into the apartment, called out for Marcus and was about to get angry when she noticed the note on the table. *Mom*, it said, *I'm spending the night at James's so we can watch a Star Wars marathon. You forgot, didn't you? See you tomorrow around noon. I'll stop at the diner on my way home. Love, Marcus.* She smiled; she had forgotten. She thanked God that she had raised her son to be such a good boy. He was still a typical fifteen-year-old, but listening to other parents at school functions, she said a little prayer that he stayed the good boy he was.

Keeping Marcus on the straight path was the only reason she had endured the slurs and criticism for staying on welfare that long from people around her. Not everyone was critical, of course, but many of the older parishioners at church had a few sharp things to say until she either told them to mind their own business or explained that her son's upbringing was more important than how she got money to live on. She assured all of them and herself at the same time that as soon as Marcus was off to college, she'd be first in line at the employment office. But now she didn't need to stand in any lines; she had a job. And one that made her feel like a real person. Fay and Brady treated her as if she were an equal part of the family at Better Than Mom's. Fay teased her about her cooking and her conservative wardrobe. Brady listened to her ideas for menu changes and seriously tasted any new recipes she suggested. It made her feel like a person, more than anything had in years, because at the diner she was no longer Marcus' mother or that lazy girl who was on welfare, she was Naomi who made the best biscuits in the county, maybe in the state, and the tastiest fried chicken anywhere.

Since Marcus was away for the night and it was only, she craned her neck to check the clock over the stove, nine-forty-five, Naomi treated herself to a bubble bath. It was not often that she had the time or the privacy to luxuriate in a tub of hot fragrant bubbles, not with an active and popular fifteen-year-old boy in the house who thought nothing of bringing over a few teammates for popcorn and movies. She felt pretty darned grubby after working all day cleaning up the mess in the diner, and a nice hot soaking bath would be just what she needed to soothe her aches and help her sleep. She rummaged in the back of her closet and unearthed a faded orange pillar candle that used to smell of exotic spices but now just smelled like fabric softener, but she plunked it in the middle of a saucer from the kitchen and lit it to lend a little atmosphere to her bath. Turning off the lights in the apartment except for the one over the sink, she drew her bath, tipping in a capful of bubble bath that Marcus had given her for Christmas the year before. She tuned the radio to a soft jazz station, stripped off her dirty, sweaty clothes, and settled carefully into the steamy water. She did her best to turn off her mind, leaned her head back on a towel and gave herself up to the sensations of the moment. The hot water seeped into her bones and made her tight muscles loosen. The flickering candlelight relaxed her, and the soft, sexy music seemed to dance along her spine, setting her toes to tapping on the faucet. She lay there breathing in the fragrant steam and imagined whirling around a starlit dance floor in a flowing gown made of dark red silk and chiffon in the arms of a graceful man in a tuxedo, palm trees swaying in the breeze. Palm trees? Where had that come from? She had never been out of the state of Wisconsin, so how had palm trees found their way into her dreams? And was that fantasy dancing partner wearing an apron? Her eyes popped open, and she glared at the cracked plaster in the bathroom corner. It wasn't until then that she realized that the station she had the radio tuned to was the same one Brady played all the time in the diner kitchen. No wonder her imaginary dancing partner was in an apron; she associated this music with Brady. She shook her head and settled back into the water, determined to keep him out of her dreams. At least until after their date.

The thought that the man in her dreams was Brady kept Naomi's eyes open and her mind whirling. She had never fantasized about a man like Brady. He was older than her by at least ten and probably fifteen years. He was shorter than she was, only by an inch or two, but still shorter, and if she wore heels that gap would widen. Did she have enough inner strength to stand up tall and endure the looks they would get? Stinson was not New York or even Chicago. Stinson was a small city of just under one hundred thousand people, and that included the surrounding rural areas some fools called suburbs. She first had to tell Marcus she was going out on Saturday with Brady, not on a real date, not a romantic date, just a friends date. Then, she would find out from Brady where he was planning to go so she could figure out what to wear, not too fancy, she hoped. She didn't like fancy food, none of that foo-foo sauce that hid the fact that the cook, oh excuse me, the chef used substandard raw ingredients. Her mama always said, Use fresh food and cook it so people can taste the goodness God put in it and you'll be fine. She didn't hold with heavy cream sauces or over-spicing her food. She liked to fix it so the person who ate it could taste what that food was supposed to taste like. Naomi often used a small squirt of fresh lemon juice, especially on fresh vegetables, to bring out the flavor. She was also a big fan of adding a pinch of a mixture of salt, ground cayenne pepper, and thyme to her dishes. It did not intrude on the food; it just brightened their flavor in ways she couldn't explain.

CHAPTER 11

Fay was curious about the bags the three old ladies carried in at lunch. The bags were flowered, typical old lady bags, but they were bulging with mysterious shapes and had wooden or metal sticks sticking out of them. The three were very specific about which table they were seated at, and each one carefully placed her bag at her feet. Fay took their orders and served them their cups of soup, each a different kind, and they asked to share an egg salad sandwich. She stood for a moment wondering how Brady would cut a square sandwich into thirds so each lady would get an equal share, but then she shrugged her shoulders thinking that was one problem she didn't have to deal with.

Two of the ladies had coffee, "high test," they both said, and the third, the oldest looking said she wanted a beer but would settle for the biggest Coke they had, and, she said, "put lots of ice in it, honey, I like to crunch ice."

Fay walked away wondering about them; they sure didn't seem like the run of the mill old ladies from the high-rise retirement apartments down the street who pinched their pennies and once a month treated themselves to a lunch at Better Than Mom's. I'm keeping an eye on those three, she thought, they're surely up to something. What three old ladies could get up to Fay was not really clear on, but she definitely thought they were suspicious. Over the course of their meal, she wondered if they hadn't stopped off at a bar for a little pre-lunch drink, especially the oldest one, who'd said she wanted a beer. The three women laughed through their light lunch, and every time Fay went past their table or stopped to see if they needed anything, she overheard or interrupted one of them telling a dirty joke. And not your average run of the mill old lady dirty joke about bathroom issues or flashers, nope, these old broads told the raunchiest jokes Fay had heard since the time she worked at a truck stop just off the Jersey Turnpike. Now, those truckers told jokes that would curl your nose hairs, but in Fay's opinion these three could have given those road-hardened men a run for their money.

She was appalled at herself when she realized she was standing next to their table, blatantly listening. Fay immediately turned away and began removing the dirty dishes from the booth at the end and wiping the table and seats. She was sure that none of the ladies had noticed until the youngest-looking one said, "Hey, miss, don't you want to hear the punch line?"

Fay, blushing bright pink, turned back toward their table, and said, "Actually, I do."

Then the woman said, "So the headwaiter says to the guy, 'With ze tongs.'" The other two women roared; Fay clapped her hand over her mouth to keep from doing the same.

She surveyed the trio of gray-haired women. "The three of you are bad." That made the customers laugh even harder. Once they had all settled down, Fay asked if she could clear away their dishes and refill their coffee and Coke. She came back with their fresh drinks, and then asked, "Are you ready for the bill?"

"Oh no, honey, you aren't getting rid of us that easy," said the oldest. "I'm Iris, by the way. I'm ninety-one," she said.

"This teenager is Dorothy; she's just seventy-six, and the baby, Patti, here is a ripe sixty-nine."

Fay nodded at each. "I'm Fay."

"We can still read, Fay," Dorothy said.

"Dotty, be nice," Patti said, "or you'll get us kicked out of here too."

Fay stood with one hand on her hip, a smile on her face. "So where have you been kicked out of, ladies?"

Iris flapped her hand as if it didn't matter. "Oh, just a couple of yarn shops run by good Christian women who wouldn't know a good joke if it jumped up and bit them in the ass and made the worst coffee in the county."

"Yarn shops?" Fay asked.

"Yep," Dorothy said, reaching into the bag at her feet and pulling out a heap of pink yarn. She sorted it out, lifted it up, and it turned into a cabled sweater back. "See? We're knitters. We like to get together once a week or so, show off our projects, complain about our problems, discuss our aches and pains, and tell a few jokes." She shook her head sadly. "Guess we're not welcome in polite society anymore. We're the current bad girls of knitting in Stinson."

Iris and Patti giggled like schoolgirls, evidently happy to be labeled bad girls.

Patti reached into her bag and showed Fay the butter-yellow seed stitch sweater she was knitting for her granddaughter. "It's going to have a cute orange ducky on the front. That is if I can figure out how this damned chart works." She leaned over and peered at the paper, frowning at what looked to Fay like a secret code.

"What does all that gibberish mean?" she asked.

"Oh, all knitting is variations on the two basic stitches," said Iris. "It's all either knit or purl or a combination of the two, or a variation like knit two together. It's not that hard."

Dorothy piped up. "Well, it couldn't be, could it, or you wouldn't be able to do it, Iris."

"Shut up, or I'll reach over and slap you silly," Iris said. "Of course, that would be redundant. You're already the silliest woman I have ever met."

Fay held her breath waiting for the explosion, but the three of them just looked at each other and started laughing again.

"Well, you ladies take your time. Have a nice afternoon. I'll bring your bill later on." She lifted the bus tub full of dishes and carted it back to the kitchen. "Hey, Brady," she said. "See those three old ladies in back?"

He nodded.

"They're staying for a while to knit. Keep an eye on them

while I grab some lunch, will you?"

"Sure," he said. "Those three come in every few months. They're a lot of fun."

Fay ladled out a cup of cream of mushroom soup and made herself half of a ham sandwich on rye. She perched on the end stool at the counter and read the paperback romance novel she carried to work in her purse.

"You are going to rot your brain reading that crap." She whirled around to see Iris standing next to her, her empty soda glass in her hand. "Do you mind if I nip back there and get a refill?"

Fay wiped her lips and hands with a napkin. "I'll get it for you, Iris."

"I don't want to interrupt your meal."

"That's okay. It'll only take me a second." She was back with the full glass in a jiffy. "Why don't you go sit down, and I'll carry this back to your table for you."

"I'm not so old and feeble that I can't carry my own drink," Iris said, but she turned to go back to her table.

"I know you're not," Fay said to her as they reached the table. "I'm doing this so I'll get a better tip."

"Oh, good one, Fay," Patti said. "Do you knit?"

Fay shook her head. "No, I never knew anybody who knitted."

"Do you want to learn how? It's all the rage these days, especially with young women like you," said Dorothy.

"Thanks for the compliment," said Fay, "but I'm not exactly young. I'll never see forty again, that's for sure."

"Hell, forty's young from where I sit," Iris said.

"From where all of us sit, as a matter of fact."

"Well, I'm working..."

Patti interrupted her. "What time do you get off?"

"Oh, two-thirty."

"If you want to learn to knit, come on over to the table after that. We'll still be going strong, and I know that among the three of us we have needles and yarn you can get started with.

How does that sound?"

"Sounds good." Fay looked at her watch. "I'll see you all in about forty-five minutes."

It was a little after two-thirty when Fay shyly sidled over to the table where the three women still sat, gray heads bent over clicking needles and mounds of colorful yarn. Only one of them was peering at a pattern; that made Faye a little intimidated.

Dorothy looked up as she hesitated. "There she is, the world's newest knitting fool."

"Well, a fool I can believe, but a knitting fool? I'm not so sure I can learn something that complicated," Fay said to her with an apologetic grimace.

"Don't be silly," said Iris. "In places like India, little, tiny children knit, and for pay too, so they can't just be goofing around. They have to earn money to support their families."

Patti nodded. "That's right. If little kids who can't even read can knit, you certainly can. Knitting is really just two basic stitches, like we said. We'll teach you the first one today, and you can practice. Next week we'll come to lunch again." She held up her hand to stop Iris from speaking. "Yes, we will, Iris. And we'll teach you the purl stitch. Once you have those two stitches mastered, you're home free. Every knitting pattern, no matter how complicated it looks, is just a bunch of variations on those two stitches." She scooted her chair over. "Here, pull up a chair and we'll get started."

Dorothy leaned across the table holding two pointy wooden sticks toward Fay. "I have some extra needles you can borrow. These are fairly inexpensive bamboo ones, so you don't have to worry about losing one; they are easily and cheaply replaced."

Fay took them. "Thanks, I'll take good care of them." She ran her fingers up and down the smooth needles. "Feels soft."

"I like how they feel in my hands too," Dorothy said. "Wait until you work with them. They're great, but you might find you like the wooden ones or even metal ones best. Every knitter is different."

Iris handed over a skein of sage-green yarn. "I had a few extras floating around at the bottom of my bag. It's a bit of wool left over from a sweater I made a while back. I don't know why it's still in my bag. It must have been waiting for today."

Fay shook her head. "Wool is scratchy. I don't think I want to knit with wool. I like soft things."

Iris pushed the yarn into her hand. "Oh, just take it. You can learn today with this and then get something softer later."

"Okay," Fay said, not wanting to hurt their feelings. She took the yarn. The three of them watched her face as she realized what she was holding, knowing smiles on them. "I, uh, Iris, you said this is wool, didn't you?"

"I did."

Fay lifted the ball of sage green yarn and smoothed it on her cheek. "It's not scratchy."

"No, it isn't."

"And it's wool."

"It's wool. Look at the label."

"Eighty-eight percent wool, twelve percent acrylic," Fay read aloud. She looked up at the faces smiling at her. "How come it isn't scratchy?"

Dorothy said, "Magic. Now let's get started. I'm so excited that you're learning to knit. Now we'll have someone else to bitch to. Iris, get her started."

Iris took one needle out of Fay's hand and pulled out a long bit of the yarn. She showed Fay how to make a slipknot and snugged it up, but not too tight, on the needle. She grasped both strands of yarn and split them with the thumb and forefinger of her left hand. "This is how you cast on," she said, doing a complicated-looking dance with the needle over, around, and through the two yarn strands, ending up with a stitch sliding onto the needle next to the slip knot loop.

"I don't think I can ever..." Fay said.

"Oh, for pity's sake, just try." Iris shoved the needle and yarn at her. She guided Fay's fingers around the yarn, then she stood behind Fay's chair and helped her learn the finger dance of casting on. "Don't pull the stitches too tight or you won't be able to get your needle in to make a stitch."

Once she understood what she was doing and why, with a few rounds of ripping out ("Knitters call it frogging, get it? Rip it, ribbit?") Fay got the hang of casting on pretty well.

"Why don't you pull it out and start over one more time?" said Patti. "Cast on twenty-five stitches and I'll get you started knitting."

The afternoon passed in a flash for Fay. After a few rows and a dropped stitch or two, she got the hang of it and had a good six inches of nearly even knitting by the time she looked up and realized that Taffy was getting the dining room ready for the supper crowd. "Holy cow, where did the afternoon go?"

Iris snorted. "See? And you thought you wouldn't enjoy knitting."

Fay turned to look her in the eye. "I'm still not convinced that I like this. I'm only doing it to humor you—and I admit I've been curious about knitting for a while. I'll practice and see how it goes." She gathered the needles and yarn, but before she put them in her capacious purse, said, "Are you two sure you want to let me borrow your needles and yarn? I can go down to the mall and get my own."

Patti piped up. "Nonsense. You have a start now. You don't want to frog that just to give Dotty back her cheap needles and Iris her leftover yarn. We'll be back next week to see how you did and teach you the next step."

Fay looked at the scrap of knitting in her lap. "Is there anything you can make with just the knit stitch?"

"Oh, honey, lots," Dorothy said. "It's called garter stitch and is probably the most used stitch. If you stop at a craft store, you'll find rows of books with beginner knitting patterns." She shoved her pink sweater into her bag. "Come on, girls, let's go. They need to get ready for the next wave of hungry people, and Fay has to go home and knit. See you in a week."

The three old ladies gathered up their knitting and

patterns, finally paid their lunch tab, and left, waving and laughing their way out the door.

Taffy watched them leave. "Who are those old bags?"

Fay straightened up and glared at her. "Don't call them old bags; they're my knitting friends."

"Knitting? I didn't know you could knit."

Fay's posture sagged. "Well, actually, they just started teaching me today, but I think I'm going to like it." She looked at the sage-green softness in her hand. "I think I'll walk over to the craft store in the mall before I go home. Bye."

"Be careful in that store," Taffy said.

"Why?"

"I scrapbook with my mom. We always spend more than we mean to over there. I think they put some sort of chemical in the air that makes you spend your money."

Fay looked shocked, but when she saw the grin on Taffy's face, she smiled too. "I'll remember. Thanks for the warning."

CHAPTER 12

Officer Norman Bates came into Better Than Mom's and asked Taffy if he could see Brady.

Brady came out of the kitchen, wiping his hands on his apron. "You need to talk to me, Officer?"

Bates looked at the diners scattered around the place. "Can we go to your office?"

"Sure."

The two men got settled in the tiny office, Brady behind the desk and Bates in the side chair.

"What can I do for you?" Brady said.

Officer Bates pulled out his notebook and flipped through the pages. "Do you know a man named Thomas Morrison?"

Brady shook his head. "No, I don't think so. Maybe I'd recognize him if I saw him. Some customers I never know their names. Why?"

Checking his notes, Bates said, "It seems he has been bragging that he and some friends wrecked a business a few weeks ago, and this is the only vandalism call we've had lately. Are you sure you haven't thrown someone out or fired someone?"

Brady kept shaking his head. "I fired my assistant months ago, but he was okay with it. He comes in for lunch every once in a while. He got another job at a gas station right away and says he likes it better than cooking. His name isn't Thomas... Morrison, did you say?"

"Yes, Morrison. What is his name just in case he's connected to Morrison?"

Brady frowned. "I don't think..."

"I know he's probably not involved, but give me his name so I can eliminate him."

"I gave it to you the day of the vandalism, but I'll give it to you again. Ed. His name is Edward Wilson. I just don't think Ed would do something like that."

Officer Bates wrote the name in his notebook, closed it, and put it away.

"So, you think this Morrison might have had something to do with my vandalism?" Brady asked.

"Maybe. It could just be big talk, taking credit for someone else's crime, but I'll keep at it. Thanks, Brady." He got up to leave and paused in the doorway. "Say, when does that redheaded waitress work?"

Brady's head came up, and he kept his face blank. "Fay? Fay works from open at six until two-thirty in the afternoon. I think she's still here at the back table with a group of older ladies. You could walk back to see her if you'd like."

Officer Bates brushed aside the offer. "No, I was just curious, that's all." He hitched up his belt and walked back through the swinging doors and out of the diner.

Brady walked over to Naomi. "Well, I'll be darned."

'What? Did he solve the crime?"

"Maybe, but he asked about Fay, so maybe he's interested in her."

"Wouldn't that be something?"

Taffy came to the pass-through. "Order up."

Brady got back to business.

Friday came, and Fay wondered what had happened between Brady and Naomi after she left the diner when they got done cleaning up the vandalism mess. They had opened the next morning as Brady had hoped, but it seemed to Fay that the two of them were treating each other with kid gloves, like they'd had a fight or something.

She leaned over Naomi's shoulder as she worked on chopping celery and carrots for the day's soup. "Did you and

Brady have a fight?"

"No. Whatever gave you that idea?" Naomi glanced at her without missing a beat.

"I don't know. You two have seemed different since the other night, that's all. I thought maybe you argued about something or something."

"No, we didn't." Naomi looked around to make sure Brady couldn't hear her.

Fay went through the swinging doors into the diner to get set up for the day.

Brady turned to Naomi. "What's gotten into her?"

"I think she has the hots for Officer Bates. She was just telling me how cute she thinks he is."

"Bates?"

"Yep. No accounting for taste, is there?"

"So, what's so funny about his name?"

Naomi smiled so that her eyes twinkled. "Remember the movie *Psycho*?"

Brady shook his head. "Never saw it."

"Well, the main character is named Norman Bates; he keeps his mummified mother in the basement, and murders Janet Leigh. We'll have to watch it sometime; it's a classic Hitchcock film."

"Oh, okay." Brady walked over to the stove and stirred each kind of soup, stopping right next to where Naomi was working. "I was thinking we should go to Prime Quarter tomorrow night. They have great steaks, you get to grill them the way you like them, it's not too expensive, I knew you'd object to a fancy place, and we can wear jeans. Okay?"

Naomi's shoulders relaxed; she didn't even know she had been tensing them. "That'll be fine. You're right, I worried that you'd choose someplace too fancy, and I wouldn't have the right clothes."

"I thought we'd have a better time if we just got to know each other better, you know, talked, before we went someplace fancy."

"What time?"

Brady looked at the clock as if he would find a hint there. "Oh, how does six o'clock work for you?"

"Works fine. Marcus should be here working, so he won't be lurking around the apartment when you come pick me up. You are planning to come to the door, right?"

Brady looked offended. "Of course, I am. A gentleman doesn't ask a lady out on a date and then sit in his car and toot the horn, so she comes running out. A gentleman rings the bell and escorts her to his car."

"Good. I'll see you around six o'clock tomorrow then."

"Six o'clock."

Naomi got back to her chopping, and Brady went back to the grill, both of them feeling much better about their date later.

It took Naomi an hour to decide what to wear. Even though Brady had told her where they were going, even though she knew it was not a fancy place, even though she saw Brady five days a week at four-thirty in the morning when no one was at their best, she still was nervous about not being dressed right.

On Friday night, she told Fay that she and Brady were going to dinner on Saturday. She had gone down to Fay's apartment with a plate of barbecued pork fried rice for Fay's supper, and when Fay answered the door, she was amazed to see her friend's hair all messy. Fay's hair was never messy. Naomi was convinced that she used an entire aerosol can of Aqua Net every single day to glue her hair into its retro sixties party curls 'do. No amount of weather could force that hair to move; it stayed put through humid days and downpours, through blizzards and driving winds. Naomi wondered if there was so much hair spray on it that it might not burst into spontaneous flames in the heat of summer.

"What are you doing to yourself?" she asked in amazement when she saw Fay's disheveled appearance.

"I'm knitting." Fay stepped back from the door, and Naomi could see that she held a pair of metal knitting needles and trailed a long string of fuchsia, orange, and blood red yarn behind her. "Come on in."

Naomi waved the food under Fay's nose. "I made fried rice; come eat before it gets cold." She walked into the kitchen, assuming that Fay was following her. "You got any soy sauce? If you don't, I have some in my pocket."

No one answered. She couldn't hear footsteps behind her.

She turned to see that Fay had sat right back down on the ratty couch and was hunched over the yarn and needles, chanting through gritted teeth, "Knit two, purl two, knit three, slip, slip, knit the slipped stitches together..." as she read out the instructions from a book laying open on the coffee table; then, "dammit," and ripped out the stitches she had just made and start over.

Naomi stood in the doorway, hands on hips, shaking her head. "You're going to break a tooth if you keep grinding your teeth like that. Come on in here and eat the supper that I made for you."

When Fay didn't get up or even acknowledge that she had heard, Naomi walked over to her and put her hand gently on the pattern. "Honey, step away from the knitting. You're going to give yourself a stroke."

"I have to get this first."

Naomi sat down next to her friend, put her arm around her shoulders, which felt as tight as guy wires, and said softly, "This is not how knitting is supposed to be. Those ladies in the diner were laughing and joking, not gritting their teeth, and swearing."

"I know I can get this; I know I can. Just give me a minute."

"No, no more minutes until you eat something." Naomi gently took the metal knitting needles away and laid them on the coffee table, careful not to disturb the three stitches that were all that was left from Fay's latest knitting attempt. Then she slid her hand up under Fay's arm and lifted her to her feet as she stood up. She kept her hand on Fay as she led her, almost like a sleepwalker, into the kitchen and deposited her in the chair in front of the still steaming plate of food.

Fay's nose dipped into the fragrant steam. "Mm, that smells great. What is it?" Naomi got a pair of Cokes from the refrigerator and opened them both, placing one in front of Fay and keeping the other for herself.

"It's barbecued pork fried rice, just like I said when I came in."

"Oh, I didn't hear you."

"I know you didn't. You were too busy swearing at that poor defenseless yarn. You need soy sauce?" She dipped a hand into the pocket of her shirt and took out a few soy sauce packets left over from her last visit to Yong Foo's Chinese Takeout down the street.

"Mm, yeah." Fay dropped her fork and squirted one packet onto her plate of food. "This is terrific. How did you learn to make such good Chinese food? You don't look Chinese to me."

Naomi sipped her Coke. "Ha, ha, very funny. But wouldn't you feel silly if it turned out I was adopted, and my daddy was Chinese?"

Fay looked up, a frown creasing her brow. "What…?"

"Oh, get serious. I was only kidding. So, tell me about learning to knit. I see you're having a lot of success with it."

Fay swallowed her mouthful of food and sipped her Coke. "Well, I stopped at the craft store on my way home from work the other day, and they had all their knitting needles and books and yarn, well, some of the yarn, on sale. I looked through the books to find a beginner's book and found this one, *The Cool Girl's Guide to Knitting,* by this woman, Nicki Trench. The whole front half of the book is full of how to make all the stitches with pictures that make it look so easy, and the back half is patterns of how to make stuff." She forked some more rice. "This is really good, Naomi. Anyway, I was already getting tired of just knitting back and forth, so I decided to find the easiest pattern possible and get some yarn and some needles and try it."

"Couldn't you use the yarn and needles you got from the knitting ladies?"

Fay shook her head. "Nope. First off, I didn't want them to know I was doing it because Patti told me to just practice the knit stitch all week and next week, she'll teach me to purl, but it was boring just going back and forth, knit, knit, knit to the end, swap hands, scoop up the yarn, and knit, knit, knit back. Besides, they have all kinds of yarn that is way cheaper than the wool stuff Iris gave me. Did you know that?" She didn't wait for Naomi to answer but kept on talking. "I found all sorts of multicolored stuff, knitters call it variegated, in a zillion colors. I picked out a few skeins of acrylic, it goes in the washer and the dryer, which is much better, I think. And then I read the pattern I picked out and got the right size needles, but instead of the expensive bamboo ones (they are six dollars a pair, if you can believe it, for bamboo sticks!), I got metal. They are way cheaper, two forty-nine a pair, and they come in bright, pretty colors. You know I like bright colors."

"Yes, I know you do."

"I just loaded up my cart with all these skeins of colors and the book and a couple different sizes of needles."

"So, what's the problem? Did you pick a pattern that was too hard?"

Fay shook her head as she finished the last bite of her supper and cleared her mouth with a sip of Coke. "No, I don't think so. It's just rows of knitting with a few variations that the Cool Girl explains clearly. No, I'm coming to think that the problem is the yarn or the needles. The needles are too slick; my stitches keep jumping off when they get close to the tip, and the yarn feels kind of sticky in my hand, not smooth like the wool. I don't know. Maybe I'm just too stupid and awkward to knit. But I think I might like it if I ever learn how. I could make mittens, or hats, or scarves for winter. I could even make some for the women's center. Those ladies you are always going on about lately could probably use something warm that somebody made for them or their kids." She peeked at Naomi from under her lashes as if afraid she had said something wrong.

Naomi looked at her with a big smile on her face. "That's a

wonderful idea, Fay. I'm sure the ladies down there would really appreciate a handmade knit hat or scarf. I don't think you are stupid at all, and I'm sure everyone feels like you do when they start. Those ladies had a good reason to start you off with quality equipment; it sounds to me like it's easier to work with. Maybe you should put your purchases aside until you have learned a little more and practiced with the good stuff. Then you might make the stuff you can afford work. Now, I have something I want to tell you."

She looked around the room as if checking for bugs.

Fay was intrigued. "What?"

Naomi twisted her hands as if she were opening a jar. "Well, you remember the other night after we cleaned up the diner?"

Fay nodded.

"And you left, but I stayed to help Brady finish up?"

Fay nodded again.

"Well, he, um, I, um…"

"What? Don't keep beating around the bush. I imagine all sorts of awful stuff. Is what you have to tell me awful?"

"Oh, no. No, it's good. I think." She paused.

"Well? What is it? I'm dying of curiosity here."

Naomi drew a deep breath and sat up straighter. "Brady asked me out to dinner tomorrow night, and I accepted."

Fay whooped. "I knew it. I knew it. I knew you two were eyeing each other up. Oh, I wish I had made a betting book on this. I was sure the two of you would end up dating." She jumped out of her chair to dance around the kitchen for a minute, then she sat back down and leaned across toward her friend. "So? Where is he taking you? What are you going to wear? Tell, tell."

Naomi had watched Fay's gyrations with amazement. Now she found it hard to know what to say. "Well, he wants to go to the Prime Quarter…"

"That's not a very fancy place," Fay interrupted.

"We don't want to go to a fancy place for a first date. We decided, well, he decided Prime Quarter is more a place to go and get acquainted, you know, like friends. If we decide to go on more dates, we can find someplace fancier. This way we can wear jeans and a nice shirt and be comfortable while we grill our steaks and have a drink or two. Plus, it's not very expensive; we can afford it."

It did not escape Fay's attention that Naomi had just said "We can afford it." That little "we" stood out a mile, as if Naomi was already thinking of Brady and herself as a couple. She couldn't help but chortle at the deliciousness of a new romance growing right under her nose. "This will be fun to watch," she said, rubbing her hands together.

Looking at her friend, Naomi thought she might have made a mistake in telling Fay about her date before it happened.

"I don't want you spreading around the news that Brady and I are going on this date, Fay. I don't want to listen to lip from Raymond and the rest of the coffee codgers every time I poke my head out of the kitchen, okay?"

Fay was too excited to really hear what Naomi said; she was already planning how she could let everyone know without Naomi finding out. "Yeah, yeah, I won't tell."

"Promise?"

Fay stopped rubbing her hands together and looked, really looked at Naomi. "Um, yes, I promise." Fay wracked her brain for a way to phrase what she wanted to know most of all. "Do you plan to make a night of it?"

Naomi looked at her as if she were nuts. "Well, I'm not going to schedule another date for after ten o'clock. What are you thinking?"

"Oh, no, no, I don't mean, are you going to have another date."

"Well, what do you mean then?"

Now it was Fay's turn to wring her hands. "I, well, I, uh, was just wondering if you and Brady were going to, well, you know…"

Naomi drew herself up to her full height, seeming to tower over the table and the now abashed Fay. "If you mean, am I planning to sleep with Brady, my boss, on our first date, all I can say is you should be ashamed of yourself." She raised her fist and shook an admonishing finger at her friend. "Shame on you, Fay, for even thinking that a moral, upstanding woman like me with a young, impressionable son in her house would even consider acting like that. How would Marcus feel to see his mother, his mother for Pete's sake, having such a low opinion of herself that she would be so trashy as to have sex with a man on their first date? This isn't the seventies, you know."

A nervous giggle escaped Fay's lips. "You wouldn't sleep with Brady? He's awfully cute sometimes. And you like him."

Naomi sorrowfully shook her head at her friend. "No wonder you have problems keeping a man. If you're giving it away on the first date, what motivation does a man have to be on his best behavior?"

"None, I guess."

"Exactly. None. My mama, God rest her soul, always said a woman needed to have enough self-control and self-respect for both her and whatever man she was keeping company with."

"And you always listened to your mama, right?"

"You know I didn't, otherwise I wouldn't have Marcus. But even then, I didn't put out on the first date."

"Second?"

"No, Miss Smarty Pants, not even on the second. It was at least three months into our relationship when we made love."

Fay leaned back and crossed her thin arms across her narrow chest. "Made love, huh? Not had sex in the back seat of his Chevy?"

"No, Marcus was not conceived in the back seat of a car. We were in a proper bed in his apartment."

"After he got you drunk?"

"Good grief, you have a low opinion of me."

Fay was honestly astonished. "What do you mean?"

"I mean, you think that I would have had to have gotten drunk before I would have had intercourse with a man I loved and who I thought loved me. That you have an image of me as an uptight woman who doesn't know how to have fun."

"Well, the only fun I've ever heard you talk about was how much you enjoy choir practice at church. Boy, that sounds like loads of fun."

Naomi laughed at how disgusted she sounded. "You've never been in a choir, have you?"

Fay shook her head no.

"Well, they're just like any other group of people; there are all sorts, quiet ones and loud ones, devout ones and profane ones, idealists and cynics, and every choir has to have at least one woman who can't carry a tune in a bucket, and ours is Glory Bea Sweeney."

"Great name."

"Yeah, she's a piece of work. She volunteers to be the director, and she's tone deaf. Personally, I think she has a big crush on Pastor Lawson."

"Oh yeah? Is he cute?"

Naomi thought about the question for a minute. "I suppose he is if you like tall, skinny men who can only talk about the Bible and have no other conversation. I mean, I like the man, but can you say, 'one dimensional'?"

"So, you still haven't said what's so fun about being in a choir."

"Well, someone is always telling a joke or making fun of someone. Usually, a couple of the men sing different lyrics from what is written."

"Oh, big whoop."

"No, you don't understand; the lyrics they make up are, uh, slightly, oh, let us say, suggestive."

A big smile lit up Fay's face. "You mean some guys in the choir make up dirty words that they sing? In church?"

"Yes, they do sometimes."

"And no one gets angry about it?"

"Oh, Glory Bea gets mad every once in a while, but even she has a little sense of humor and will crack a smile sometimes."

"What does the pastor say about that?"

"The pastor does not attend the choir practices. He hears us only during the service or if he stops over at the church when we are there." She snorted. "Or if Miss Glory Bea specially invites him to come over. Then she simpers around him like he is the messiah, smiling up at him like the sun shines out of his hind end, and braying out her annoying laugh at every even remotely funny thing he says. It is enough to give me gas."

"Well, that sure sounds like fun. How did I ever miss the good times of choir practice? Oh, maybe because I have been in a church only once in my entire life."

Now it was Naomi's turn to be astonished. "You've only been to church once in your whole life?"

"That's right. Once."

"I feel like I have spent over half of my life in church. I hated it when I was a child, getting all dressed up on Sunday morning in a scratchy dress that I couldn't play in. Mama always bought me the frilliest dresses with lots of petticoats and a lace collar that she would starch until it felt like barbed wire around my neck. She would braid my hair on Saturday night, pulling on it so hard to get it just right that I thought she was going to pull it out. She wrapped each braid in toilet paper before I went to bed, so all her work did not fuzz out while I slept."

"Holy cow."

"Exactly. I had socks with lace ruffles and black patent leather shoes that showed every speck of dust. Mama was always handing me her hankie to wipe them off, so they stayed shiny. Drove her nuts that I couldn't walk the seven blocks to church without getting dust on my shoes. We lived in rural Wisconsin, for God's sake. There was dust everywhere."

Fay shook her head as if she could not even imagine a life like that.

"What was it like when you were a girl?" Naomi asked.

Fay rubbed her hand over her lips. "Well. Are you sure you want to hear about my childhood?"

"Yes, I do. Why?"

Fay shrugged shoulders that looked a lot like a wooden hanger in a t-shirt. "No real reason. I just never thought it was very interesting. But here goes. We lived in a small mill town in upstate New York, where my dad worked as a mechanic in the mill and Ma was a slut."

"What?"

Fay stuck her chin out in defiance of her friend's amazement. "My ma was the town punch, the slut, round heels, mattress back, whatever you called them where you grew up. Dad worked at the mill odd hours, sometimes around the clock, and when he got off, he went out drinking with his buddies. He usually drank up most of his paycheck, so Ma took up hooking to pay the bills. There weren't any jobs for uneducated women in our town that were not in the mill, and Ma always said that one person in the family spending his life in that hellhole of a place was enough."

Naomi's voice was very small. "And your dad didn't know? About what your mom did, I mean?"

Fay's laugh was harsh. "Of course, he knew. He chose not to mind. And he didn't want his buddies to know that his wife had signed up for the dole. That is what we called welfare where I'm from. So, he pretended Ma was especially popular, and she pretended that the money she got for it was gifts. Gifts from admirers, she always called it. Filthy dirty money that cost all her self-respect and paid the bills. That filthy money bought my school clothes and Christmas toys and my one and only prom dress. It even paid for Dad's funeral when he had a heart attack at the tavern one night." She swiped her hand across her face, smearing the mascara that was running down her cheeks. "Ma was mad that he had waited to die until he got to the bar. 'Why the son of a bitch couldn't croak at the mill so they would pay for his funeral, I do not know,' is what she said after we got home from the cemetery. That was the last time I ever saw my Aunt Eunice and Uncle Arnie; she was Dad's sister. I guess she overheard Ma, or someone told her about the hooking, because when she left that day, she gave me a hug and slipped me a fifty-dollar bill. 'Don't tell your ma you got this, you hear?' she said. 'Yes, ma'am,' I said. I knew why. She hugged me again, and they left. That was the last time I saw them, and the funeral was the only time I was in a church."

CHAPTER 13

Officer Bates parked his truck outside Better Than Mom's. He noticed Brady had replaced the broken planters, and that there were new geraniums blooming happily in them. He also noticed, and approved of, the metal grids that had been bolted over the windows; the bars were far enough apart that customers wouldn't feel like they were in jail but close enough together that Officer Bates thought that even he, skinny as he was, would have trouble getting through them. Norman hitched up his pants and went inside, hoping that Fay had not gone home for the day. As soon as he got through the door and dodged a clutch of gray-haired ladies leaving, he saw the flash of her piled-up red hair and gave a sigh of relief. He had wagered with himself that she worked through the lunch hour until the supper waitress got off from college. He had stopped in a few days after the break-in to see Fay, but he was too late. A week passed, and he couldn't think of any other way to bump into Fay so he could maybe ask her on a date. A date. He hadn't been on a date in years. He gave up trying to find Miss Right when he hit thirty-eight years old and since then had settled for a series of Miss Right for Now's, each of whom had something he wanted in a wife, but none of them came close to having it all. Or maybe all his years as a cop had made him a cynic, and he would never find the right woman to spend the dwindling rest of his life with. He shook his head and found a seat at the counter so he could watch Fay work without looking like a stalker.

She was busy at the cash register talking to a geeky-looking guy carrying a briefcase. They sounded pretty friendly; he wondered if they were dating. There, that sounded like an inside joke laugh. Yeah, they were probably dating, even though the guy didn't look like Fay's type; that pals-y laugh made it sound like it. He was sitting there brooding about maybe missing his chance to ask her out when she suddenly appeared right in front of him.

"Well, if it isn't Officer Norman Bates, the super sleuth." She slapped a menu down in front of him; the metal corners of the plastic holder sounded like caps when they hit the Formica counter. "Rustled up any good clues lately?" He picked up the menu and didn't look at her.

"Nope, and call me Norm."

He frowned at the plastic-covered paper in his hand as if it had offended him. Stupid, he thought, stupid line. How dopey can he get to just say 'nope' when she gave him the perfect opening? He could see, if he peeked up under his lowered brows, that she was standing in front of him, order pad and pencil ready to take his lunch order.

"Mm, I think that today I'll have a bowl of soup and a turkey club."

"What kind of soup would you like, sir? We have cream of mushroom, which is the cream soup of the day; hearty beef and tomato made with the freshest tomatoes handpicked before dawn; and chunky vegetable, which is our vegetarian selection of the day."

"Is the cream of mushroom homemade?"

She drew herself up in offense. "All our soups are homemade every day, sir. Indeed, all of our menu items are made fresh daily."

"Oh, okay."

"What variety of bread would you like? We have white, whole wheat, and marble rye for your pleasure today."

"Rye, please."

"And to drink?"

"I will have a glass of iced tea, no lemon."

"Sweet or regular tea?"

"Sweet."

She turned away to put in his order, pushing her pencil behind her right ear as she went.

Norman stared after her as she swung her hips as she walked like she knew he was watching. He snapped back when someone elbowed him in the ribs.

"Don't mind Fay," Raymond said. "She's been spending time with Stevie the scribbler these days."

"What?" Norman felt as if he were coming in in the middle of a conversation.

"You were wondering why she was talking all formal like that, weren't you?"

Norman had not noticed, being too busy trying to keep his cool. "Yeah. How come she was talking like that?"

Raymond made a disgusted sound. "I told you; she's been sitting back there talking to Stevie. Steve's a writer; it turns out he writes some popular historical romance novels. Fay pried it out of him a couple of weeks ago, and she and he have been kind of chummy ever since. I sit here and watch the two of them in that back booth, and I don't think I ever saw old Stevie talk so much." Raymond nodded toward the back of the room. "He used to work for me when I was president of the mill, you know."

Norman looked at the older man with a small understanding smile. "Yeah, I know."

He remembered how hard it had been for his old man when he retired from being a cop. One day you're patrolling town with a gun on your hip, keeping the world your family lives in safe, and the next day you are shuffling around the house in slippers and a stretched-out cardigan getting in your wife's way. He had heard that Raymond's wife had only stood about a month of him being retired before she divorced him, took half of his money, most of his furniture, and all of his brand-new pearl-gray Lexus four-door sedan, and skedaddled off to Arizona. So, he supposed old Raymond still hadn't gotten over being in charge of everything around him, especially now that he didn't even have a wife to boss around.

"Do you think that Fay and Steve are dating?" Norman

asked Raymond.

"No, I don't," Raymond said. "I think if they were Fay wouldn't be as nice to him as she is."

"What do you mean?"

"I mean, I think Fay is the kind of woman who is all peaches and cream when she's flirting with you and once she has you good and hooked she turns into a, well, a witch, if you know what I mean."

Norman looked at Fay striding around the diner, refilling water glasses and coffee mugs, delivering plates of food or clearing dishes off tables. She seemed good-humored with all the customers, not witch-y at all.

"Really? I thought she was a little witch-y all the time, especially with me, but nice to everyone else."

Raymond leaned back as if he needed to get a better look at Norman. "She has already started being a witch to you?"

"Well, she had some pretty sharp things to say to me when I was investigating the break-in here. And you heard how she ribbed me about not finding any clues when I came in."

"Yeah."

"So, I was thinking she didn't like me."

Raymond chuckled. "Oh no, my friend, I think from what I've learned about Fay since she started working here that it means she finds you interesting. I'd think about asking her out if I were you."

"I just might," Norman said as he saw Fay coming toward him, a bowl of steaming soup in one hand and a plate with a sandwich on it in the other.

She plunked them down in front of him and said, "Can I freshen your tea?"

"That would be fine," he said. "This smells wonderful. Did you make the soup?"

Fay laughed. "No, micro zapping frozen burritos is about the extent of my culinary talents. Enjoy your lunch."

Norman dug into the soup; it was as tasty as it smelled, and the turkey club sandwich was excellent.

"Nice start," Raymond said quietly.

Not wanting to spray the old guy with food, Norman finished chewing and swallowed before he said, "What?"

"I thought that your complimenting her on the food right away was a good start to getting up the guts to ask her out, that's all."

"Ah, thanks. I'll keep working on it."

CHAPTER 14

Norman stopped at the diner for lunch two more times that week and a couple more times the following week. Each time he sat in a different place at the counter, away from where Raymond sat, and each time the old man picked up his coffee mug and moved to sit next to Norman. After the first time it happened, Norman tried to think of a way to tell Raymond to leave him alone, that he'd never have the nerve to ask Fay out with him sitting right next to him, ears flapping like Dumbo to hear every word. Finally, at the end of the second week, Norman was relieved to see that Raymond was nowhere in sight when he entered Better Than Mom's. He sat down at the counter, more relaxed than he had been in days. With a slight smile on his face, he watched Fay zooming around at the tail end of the lunch rush. When she finally got to him, she was just slightly out of breath and her cheeks were flushed.

"Well, you're a little early today, Norman."

He chuckled. "The chief hired a new patrolman, and he's eager to get on the road. He came to work a whole hour early today, so they let me leave early because I have seniority."

"Well, that's nice of them. What'll it be?"

He glanced at the chalkboard over the pass-through to see what the soups were that day—creamy broccoli and cheese, chicken vegetable noodle, and Jamaican pumpkin soup. "I'll have a bowl of the Jamaican pumpkin soup and a chicken salad sandwich on whole wheat toast."

Fay was writing on her pad. "Sweet tea today, as usual?"

"That'll be fine," he said, feeling that today would be his lucky day when she flashed him her biggest smile as she turned to put in his order.

His bowl of Jamaican pumpkin soup and chicken salad sandwich were as excellent as always. The soup was rich with butter and cream and fragrant with butternut squash.

"Hey, Fay," he said when she came to ask how his food was. "I thought this was supposed to be vegetarian soup." He raised his soup spoon as if she might not know what soup he referred to.

"It is, there's no meat in there."

"But doesn't it have butter and cream, which come from animals?"

She smiled at his persistence. "Yes, as a matter of fact, it does. This is vegetarian soup, no meat, not vegan soup which would have no animal products at all." She filled his glass with tea. "How is everything?"

He smiled what he hoped was a winning smile. "Everything's delicious."

"Good."

She turned away and worked her way down the counter on his side and back up the other side, handing out bills, filling glasses, and flirting her way to bigger tips as she went.

Today, without the intimidating presence of Raymond, Norman felt as if he could finally ask Fay out. He waited until he was finished with his soup and sandwich and had devoured a piece of the best blueberry pie he thought he had ever had, before he sat back from the counter, drained his glass, and signaled to Fay that he would like a refill. She leaned on the counter after filling his glass, like she was ready to talk a while. The lunch rush was over; there were only two other diners in the place, and, to Norman's relief, they were sitting in a booth far down the length of the building talking in low tones, too far away to hear what he planned to say.

"How'd you like the pie?" she asked.

"I have to say that was the best blueberry pie I have ever eaten," he said.

She smiled and said, "I'll tell Naomi how much you liked

it." She motioned to the stack of go boxes on the counter under the pass-through. "I could box a piece up for you to take home for after supper if you'd like." She straightened as if to do as she proposed.

Norman saw his opening, and for the first time in his life, slid gracefully into it. "Well, I was wondering if you might like to have supper with me tonight. I know it's late notice, and I'll understand if you have plans, but I thought we could grab a bite and maybe a drink or two. Get to know each other a bit."

Fay looked him up and down as if he were a side of beef or a used car she was considering buying. She looked at her watch as if she had some place to be right at that very minute. "Man, it is kind of late, almost two o'clock." She crossed her arms and looked appraisingly back at him. "I don't have any plans tonight. I suppose I could be convinced to have supper with you." She glanced over her shoulder to check how the diners in the far booth were doing. They were still leaning toward each other, immersed in their conversation. She shrugged her shoulders as if to say, no problem over there, and turned back to face Norman. By now the suspense was killing him. "Yeah, sure, let's have supper together tonight. I guess that's not really the way it is supposed to go, but yes, I'd like to have supper with you, Norman."

"What do you mean it's not the way it's supposed to go?"

"Well, isn't the lady supposed to play hard to get before she agrees to go out with the man? Isn't she supposed to be busy, even if she has to pretend, the first few times he asks her out?"

Norman smiled back at her. "I don't know, Fay. I didn't get the dating handbook that I was convinced the girls got in health class in high school. None of the boys I knew had any clue about dating and what girls were thinking. The girls always seemed to share some secret knowledge and knew how to string us along."

Fay laughed as if what he said was the funniest thing she had heard in weeks. "You know, you might be right. All of us girls talked about was boys and how to get them to notice us and how to behave to make them take us out and still respect us. I suppose all the boys talked about was sports."

Norman leaned across the counter to whisper. "And we also talked about ways to peek into the girls' locker room when Elsie May Brown was changing. My, my, she was every boy's dream. A knockout in a sweater and everyone was panting to know what she looked like in her underwear."

Fay could hear the wistfulness in his voice. "And did you ever get that peek?"

He looked at her expression to see how she was taking this conversation subject. She looked amused rather than offended, so he continued. "You know, I did once. I was passing her house on my way home from a friend's one night when I was, oh, probably a junior, and Elsie May was in her bedroom changing. The curtains were drawn, but there was a gap where one had caught on something. I glanced in and stopped dead right there on the sidewalk. There she stood in all her blond glory, stripped down to her bra and panties, brushing her hair." He sighed.

Fay laughed and said, "I'd bet ten dollars that her curtain had not caught on anything. That she had arranged it like that in case someone just like you would walk by so that they would get an eyeful."

"Do you really think so?"

"I do. Norman, women are sly, calculating creatures who plan and manipulate men to their own ends." She crossed her arms over her chest. "Do you still want to go out with me after I said that?"

Norman reached out and ran his hand softly down her upper arm and stopped, holding her arm lightly just above the elbow. "Of course, I do. It's taken me nearly three weeks to muster up the guts to ask you. I won't let a few words get in my way." He could feel her muscles relax. It surprised him to discover that she was nervous too.

"Good. What time?" They spent the next few minutes discussing what time she got off work and where they would go. They settled on a small country bar and supper club that had live music on Saturdays; the place was well known for having great pan-fried steaks.

Norman tossed a couple of bucks on the counter for a tip, paid his bill, and stuck a toothpick between his teeth. "See you at six-thirty, Fay. I'm looking forward to finally having the chance to get to know you better." He winked at her, a surprisingly attractive wink that accentuated the twinkle in his eye that Fay had never noticed before.

She felt herself blushing, and she peeked at him from under her lashes. "Bye, Norman, see you at six-thirty."

CHAPTER 15

Brady stood outside Naomi's door trying to muster up the guts to ring the bell. How foolish he felt being nervous to go to supper with a woman in whose company he spent most of his days. He wiped his hands down his jeans once more, took a deep breath, and pressed the bell. He could hear the buzz inside and Marcus yell, "I'll get it, Mom." He heard the deadbolt snap open and the rattle of the security chain as it was removed from the door.

Marcus was frowning as he opened the door to Brady, his boss too. "Have you come to pick up my mother, young man?" he said in imitation of the stereotype of a father greeting his daughter's date.

Brady was too nervous to do more than smile.

Marcus opened the door wide and said, "Come on in, Brady. I'm glad to have this opportunity to talk to you about your intentions." He motioned for the older man to sit on the couch and sat down himself in a recliner. He picked up the remote and muted the sound on the television. "So," Marcus said, "where are you planning to take Naomi for supper? Someplace nice, I assume?"

Brady sat, like every other man/boy on his first date confronted by the son/father of the girl he liked, on the edge of his seat, his forearms resting on his thighs and his hands clasped so tight that his fingers were white. "I thought we'd go to the Prime Quarter; I heard they have very good meat there, and I thought we could get better acquainted in a place that doesn't have loud music and... oh for heaven's sake, Marcus, what are you doing to me? And why aren't you at work?"

Marcus laughed. "I'm on my supper break. I'm just jerking you around a bit, Brady. Too bad you never had a daughter; you'd recognize the third degree when you saw it. I can't count the number of times I've sat with some girl's daddy letting him think he was intimidating me so that I would behave respectfully to his daughter. As if my mom would tolerate my not being a gentleman."

"You go on dates?"

"Of course, I do."

"But you are only fourteen, right?"

"I'm fifteen now, remember? You made me wait until my fifteenth birthday before you would let me come to work for you."

Now Brady sat back and unclasped his hands. "It wasn't me; the city has an ordinance that you have to be fifteen to get a work permit; that's why I made you wait."

It was Marcus' turn to fold his arms over his chest. "What time do you plan to have Naomi home by? You know she needs to get up in time for church tomorrow. Don't be keeping her out until all hours or buying her too many drinks."

"I won't, I won't. Hey, what kind of drink does your mom like, anyway? I could impress her by already knowing that about her." He looked around. "What's taking her so long? You don't think she changed her mind about going out with me, do you?"

"Nah, she has been talking about nothing else for the past few days. Man, you don't know much about girls or women, I guess I should say, do you?"

Brady shook his head. "Not really. For most of the years I was in the navy, they kept the male and female sailors pretty segregated. It was only on my last few cruises that there were women on board ship."

"How did you like being in the navy?" Marcus asked.

"I liked it fine. I went in right out of high school and stayed in for twenty-three years."

"Did you always want to be a cook?"

"No. I never thought of it, but they give you a whole

battery of aptitude tests when you enlist, and cook is what the tests said I should be. So, they sent me to navy cook school in Fort Lee, Virginia, after boot camp, and the week after I graduated, I was on a carrier headed to Southeast Asia."

"Did you see any combat?" Marcus leaned forward.

"Not unless you count fights in the mess. A few times we were on alert when an enemy plane got to within fifty miles of the ship, but most of the time, I was too busy making meals for a couple thousand men to worry about the enemy. And then after Vietnam there was no real enemy, besides the Russians of course, so we basically just sailed around the seven seas, and I served coffee to the captain on the bridge in every one of them."

"Awesome."

"You ever think about joining the military?"

Marcus looked at him as if he were crazy. "Nah, man, I'm going to be a football player. First in college, then the pros."

"What if you get hurt or don't make it or get cut? There are a lot of things that might come between you and that dream. It's always smart to hedge your bets a little, to have a Plan B to fall back on if Plan A falls through."

"What are you two planning out here while I'm getting ready?" Both Brady and Marcus jumped and stood up when they heard Naomi's voice.

"Nothing, Mom, me and Brady were just passing time waiting on you. You took long enough. It's not as if you don't see Brady nearly every day."

"Hush up," she said. "A girl still has to make herself beautiful before a date even if the man sees her all sweaty and covered with flour at work every day." She turned to Brady. "Hi." Her voice softened as she said it.

"Hi," he said back, his ears reddening as he looked at her. "You look pretty, Naomi."

The three of them stood there for a few minutes, awkward, not knowing what to do next.

Naomi broke the silence. "We should probably get going."

Brady snapped to awareness too and clapped his hands

together. "Yeah, let's go." He followed Naomi to the door, where he held her jacket for her.

She turned to Marcus, who had also followed the couple to the door. "Now, no crowds of boys in here while I'm gone. James only if he stops over when you two get off work. Don't eat everything in the fridge either. That cake is for the fellowship after church tomorrow."

"Okay, Mom, you told me twenty times already."

"Well, telling you twenty-one times won't hurt. You seem to have a very convenient memory where cake is concerned." She leaned over and kissed her son on the cheek. "Have a nice evening. I shouldn't be too late." She turned to look at Brady. "Right?"

He shrugged. "It's up to you. We can play it by ear once we're done eating."

Naomi opened the door, and Brady held it for her. "Good night, Marcus," Brady said. "I'll see you at the diner in a day or two." He winked at the young man as he gently closed the door.

Brady and Naomi walked in silence to his old blue Ford pickup. He opened the passenger door for her and gently closed it when she was settled in the seat. He pretended not to notice her fumble to buckle her seat belt until she asked him to help.

"I don't have any trouble buckling these darned things when I am in the driver's seat, but they're forever getting the best of me in the passenger seat," she said. "Will you help me?"

"I'd be happy to," he said and reached over to take the buckle from her.

For the second time, their hands met, and both of them felt the jolt of electricity. Naomi moved her hand away as from a shock, and Brady fumbled with the buckle a bit, taking a while to get the end of the seat belt in the buckle straight so it slid into place. "There you are."

"Thanks."

Both of them were glad that there was good music on in the truck. After agreeing that it was indeed good music, neither of them spoke until they arrived at the restaurant. It took a few minutes of searching to find a parking place.

"Popular spot," Naomi said.

"Well, it's down here where all those national chain motels are, and this end of town is much closer to the interstate than we are at Better Than Mom's," said Brady as he opened her door for her and helped her out.

The place was packed when they walked in. The hostess took their name and invited them to "enjoy a cocktail in our lounge" while they waited. She said that their wait should be about forty-five minutes.

"Which means at least an hour," Naomi murmured in Brady's ear as he helped her off with her jacket and they walked into the lounge, which looked to both of them a lot like a plain old bar.

CHAPTER 16

Norman swung by the car wash on his way home from the diner and had his pickup cleaned inside and out. He even paid extra to have a squirt of lemon air freshener put under the seat. He polished his favorite shoes and pressed his Levi's. Norman sent his shirts out to be washed and pressed so he didn't have to worry about finding a clean, unwrinkled shirt to wear. He debated about what color shirt because he didn't want what he wore to clash with what Fay was wearing. Don't be foolish, he thought as he went into the bathroom to shave and shower for the second time in the same day. He caught himself humming as he shaved. He grinned at himself in the mirror when he thought about the adage that went, old men shave in the morning, young men shave at night. How true, he thought. It had been years since he had shaved after he got home from work. Usually, he pulled on a baggy pair of jeans and an old ratty flannel shirt, made himself a TV dinner and sat eating it in front of the television as nature intended. He favored science programs and documentaries rather than the pseudo-cop shows so many of his fellow officers watched. He had had quite enough of police work over the years, so he didn't want to spend his off time watching it as entertainment. He didn't think it was entertaining anyway. Who wants to watch bullets and blood spray across the screen or bodies falling or, worse yet, forensic geniuses pulling clues out of thin air and solving a crime in fifty minutes? It was shows like that that made the public lose respect for their local police force. People were always expecting miracles when they were the victims of crimes; now with those silly shows it was much worse. But Norman was not thinking about work or how frustrated he got over people's expectations as he stepped into the steamy shower. He was thinking about Fay and how pretty she had looked that afternoon, flushed from work, when she stood across from him and said she would go out with him tonight. Tonight! Just like that, she had said yes. That must mean she had been thinking about it, right?

Women were always two or three steps ahead of men, more probably, and Norman just hoped he could keep up, or at least not make a total ass of himself before the evening ended. He dried off and splashed on a little cologne, not too much, he didn't want to overpower Fay; he just wanted to smell good for her.

For her part, Fay was not quite as excited about the coming date. When she got off work, she walked the block to her apartment and immediately took a shower to wash the grease smell out of her hair and off her skin. She always felt as if she had been lightly sprayed with vegetable oil, and her work clothes frankly reeked of French fries. Not that that was a bad thing. She loved her job, loved being a waitress. She met the most interesting people and made pretty good money. Oh, there were some assholes that made some days long, but she was certain there were assholes that everyone in every job had to deal with.

After her shower, she dried off, shaved her legs and armpits, dried her hair, and let it flow down her back. She leaned close to the mirror to check that she didn't have any gray roots showing. Not more than a year ago, she would have been checking for brown roots, but suddenly what grew out of her scalp was unfortunately more gray hair than brown. Then she stood in front of her closet, glaring at her wardrobe. She would have called Naomi to come and help her decide what to wear, but Naomi and Brady were out on their own date, so she was on her own. Fay knew she would wear her favorite pencil-legged jeans; she was slim, even skinny, so she could get away with tight tapered jeans that made other, plumper women envious. She kind of enjoyed being the target of that envy.

But what top to wear? It was fall, so she supposed she could wear a sweater, but she was reluctant to give in to autumn just yet. It was too chilly at night to wear a tank top, and at forty, oh all right, forty-two, she was getting a little old to wear them, anyway. Wait a minute, she could wear a tank top, one with spaghetti straps, and put her new boat neck sweater over it. She had gotten the sweater at the thrift shop down the road, and she loved it. It was heavy cotton knit, almost hand-knitted looking, in dark rose and teal, colors Fay loved. It had three quarter length sleeves, which were perfect for the warm evenings and cooler nights of this time of year.

Now, which shoes? She didn't have to worry about any of her heels making her taller than Norman; he had to be six foot four at least, and she was barely over five foot seven, so that was no problem. But what if he wanted to dance? Nah, he probably wouldn't. Few men liked to dance, so she didn't have to worry about wearing shoes that would hurt her feet. Besides, they were headed to a country supper club with live music, which probably meant either a twangy country combo, somebody's aunt who sang out of tune and imagined herself a lounge singer, or an oompah band with an accordion. Yeesh.

Okay, if Naomi will go out on the night I really need her, she'll just have to find out with the rest of the world. Fay decided to leave her hair down for once, to give Norman a little surprise. She went easy on the cologne and put on her makeup with a much lighter hand than she did every day for work. She wriggled her way into her favorite skinny jeans that made her look like she actually had an ass, and carefully lifted her breasts into a lacy cupped bra she had spent a week's tips for in Victoria's Secret when she was still trying to compete with Butch's pool cue. Over it, she slid into her white spaghetti strap tank and over that she snuggled into her new sweater. She looked at herself in the mirror on the back of her closet door. She looked good. Fay took off the sweater and brushed her teeth for the second time, and rinsed with some store-brand mouthwash that tasted a little like kerosene and burned like hell. She put her sweater back on, hooked some sparkly, dangly earrings in her ears and picked through her jewelry box to find a necklace that hung in just the right place. She settled on a choker with a piece of rose quartz that she thought looked great with the dark rose stripe in her sweater.

One look at the clock on the stove, it was two minutes before six-thirty, and she stopped fiddling with her jewelry, hair, and sweater, slid her feet into her favorite sling back heels, and transferred her wallet, makeup bag, and cheap pay as you go cellphone to the matching bag. She knew Norman would be punctual, and he was. He rang the bell, and when Fay opened the door, he just stood there staring at her.

"What?" she said. "Do I have dirt on my face?"

He opened and closed his mouth like a perch in the bottom of a skiff. "Uh, no. Uh, holy shit, Fay. Oh, sorry I swore, but you look…"

"I look?"

He stood transfixed and silent in the hallway.

Finally, she lost patience. "Oh, for heaven's sake, Norman, come in."

He stumbled over the threshold, never taking his eyes off her. Eventually he found his tongue. "Fay, you look beautiful. In my wildest dreams, I never imagined you would look like this tonight."

She smiled at the look of wonder on his face. "Are we ready?" she asked.

"Bring a jacket or something," he said. "It gets kind of chilly out in the country."

She pulled a jacket off the hook next to the door and said, "Okay, I'm ready. Let's go."

Fay felt contentment or relaxation come over her as they walked down the hall and out the door to his pickup. Norman unlocked and opened the door for her and waited until she was settled before gently closing it. She reached across and pulled up the lock knob for him. He was surprised.

"Thanks."

Both of them were mostly quiet on the fairly long drive to the country bar and supper club. Fay was surprised to see the number of cars clustered around the place.

"Quite the crowd," she said as Norman pulled into the parking lot.

"Yep, there is. A lot of people like the food, and I hear the band is great."

Fay reached for the door handle to get out, but Norman said, "Wait. Let me come around and get the door."

"Okay."

She was surprised when she stepped inside to hear the four man, well, three men and one woman, combo playing *Stardust*. As soon as Norman had closed the door and heard the music too, he grabbed her hand and twirled her into his arms.

"Let's dance," he said to the surprised woman he held. "*Stardust* is one of my favorites."

Even with her purse swinging out and back, slapping her in the side, Fay enjoyed it. She could tell Norman was a good dancer. She also realized that she was learning a lot about Officer Norman Bates just by being in his arms. He was light on his feet, graceful even; he smelled really nice; and the way his hand felt holding hers, with the other resting lightly just under her shoulder, telegraphed how he was feeling about being there with her. As the song ended, Norman swung them around, holding her closer than he had, and bent her backward in a dip. Couples who had been listlessly swaying back and forth alongside them stepped away from them as if they were about to spring—or fall, but Norman gently lifted Fay back to her feet, his hands caressing her shoulders before letting go to join in the applause. The combo leader announced a break, so everyone left the floor. Norman steered Fay toward the hostess, who was standing at her station, a pair of menus in her hands, staring at them as if she didn't quite understand what they were doing.

When they reached her, Norman said, "Sorry, but I can't resist *Stardust*. It just begs you to dance to it."

The teenage girl just nodded and said, "Okay. Two?" She

led them to a table in the small dining room off the bar, plunked down the menus at the seats across from each other, and said, "Mom, um, Beth will be your waitress." Then she turned and left, shaking her head as if she were thinking, grownups. Norman pulled Fay onto the dance floor once more before their dinners came.

She couldn't believe her eyes at the bounty of food their waitress brought. There was a cup of good homemade French onion soup topped with a slab of baguette toasted and hidden under melted Swiss cheese to start. Then came a tossed salad made with mixed greens and a light balsamic vinaigrette. Their entrée of tenderloin, the dish the place was famous for, looked to Fay like she was being served the entire tenderloin, not just a slice. The meat was cooked to perfection and rested on a bed of sautéed mushrooms, not a white button in view. When Fay declined a potato, their waitress asked if she was interested in the vegetable of the day. When told that it was parsnips, Fay wasn't sure she would like them, but agreed to try them. Her eyes widened when the plate of them was set down next to her.

"I didn't order fries," she said to the waitress.

"They're not potato fries," Beth said. "They're parsnip fries. Try them." She nudged the plate closer to Fay's hand.

Fay looked at Norman, who had also ordered the parsnips, to see him smiling like she was going to uncover a secret. She shrugged and picked one up.

"Careful," Beth said. "They're really hot." Fay gingerly bit the tip of the parsnip fry she held. The inside was creamy and firm at the same time; the outside was crunchy and had some mild herbs on it. The whole thing was heavenly.

Fay pushed her empty plate away. "I'm stuffed," she said. "Do they think they're feeding field hands?"

Norman laughed. "Of course, they do. This is farm country. Almost everybody is a field hand or something. People work hard, so they have to eat to keep up their strength."

Fay looked around at the room. Dim lights around the

ceiling illuminated pine paneling dotted with stuffed deer and moose heads interspersed with a bear roaring down at the laughing diners. Sometimes over, sometimes under the hum and laughter, Fay heard the jazzy strains of the band.

They found a table in the bar and spent the rest of the evening dancing to every song.

CHAPTER 17

Brady kept his hand at the small of Naomi's back as he followed her through the crowd in the bar. She spied a table near the cold fireplace and veered that way, excusing herself when she needed to pass between people talking. When they stood in front of the table, they saw why it was empty—there were no chairs.

"Well, hell," she said, surprising Brady into laughter.

"Oh, Naomi, you're in trouble now."

"Why? Because I said hell?"

"Yes, ma'am. Hell's a swear word; my mama told me it was. And you a churchwoman."

She laughed right back at him. "I may be a churchwoman, but I get frustrated just as much as the next person. I don't think even Pastor Lawson would say I'm going to hell for saying hell."

Brady looked around to see a foursome leaving a nearby table. "Hey, grab a couple of those chairs there. I'll go to the bar; I think we'd die of thirst waiting for the waitress. What would you like to drink?"

Naomi shrugged. "I'm not much of a drinker. A rum and Coke, maybe?"

Brady turned to go up and order, and then turned right back to her. "You want a slice of lime in it?"

Naomi was shoving two chairs from one table to the other. "Sure, that'd be good."

"One Cuba Libre coming up."

By the time Brady was back with the drinks, Naomi had wiped off the table with a couple of napkins left behind and removed the empty glasses and put them on the mantle of the stone fireplace behind her. She had also gotten a basket of pretzels and some spicy mustard dip from a small hors d'oeuvre bar against the wall.

He set the drinks down carefully and then sat beside her. "Man, it's a zoo in here. I wonder what's so special about the place," he said as he sipped his drink. "It can't be the ahm-bee-ahnce."

The disdainful tone in his voice and the fact that down-to-earth ex-navy cook Brady even knew the word "ambience"—and used it correctly—made Naomi snort her sip of drink.

"Ambience? Are you kidding me? People around here want a lot of food, cheap, and they get a slab of beef, a gigantic baked potato, an all-you-can-eat salad bar, and Texas toast for $19.95. It's a cheapo's dream."

"I guess you're right. Everybody always complains when I raise prices, especially the codgers. I have to soothe them with explanations of rising production costs and shipping prices. Raymond's the worst, but then he's the worst in just about every way. No wonder his wife lit out for Arizona when he retired. I can't imagine working for him."

Naomi swallowed the bite of pretzel in her mouth. "Me neither. Fay tells me about the stuff he says, all racist and intolerant. It's a God's wonder someone hasn't taken him out behind the woodshed and taught him a lesson."

Brady toyed with the narrow little straw in his bourbon and Coke. "We shouldn't spend the evening talking about the diner, should we? Tell me about you."

As they talked, Brady and Naomi realized that even though they worked together every day, they knew little about each other's personal lives, and they knew even less about the other person's hopes and dreams. They spent a long time lingering over that one drink, each of them pleased to find that the other wasn't a big drinker.

Naomi was right, it was an hour before the hostess came to show them to a table. After she took their drink orders, sweet tea for both of them, she invited them to help themselves at the salad bar and grill.

"Are you hungry?" Brady said.

Naomi nodded. "I'm starving; let's get a salad to start."

They ate their way through their salads and then chose steaks, both ribeye. They agreed it was the tastiest one.

Brady asked, "How do you like your steak?"

"Grilled myself," she said, brandishing long tongs at him. "Just because you cook at the diner doesn't mean you need to cook my meat."

"Okay," he said in a small voice.

They didn't run out of things to talk about. All the places Brady had sailed to in the navy fascinated Naomi. It was after eleven o'clock when Brady pulled into the parking lot of the apartment complex.

"I had a good time," he said to the windshield.

"I had a good time too," she said to her lap.

Brady got out and went around to open the door for her. He offered his hand to help her out of the truck, and she took it. Neither let go as they walked into the building and up the stairs to Naomi's door.

"I guess I'll see you in a few hours," Naomi said.

Brady's head popped up. "Yeah, see you in a few hours." He leaned up and kissed her cheek. "Goodnight, Naomi."

"Goodnight, Brady. Thank you for a lovely evening." He smiled, gave a little wave, and headed back to his truck.

Naomi pushed the door shut, and a voice behind her said, "So, how was the date?"

She put a hand on her chest. "Good grief, Marcus, you scared me to death."

"Sorry. Did you have a good time?"

She hung up her jacket. "I had a good time. We talked the whole time, and now," she yawned, "I'm off to bed. We have church and then I have to work tomorrow."

"G'night, Mom."

It was close to midnight when Fay and Norman left the supper club. They had danced every dance once their meal was finished.

"I wouldn't have pegged you for a dancer," Fay said.

Norman looked offended. "What did you think?"

"I thought you'd be a watcher and maybe a toe-tapper, but not a dancer. I got the feeling you toned it down for me."

"I did." He pulled onto the state highway that would take them back to Stinson. "Did you like dancing?"

She turned in the seat to face him. "I loved it. I wish I had on better shoes and a dress with a skirt that would swirl out like in those old Fred Astaire and Ginger Rogers movies. Maybe I can find something at the thrift store for next time." She covered her mouth with her hand. "If you want there to be a next time, that is."

Norman let out a breath. "I definitely want there to be a next time." They drove in silence for a while. "Would you be interested in taking some lessons? The Park and Rec Department has dancing lessons on Tuesday nights. We could go." He waited for her response. "It isn't very expensive. What do you think?"

"I think dancing lessons are a great idea." She paused, then asked, "Can I wear a swirly skirt?"

He smiled at her little-girl voice. "Of course, you can wear a swirly skirt and see if you can find shoes with a strap, so your foot stays in them. You don't want to twist an ankle coming out of your shoes."

Fay reached across the seat, took Norman's hand, and held

it all the way to her apartment.

When they got to Fay's floor, the hall light was out. Only the exit sign shed its feeble light in the space. Fay counted the doors to her front door and fumbled her key into the lock. "I had a good time, Norman. Thanks for supper and the dancing. I loved dancing. Sorry it's so dark in here."

Norman's breath touched her cheek. "I don't mind the dark," he said and kissed his way from her cheek to her lips. "I don't mind the dark one bit."

Fay's breath caught in her throat as he kissed his way to her mouth. Then their lips were touching, and everything else faded away. Her hands reached to hold his shoulders, and his hand slid up behind her head.

He broke the kiss, dipped down for one more, and then said, "Good night, Fay, I had a wonderful time. I'll see you tomorrow." His hand lightly squeezed her neck, and then he was gone.

Fay closed her door and leaned against it. "Oh mercy," she said aloud, "that long, tall policeman sure can kiss."

CHAPTER 18

It was Sunday afternoon, and Fay was still walking on air. Her date with Norman had exceeded all of her hopes for the evening. He had been easy to talk to, and they had danced. She needed a swirly skirt. Maybe Naomi could be persuaded to drive down to the thrift store with her to flip the racks. That was a good idea. Naomi and Brady had gone on their first date last night too. Fay was dying to know how it went. Before she could talk herself out of it, she scooted down the hall to knock on Naomi's door.

Marcus answered it. "Hey, Fay, come on in. Mom's on the couch."

She was surprised to see Naomi stretched out on the couch with her forearm over her eyes. "Are you okay?" Fay said.

Naomi moved her arm and blinked at her friend. "I'm fine. I stayed up too late last night and got up too early today, that's all." She swung her feet onto the floor and sat up to make room for Fay. "What's up?"

Fay smiled at her. "Well, I was thinking maybe you'd like to take a little trip to the thrift store this afternoon. Norman and I danced all night last night, and I need a skirt that swirls before our next date. What do you say? Do you want to come along?"

Naomi looked at her as if she couldn't believe her ears. "Norman is a dancer?"

"Yes, he is. A good one, too."

"Well, I'll be." She turned to her son. "Marcus, how's your homework coming?"

He heaved a sigh. "Almost done, General, I just have a History chapter to finish."

Naomi pushed herself to her feet. "I'm going to the thrift store with Fay, and you'd better have your work done when I get back. No goofing off with James until you're done."

"All right, Mom. You've said it a million times, homework comes first." He bent his head over his books.

It took Naomi only a couple of minutes to run a comb through her hair and put on a little lipstick, and she was ready. In the meantime, Fay went to her apartment to do the same. They met in the hall in ten minutes, ready to hit the thrift shop racks. The store was almost deserted when they arrived, so it was easy to fall into conversation while they shopped.

Fay, ever the impatient one, started right in. "So," she said, "how was your date with Brady?"

"Good."

"Where did you go?"

Naomi looked at her. "I told you; we went to the Prime Quarter for steaks."

"How was the food?"

"Good. Plentiful. Good." Naomi pulled a green skirt off the rack and held it up for Fay to see.

Fay shook her head. "Not green. Green makes me look like I'm going to be sick. So, what did you talk about?"

"Oh, work, the customers, Marcus, his time in the Navy, you know, getting to know you stuff."

Fay shook her head and pulled a purple paisley broomstick skirt off the rack. "This might do." She put it in her cart. "Didn't you talk about your hopes and dreams, that kind of stuff? Man, getting you to talk is tough. I hope you weren't this quiet last night."

Naomi clicked her tongue. "I don't think I was quiet last night, but I'm not about to recount our whole conversation. We talked all night; it was nice. How about you? Did you spend the whole night dancing?"

Fay tucked a pale pink skirt into her waist and turned around to watch it swirl. "I like this one. We mostly danced. The supper club, Bricks, is out of town about twenty miles so we had a nice long drive to talk, then as soon as we got into the place Norman swept me onto the dance floor because they were playing *Stardust* which he said begs to be danced to. We ordered tenderloin and parsnip fries, oh they're so good, and even before the food came, we danced again. Norman's a real good dancer. We're going to take lessons at the Park and Rec starting next week. That's why I need a swirly skirt." By then she had a pile of skirts in her cart in every color except green and went to try them on. Her voice came from behind the changing room door. "So do you think you and Brady will go out again?"

Naomi leaned on the cart, putting the rejected skirts back on their hangers. "I sure hope so. I had a good time. I like Brady."

Fay peeked around the door, her eyes sparkling. "Did he kiss you?"

Naomi blushed. "What a question. Fay, you have no boundaries."

"Okay, but did he kiss you?"

"We had a goodnight kiss at my door. Satisfied?"

Fay grinned. "Norm kissed me too, thoroughly. That beanpole of a policeman can really kiss."

Naomi shook her head. "That's more than I need to know."

Fay ended up with three skirts and lucked into a pair of t-strap pumps in her size in the shoe department. "Norm said that I need strap shoes, so I don't dance out of them. Maybe I should invest in some real dancing shoes."

The next time the bridge ladies came in to play cards in the back of the dining room, Raymond smoothed his hair back and say hello to the lady with the reddish, curly hair. "Hi, Maralee," he said.

"Hello, Mr., uh, Raymond," she said.

"How are you doing these days, Maralee?"

She motioned to her friends to go on to the table. "I'm doing well, thank you, Raymond. How are you?"

"Fine. I'm just fine."

They looked at each other, both seeming to be stuck for what to say next.

Finally, Maralee moved away. "I've got to join my friends for lunch and then cards. Nice to see you, Raymond." She turned to walk away.

"Maralee," he said. She turned back. "Would you like to go out to the movies some evening?" he said before he thought about it too much.

The blush started at her collar and spread up to the roots of her hair. "I'd like that." She turned again and walked back to meet her friends.

On the following Thursday, Fay put her knitting into a tote to take to the diner. The knitting ladies had said they'd be back this week to show her how to purl, and she wanted to be ready. She had struggled for days with the metal needles, acrylic yarn, and the pattern she had picked out and finally gave up and went back to just doing the knit stitch on the bamboo needles and wool yarn from Dorothy and Iris. Fay debated taking it all along but settled for taking the book alone. She figured she could make notes on the page when they showed her stitches so she could make them again when she was by herself.

The morning went by in a whirl of coffee mugs, plates of eggs, and smart talk from the coffee codgers, especially Raymond. Raymond was different somehow. Taffy had said that he was in one evening with a lady friend for pie and coffee. Fay wondered if the lady was anyone she was familiar with. She remembered that one of the bridge ladies had given Raymond a calling card when he helped her pick up a dropped deck of playing cards. Hm, that could be interesting.

At the end of the lunch rush in came the three knitting ladies. They asked to be seated at the table at the back of the restaurant so they could knit all afternoon and not disturb anyone eating. By then, Stevie the scribbler had packed up his briefcase of manuscript pages and gone home, so that end of the diner was empty. When Fay delivered their drinks, Patti reached up to touch her forearm. "Did you bring your knitting, Fay?"

Fay nodded. "I sure did. I'll be over just as soon as I'm through. See you around two-thirty." She took their lunch orders and went to put them in.

For the last hour of her shift, Fay cleaned and sanitized the tables, booths, and chairs. She wiped down all the condiment containers, the dessert menus, and the napkin holders. She kept an eye on the few scattered customers and made sure that they had what they needed. When the knitters were finished eating, she cleared their dishes and cleaned the table so that they wouldn't get food on their knitting.

Taffy was on time, so Fay could join the knitters as soon as her shift ended. She picked up her tote of knitting and her purse from Brady's office and went to join her new friends.

"There she is, Stinson's newest knitter," Iris said. "Come sit by me, Fay." She scooted her chair over even though there was an empty chair next to her. "So how did the knitting go?"

Fay got settled and pulled out the long, wavering strip of garter stitch. "It went okay. I think I did something wrong because the edges go in and out."

Dorothy flapped her hand. "Oh, that's just newbie knitter tension. Sometimes your stitches are loose, and sometimes they are tight. It'll all even out once you've got a bit more experience under your belt."

Iris looked at Fay's work and said, "Show me how you've been knitting."

"Okay," Fay said, and bent her head to her needles.

She had knitted across the row when Iris said, "Good. Now it's time to learn to purl."

Fay blushed. "I bought this book." She reached into her tote and pulled it out. "And I tried purling. I don't think I did it right because it felt so awkward." She handed the book to Patti across the table. "It's the *Cool Girl's Guide to Knitting,* and I want to be one of the cool girls."

Patti was paging through the book. "Oh, this has nice diagrams and pictures of the stitches. I think you made a wise buy. What else did you buy?"

Fay confessed to buying variegated acrylic yarn and metal needles because they were on sale. She told them how much trouble she had getting the yarn to behave on those metal needles. They all nodded their heads as she spoke.

"Metal needles are slick, and acrylic yarn isn't as springy as wool is. That's why we started you on bamboo and wool," Dorothy said.

"But these needles and this yarn are so much more expensive than what I bought."

Iris patted her hand. "Those bamboo needles are about the least expensive ones around. Some of the fanciest needles are between twenty and forty dollars a pair, and really good yarn can be at least twenty a skein. The yarn we gave you is eight bucks a skein, cheap for decent yarn."

For the next hour, Fay struggled to make her yarn, needles,

and fingers master the purl stitch. There was a lot of jaw clenching and just a little under-the-breath cursing as she tried to master the other basic knitting stitch. She had the *Cool Girl's Guide* open on the table in front of her with a butter knife holding the pages flat, and Patti sat beside her coaxing her through the motions of the purl stitch. By the time they packed up to leave, she had a good inch of purl stitches added onto her knitted strip.

"Now keep working on the purl one row then knit back and see what happens," Dorothy said. "We'll see you next week and help you start that pattern you like so much."

Fay held up her strip of green knitting and smiled at it. "I did it. I might be a knitter after all." She tucked her book and knitting into her tote. "I'll see you next week."

The three older ladies paid their lunch tabs and left, waving, and calling their goodbyes.

CHAPTER 19

During the first dancing lesson, Fay and Norm struggled. He would zig and she would zag, both of them trying to lead. The instructor split them up in the second lesson, asking them first to dance the steps alone, then pairing them with a more experienced partner. It was hardest for Fay because she kept wanting to move forward when she should have moved back.

"Back, Fay, back," the instructor would say, "let Mike lead you into the steps."

But she kept charging into the dance steps, so the instructor partnered her himself.

"Slow and easy," he said, as he steered her into a turn. "Did you ever watch Fred Astaire movies?"

"Yes, I did. I loved Ginger Rogers' dresses and shoes."

"Don't watch your feet. And do you remember her mostly moving backward?"

"I guess," she said.

Progress was slow, but when he said, "If you lead, your skirt won't swirl like Ginger's did," that did the trick.

Fay wanted her skirt to swirl in the worst way, so she slowed down and let him lead. She got it. "Oh," she said, "that feels better."

By the end of that lesson, Fay and Norm were back dancing together, doing a creditable waltz.

"Next week, swing dancing," the instructor said.

As he helped her on with her jacket, Norm said, "If we hurry, we can get to the diner for a piece of pie."

Fay smiled at the hopeful note in his voice. "Okay, I could eat pie."

She was surprised to see some of the morning regulars at the diner when they arrived.

Taffy hurried toward them with menus in her hand. "Anything wrong?"

"No," Fay said, "we've been at dance class and need pie. Is there any blueberry left? Norm likes blueberry."

Taffy showed them to a booth. "What kind of pie would you like, Fay?"

Fay craned her neck to see the pies in the bakery case. "I'll have a big slice of banana cream."

Taffy left to collect their pie, and Marcus came up to the table. "What are you doing in here at night?" he said.

"Getting pie," they said in unison.

"Oh." He carried a full bus tub into the kitchen. They heard him say, "Hey Brady, Fay and Officer Bates are here."

Brady's head poked out the swinging doors. "Everything okay?" he said.

Fay threw up her hands. "For Pete's sake, can't two people get pie in the evening without all these questions?"

Steve walked up from the back booth, briefcase in hand. "I'm here because I have a deadline and it's my favorite place to write. I had lemon pie."

All three of them laughed.

Taffy reached around to serve their blueberry and banana cream slices. "Coffee?"

Fay shook her head. "Nah, it'll keep me awake."

Norm said, "I'll have decaf. It's too late for that high-test stuff."

They lingered over their empty plates, Norm drinking coffee and Fay going over every step they'd learned that night.

As he walked her to her door, he said, "You called me Norm."

"Yeah. Like it?" She intertwined her fingers in his.

He brought their linked hands to his lips and kissed her fingers. "I like it."

When the six lessons were finished, neither Norm nor Fay was ready to quit learning. They signed up to repeat the class but also checked out the local ballroom dance school and signed up for a beginners' class. In the first ballroom class, they found a well of gracefulness that made them look like they had been dancing together for years. The too-tall policeman and the skinny waitress were the envy of the other students.

"Where'd you learn that?" one woman asked.

"Oh, we took the Park and Rec classes; that's where we started," Fay said, her face glowing at the praise.

At the end of the session, the instructor announced that couples might think about signing up for the local amateur competition being held in a month. He spoke to Fay and Norm about it. "You two should definitely sign up. You're both so tall and slender, you look like something out of *The Great Gatsby*. Sign up. I'll help you get ready."

Norm looked at Fay. "What do you think?"

"Can I have a dress with feathers around the hem?" she said.

He smiled at her enthusiasm. "You can have a dress with feathers if I have to sew them on myself. Let's check the thrift store after work tomorrow to see if we can find something that will work."

They danced hard the next month, working on a couple of routines for the competition. The instructor was as good as his word, stayed after class, and scheduled extra rehearsals to help all the students get ready.

Fay and Naomi found a rose-pink dress with a full skirt and rhinestones on the bodice at the thrift store that fit Fay perfectly. They bought pink and silver feather boas at the craft store that they hand-sewed around the hem. On the night of the last rehearsal before the competition, Fay took the dress along to practice in it.

When she came out of the changing room, Norm was speechless.

Fay smiled. "Do I have dirt on my face?" she said.

"No," his voice came out in a croak. "You look like an angel."

She walked over to stand in front of him, reached up to touch his cheek and said, "Sweet."

Fay was a bundle of nerves at the start of the competition, but Norm was calm. "All we have to do is dance like we did last night at rehearsal, Fay. We know the music, we know the steps, let's just dance," he said.

And they did.

They came in second in their division and resolved to continue taking lessons and entering competitions. "Next time we'll really kick dancing's butt," Norm said.

CHAPTER 20

"You should do it," Brady said one afternoon while they chopped and prepped for the next day's menu.

Naomi looked at him out of the corner of her eye. "Are you trying to get rid of me? You could just fire me, or I could quit."

"No," he said, "I'm not trying to get rid of you, but you should follow your dream of becoming a nurse. You can do it right here at the college in Stinson, so you won't have to go someplace new."

She sighed. "Yes, but I don't want to go back on welfare while I'm in school. I can't keep working here full time and go to school full time; it wouldn't work. I'd be shortchanging both you and my studies. And what about Marcus?"

"What about me?" Marcus came in the back door for his afternoon shift.

"You're early," Brady said.

Marcus smiled at him. "I'm trying to impress my boss. School got out early for some teacher meeting."

"Is your schoolwork done?" said Naomi and Brady together.

Marcus turned from hanging up his jacket in Brady's office. "Yes, my schoolwork is done." He came toward them, tying his apron behind his back. "Now, what about me?"

Naomi put down her knife and folded her arms across her chest. "Brady is trying to convince me I should go to nursing school. I told him I can't work and go to school and keep you out of trouble all at the same time."

"You want to be a nurse?"

"I did when I was in high school, but now I'm too old. I have too many responsibilities and not enough money to run off and go to college. Especially not when I'm trying to get you ready to go to college in a couple of years." She turned and started browning cubed beef and onions for tomorrow's stew.

"You could get financial aid," Brady said in a quiet voice. "I could go with you and help you navigate getting registered and all that."

Marcus put his Better Than Mom's ball cap on backwards and got ready to carry a tub of clean dishes out into the diner. "You should look into it, Mom. You're always telling me to keep my eyes on my dreams, so maybe we can chase our dreams together.

She looked at the two men in her life through the steam rising from the stew pot. "I'll think about it."

Less than a month later, Naomi and Brady walked out of the registrar's office on the University of Wisconsin-Stinson campus on the other side of town. Naomi held a bulging folder against her chest. "I can't believe I just did that." The hand holding the folder shook. "I can't believe that my financial aid grants are more than welfare would be, so I don't have to go back on it ."

"You did it," Brady said, "and I'm so proud of you. You're a real college coed now. Let's go find the bookstore. You need textbooks."

"No, not now. One step at a time. School will start in three weeks, and I have time to get my books." She turned to look at him. "Don't I?"

He put his arm around her waist. "You have time, not a lot

of time, but some time. Let's just find the bookstore so you know where to go when you come to buy books." He saw a campus map on the wall and steered her over to it. "Look, we don't even have to walk outside in the heat to get there. We follow the blue tunnel." He turned and walked away; Naomi followed, dragging her feet.

It was Naomi's last day at the diner. School was starting tomorrow, so she couldn't be in the kitchen at four-thirty in the morning and then in the classroom at eight o'clock. Tears rolled slowly down her cheeks as she chopped celery and carrots for the day's soups.

"Hey, don't cry," Brady said, wiping her cheeks with the corner of his apron. "You're only going across town to school, not into the navy to sail away to foreign ports."

"I know," she said, "but I love it here. I love everyone, even Raymond, so why am I leaving?"

Fay pushed through the swinging doors from the front end, where she was getting coffee made and everything set up for the morning rush. "You're leaving to follow your dream. You'll still live down the hall from me. You'll still come here to sit in the back and study. You're not getting away from us, just changing things up a bit."

"Yeah," Brady said, "changing things up a bit, that's all. Marcus and I have it all worked out. He'll come here straight from football practice; Coach will drop him off. He can do his homework at a back table, and then when I see his work is done, he can bus tables for a couple of hours before you get home from school. We'll keep him on the straight and narrow."

Marcus piped up from the pass-through window. "And I'll be saving money for college since I'm not a returning woman student who will get a boatload of grants to go back to school." He waved to the three in the kitchen. "I'm outta here. Practice starts, and I've got to get going. See you all later." And he was gone out the front door.

As soon as Marcus was out the door, Raymond was in and on his regular stool. "I need coffee," he said. "Is anybody working today?"

Fay looked at the other two and smiled. "Ah, it's the call of the Raymond-bird squawking for its coffee."

Naomi reached into the oven. "Tell him the biscuits are done."

CHAPTER 21

Fay and Norm were in the district competition, dancing the waltz. Fay wore a mint green dress with peach feathers around the hem that perfectly matched her hair. Norm wore his usual tuxedo with a mint green vest and peach bow tie. They looked like a spring garden. Fay's rhinestone earrings glittered in the ballroom's lights, and her shoes were silver glitter.

"I feel like a princess," she said to Norm.

He looked down at her pressed to his side and twisting her hands together. "You look like a nervous princess," he laid his hand over hers. "Stop fidgeting; you'll ruin your manicure."

She shook her fingers out and grabbed his hand. "What if I stumble? What if I fall?"

He smiled down at her. "You go through this every time. You won't stumble. You won't fall, and if you do, we'll survive." He took both of her hands in his and turned to face her. "We've done this before. We've practiced as much as we could; now it's time to dance." He touched his forehead to hers. "Follow my lead, you'll be fine."

She took a deep breath and nodded.

Just then, the announcer called the waltz dancers to the floor. "That's us," Norm said, and he led Fay out onto the dance floor where the other couples were assembling.

"Ladies and gentlemen, the waltz," the announcer said in his smooth voice. The lights around the room dimmed, and the dancers faced each other, ready to begin. As the music began, Fay started to move, but Norm held her still.

"Two-three-four," he said in a bare whisper. On the four count he stepped into the waltz, and Fay followed. She locked her eyes on his, and he smiled at her. She smiled back, and he felt her relax into the steps. Soon she was enjoying herself, hearing only the music, being aware of only Norm and the steps. The rest of the dancers might have disappeared. In what seemed like a heartbeat, the music came to a crescendo, and they stopped dancing in a waltz pose. There was a moment of silence and then applause. They had done it.

Fay was beaming at Norm as he lifted her to her feet and they took bows, bowing to the judges first and then to the crowd.

"One-twenty-two," called a voice from the audience.

"That's us," Fay said to Norm. "Someone liked us."

"Of course they did; we did well," Norm said as he led her off the dance floor to await the eliminations.

It was a tense few minutes until the announcer came back on to call couples back for a second round.

"One-eighteen, one-twenty-one."

Fay bounced on the balls of her feet in suspense. "One-twenty-two..."

Norm's hand gripped her elbow as he escorted her to the center of the dance floor. They bowed to the judges again and took their stance. Three more couples joined them on the floor, the crowd lights dimmed, and the music began.

Once again, Fay felt like she had wings on her feet. She followed Norm's lead, kept her eyes on his, and smiled. Voices called couples' numbers from the darkness, but Fay and Norm were too focused to hear them. Once again when the music ended, they bowed to the judges and then to the crowd. The six couples clustered together at the edge of the floor to await the judges' decision. Three couples would get ribbons and three would be disappointed.

"I hope we get a ribbon," Fay said into Norm's shoulder.

He leaned down and kissed the top of her head. "I hope we do too."

The announcer's voice rang out, "And now the results of the waltz competition. In third place, couple one-twenty-seven." Dancers in royal purple rushed past Fay.

"In second place, couple one-twenty-two."

For a heartbeat, Fay and Norm stood still until a hand touched her. "That's you, honey," said a soft voice from behind.

They joined hands and hurried out onto the floor to applause. They had come second. All of their lessons and practice had paid off.

Norm leaned down to her ear. "Next time we'll take first."

She looked up, with tears glittering in her eyes. "Okay."

They got back to Better Than Mom's before it closed. A few of the regulars were there, and Naomi was in the back of the room, her textbooks spread all over a table. When she saw Fay and Norm come in, she put down her pencil and came to greet them.

"How did you do? I wish I had been there."

"I'm glad you weren't," said Fay. "I would have been too nervous."

Norm laughed. "I don't think you could have been more nervous." He brandished a red ribbon and a small trophy. "We came in second. And we need pie."

"Coming right up," said Taffy. "What'll you have?"

Fay ordered the French Silk with whipped cream, and Norm had blueberry with vanilla ice cream.

Naomi took the stool next to Fay and ordered a small slice of Dutch Apple, unadorned. "I need a break, and eating a slice of pie is a good excuse."

They laughed, and Naomi asked more questions about the competition. When they'd talked through it twice, she asked, "So, are you going to do it again?"

Fay looked at Norm, who looked right back at her. They turned to look at Naomi and said together, "Of course we are."

Fay continued, "We can't stop now. We got second again; we want a first."

Taffy set down their pie and poured them all a cup of coffee, decaf at that late hour.

It was Thursday, and the knitters were in the back at their usual table. Fay was embarrassed that she hadn't been knitting, but she couldn't avoid them.

"Hey, Fay," Iris said when Fay stopped to take their orders, "I hope you brought your knitting."

Fay chewed her lip. "Well, I've been kind of busy and haven't been knitting."

"That's okay," said Patti, "just come sit with us when you get off."

"My stuff is at home."

Iris snorted. "So, go get it. We know you live right behind here."

Fay felt her cheeks redden. "Okay." She took their orders: three fruit and cottage cheese plates and three iced teas, with extra ice for Iris. When she got off at two-thirty, she hurried to her apartment, grabbed her knitting, and went back to sit with the three ladies. She was ashamed that she had to ask for help to remember the knit stitch, but Dorothy patiently talked her through it.

After sitting knitting for a few minutes without talking,

Iris said, "So why haven't you been knitting? You got a boyfriend?" Her voice got higher, and her smile lit up her face.

Fay blushed. "Kind of, yeah."

"How can you kind of have a boyfriend? You either have one or you don't," said Dorothy.

Fay stopped frowning at her knitting and looked up. "Officer Bates, Norm and I have been taking dancing lessons during the week and then entering ballroom dance competitions on the weekends."

The three older women hooted with glee. "Dancing," Patti said, "you mean in those swirly dresses with lots of sequins and feathers?"

"Well, yes, that's exactly what we're doing, only Norm wears a tuxedo, but his vest or cummerbund and bow tie matches my dress."

Iris looked at the others. "We should go watch. We could knit in the stands and watch Fay and Officer Bates dance. It'd be fun."

"Yes," said Dorothy.

Patti said, "We should do that. When's the next competition?"

Fay looked at the three gray-haired ladies looking back at her with smiles on their faces and eagerness in their eyes. "Do you mean it?"

"Of course, we mean it," said Patti. "We need something to do on the weekends. We might as well come watch you dance and cheer you on."

Iris squinted at Fay. "We can cheer, right?"

Fay nodded. "Yes, you can cheer, and you can call out the number of the couple you're cheering for." She shook her head. "I can't believe that you want to come and watch us."

Dorothy leaned over and patted her hand. "You're our friend now, knit."

The four heads, three gray and one red, bent to their knitting and chatted and laughed the afternoon away.

CHAPTER 22

Brady checked that he'd locked the front door, then turned off the oven and the burners before turning out the lights and locking the back door of the diner. He missed Naomi. She was in school, and today Dicky hadn't shown up, but John had come through the door looking for a job and been hired. A few customers had groused that there weren't biscuits, but the biscuit maker was gone. Maybe Naomi could teach him how to make her biscuits, as if he didn't have enough to do in the morning. Maybe John knew how to make biscuits, he'd have to ask him tomorrow. Brady couldn't remember the last time he'd felt so lonely. It was a long drive home.

John knew how to make biscuits, not as light and fluffy as Naomi's, but adequate. John's friends and relatives started coming into Better Than Mom's, and over time John introduced a southwest flavor to the menu. Brady let him make a pan of Chicken Enchilada Bake for the buffet as an experiment, and it was gone in a flash. "Do we have more of this enchilada stuff?" Fay asked as she restocked the buffet.

John said, "No, ma'am, Miss Fay, I only made one pan."

"Dang it," she said. "I didn't get a taste, and it's all gone. People love it. Make more next time."

"Yes, ma'am."

Naomi laid down her pencil. She had been studying all

evening, and she was tired. Marcus had gone to bed an hour ago, and the apartment was quiet. Sometimes she wondered if letting Brady and Marcus talk her into going to college was a good thing. When she read some of the information, it felt like it bounced off her brain instead of sinking in. She had talked to a counselor in the Continuing Ed office, and the counselor said that it might take a little time for her brain to get back into learning mode, that she had been out of school long enough for it to be challenging to start up again.

If she'd known it would be this frustrating, she'd have told them to go peddle their papers someplace else. The young people in her classes were so quick on the draw when the teacher asked a question. Professor, she had to remember to call them professors. Anyway, she had yet to find the courage to raise her hand to answer a question in class even when she knew the answer.

She was glad that she'd had to start at the beginning with general ed classes to build up the prerequisites for the nursing classes. These classes would give her the chance to remember how to learn things, give her brain a chance to learn to absorb rather than reject new information. She sighed and looked at the clock. It was eleven-thirty and time for her to hit the hay.

Tomorrow was Saturday, and she was opening the diner with Brady. Even though she had gotten grants and scholarships that paid for her schooling and rent, she was so used to having a job that she couldn't give it up just yet. Besides, she enjoyed working with Brady. Now that school was in session, she didn't have much time for dates, so some weeks the only time she saw him was at Better Than Mom's on Saturday and Sunday mornings.

She was gathering up her papers and books when she heard voices in the hall. It sounded like Fay and Officer Bates were just getting home from a date. Naomi wondered if Norm would spend the night or if he was just dropping Fay off. Part of Naomi wanted to press her ear to the door to hear what they were saying, and part of her was horrified at the impulse.

She finished putting her schoolwork into her backpack, put the pens and pencils into the cup in the middle of the table, and turned out the kitchen light. It was time for her to go to sleep, not spend precious bedtime spying on her neighbor.

One morning a few weeks later, John said, "I'm lonely here, Mister Brady and Miss Fay, even with my cousins and friends from home. I want to have my Rosa with me in my new home. She's coming to visit me, and I'll ask her to marry me."

Fay's eyes filled with tears, and Brady cleared his throat a few times when they heard the longing in John's voice. At that moment they pledged to do whatever was needed to make John and Rosa's evening special.

Everyone in the place knew she was coming and knew how excited John was for her to come, and how much impressing her meant to him. Fay and Brady spent some time planning how to make John and Rosa's meal special. On the night they came in, Fay worked for Taffy, so she fixed a table in the back with a cloth tablecloth and cloth napkins she picked up at the dollar store. In the center of the table was a cheap vase she also got at the dollar store with a few grocery store flowers and one fern frond. The trip to the dollar store also yielded a votive holder and candle, unscented so the fragrance did not compete with the aroma of the food.

All that morning after he and Brady had the day's food prepared or prepped, John worked on special dishes that Fay would serve him and his girl. Finally, around four in the afternoon, Brady and Fay shooed him out. "Go," Fay said, "go and get ready to pick her up. We'll take care of everything. Just go." She pushed him toward to door.

As he was backing out, John said, "Now the tamales steam

for twenty minutes only, just twenty minutes, then they get garnished with cilantro, and I made a tomato peel rose for the sautéed corn. Make sure the table has a tablecloth and …"

Fay took his arm and said, "John, I know how to set a table. It's all there, tablecloth, napkins, flowers, even a candle. We got this." To stem the flood of nervous advice, Fay shoved John out the door and closed it in his face.

A few of the regular patrons were aware of the importance of the evening to John and they stayed around long after finishing their meals to offer their silent support on this night of nights and also to get a look at the woman John was so crazy about. Other patrons smelling the luscious aromas coming from John's special meal asked Fay where it was on the menu so they could order it and were disappointed. "Sorry, it's a special dinner for our cook, John, and his sweetheart from home. There's only enough for two. I'm sorry. Maybe we can ask Brady about putting it on the specials menu."

"What do you mean we can't have that? The whole place smells like it, and we can't have any? We're leaving, and you can be sure we won't be back."

No one in the place thought that it was a great loss.

Finally, everyone's waiting paid off; John and Rosa arrived.

John was almost unrecognizable. He was wearing knife-creased jeans, a green and white plaid cowboy shirt, a string tie with a thunderbird and turquoise slide, highly polished pointy-toed cowboy boots, and a white ten-gallon cowboy hat with a rattlesnake skin hatband.

Rosa was at least six inches shorter than the five-foot-six-inch-tall John. She wore a beautiful ruffled black skirt with multicolored embroidered flowers and birds all over it. Her blouse was white with ruffles around the shoulders. Her wavy black hair cascaded halfway down her back, and she had a beautiful ruby and emerald embroidered wool shawl around her shoulders with the ends clutched in her fists. Her liquid brown eyes darted around the café; it was obvious that John had told her that everyone in there was waiting to meet her. She looked nervous. John looked nervous.

Only Brady and Fay knew John planned to ask Rosa to marry him after their meal. He made a special dessert for her and instructed Fay how and when to serve it. She hoped her hands wouldn't shake when she served it, or her facial expression give it away.

CHAPTER 23

Brady was tired and frustrated. He'd worked all week and on the weekend mornings and hadn't had a minute alone with Naomi. "We need to go on a date," he said to her as she hung up her apron and got ready to head home on Sunday just after noon.

"I know, Brady, but I don't have any time that I'm not in school or doing homework or working. Neither do you. You're always in the kitchen here."

"Don't blame me for your lack of free time," he said. "I'm not the one who insists on you working the weekend mornings."

She crossed her arms over her chest. "But you are the one who pushed me to go to college. I was just fine working here and going to church and raising my son. You hauled me out to school and dragged me through the registration and everything."

He put his fists on his hips. "How can you blame me? You're the one who wants to be a nurse. You could have backed out at any point, but you didn't. You filled out the forms, you applied for financial aid, you bought the books, and you're taking the classes. Seems to me you're more to blame for your situation than I am."

"I'm to blame? Just because I said I wanted to be a nurse when I was in high school doesn't mean I want to be one now."

Brady stopped to look at Naomi's pale face. "What's the matter? I thought you were enjoying your classes."

She flapped her hand at him. "I am, oh, I am, but all the young people in my classes understand the material so quickly, and I'm struggling to learn even the most basic things."

He walked to her and held her upper arms, rubbing his hands up and down. "Aw, honey, I'm sorry you're having trouble. Those kids are just out of high school and probably had biology or chemistry a year ago. It's going to take you a little time to catch up, that's all."

She looked down. "I guess. I just feel so old and dumb. I never answer questions, and I just know I'm getting all my homework wrong."

"Have your teachers…"

"Professors."

"Professors said anything?"

She shook her head. "No, no one has said anything, but I can't believe they're not thinking that I shouldn't be in the classes."

He pulled her into his chest. "Don't be silly, I'm sure you're doing fine, but if you're worried, talk to them. They'll tell you if they think you need help."

John cleared his throat. "Uh, Mr. Brady, I need some help with all these orders."

Brady and Naomi jumped apart. They had forgotten where they were. Naomi was embarrassed that John had overheard her fears.

"Don't be afraid of not being the smartest one in your classes, Miss Naomi. I think you are very brave to go to college."

"Thanks, John," she said as she picked up her purse and went out the back door.

Brady followed her out. "Get your homework caught up and let's take a drive or a walk or something tonight after supper, okay?" She nodded and walked across the parking lot to her apartment complex.

Naomi opened the door.

Brady stood in the hall smiling at her. "Are you ready?" he said.

She smiled back. "Ready for what?"

His big shoulders raised and lowered in a shrug. "I don't know. Ready to go out with me this evening, I guess."

She stood aside and ushered him in. "I've finished my homework, and Marcus is working, so I'm ready to go out." She pulled her jacket off the coat hook by the door, and Brady held it for her to slip into. She wrote a note for Marcus, which she left on the table, and turned with her purse in her hand. "Ready."

Brady held the door for her, and they left the apartment. He opened the truck door for her and then went around to get into the driver's side.

"Where are we going?" she said.

"I'm not sure," he said. "Have you eaten?"

She nodded. "I had some pot pie leftovers, so I'm good."

"When did we make pot pie?"

She laughed. "I made pot pie yesterday. We don't eat from the diner every day; I still cook for my family."

Brady flushed. "Oh. Oh, yeah, of course you do."

She laughed and reached over to touch his hand. "Did you eat?"

He rolled his hand to clasp hers. "I had a late lunch, so I'm good too. What are you in the mood to do? Go to the movies?"

She shook her head. "No, we don't spend much time together that isn't working, and we'd just sit like statues in a movie. It's a nice night. Why don't we take a walk?"

Brady turned the key. "That's a good idea."

"Where are we going?"

"Downtown," he said. "We could walk along the river trail and stop somewhere for a drink."

"Sounds good to me."

It was a warm autumn night, and Naomi was glad to have her light jacket against the cool breeze that came off the river. They walked along arm in arm, enjoying the lights and the activity along the trail. There were still bicyclists and skaters out, but most of the traffic on the trail was people just like them enjoying an evening stroll.

Naomi leaned onto Brady's shoulder. "I'm sorry I snapped at you."

"It's okay."

"No, it isn't. I decided to go to school; you didn't force me, so I can't blame you when I feel like I'm out of my depth."

"I understand and I'm flattered that you feel comfortable enough with me to blow up like that and trust that I'll understand, and I do understand." He squeezed her arm with his. "If I went to college now, I'd be a basket case. I was never any great shakes at schoolwork and probably wouldn't be better now."

"Oh, I don't know about that. You can get credit for your life experiences these days, so I'm going to take a test to see what credits I can gain. I bet you'd do all right in the life experience part with all the places you've been."

"Yeah, locked in the steel ship belowdecks or in a metal tube a mile underwater."

"Not that. How long have you owned your own business?"

"Almost seven years."

"So, think of all the business experience you have and all the people you've served over the years. You have a lot of knowledge about a lot of things."

"Maybe, but I don't want to be a nurse."

"I'm not sure I want to be one either."

Brady stopped walking and stared at Naomi. "What? You don't want to be a nurse after all?"

"I said that I'm not sure." She tugged on his arm. "Let's keep walking. You promised me a drink." She resumed talking. "Part of me wants to be in college and be a nurse, and part of me wants to work at the diner and have an easier life. Then I think, what kind of example is that for Marcus? I can't just give up the first time I feel out of my depth. He'd think it is okay for him to give up when things got tough, and I can't let him do that. The only way he'll get ahead in life is to power through the tough times and keep his eye on his goals."

Brady was quiet for a while. "Sounds like good advice for all of us. I know you're struggling right now, but you just started. You need to give yourself time to get used to being in school and used to learning new things. If you still feel you're out of your depth in a month, go talk to a counselor about it. Maybe there's some help for returning adults. Maybe there's another woman a year ahead of you who felt the same way and can give you some advice."

Now Naomi was quiet for a bit. "That's a good idea, Brady. I think I'll go see the counselor tomorrow after class and see if there isn't someone ahead of me I can meet and get some tips on getting started. Thanks." She leaned over and planted a kiss on his cheek.

"Anytime."

He steered her onto the sidewalk area outside a bar. "Time for a drink," he said, ushering her into a chair at an empty table. "What'll you have?"

She thought for a moment. "I'll have an Irish coffee, please."

"Good idea." He turned to go inside. "Two Irish coffees

coming up."

CHAPTER 24

Fay delivered Steve's bowl of Texas Black Bean soup and glass of milk. Steve didn't look up or say thank you like he usually did. She figured he was on a deadline or in the middle of a paragraph and couldn't break his concentration, so she left the food and turned away.

"Wait, Fay," he said.

She turned back to see him motion for her to sit across from him. She checked the room to see if anyone was trying to catch her attention, but all the patrons were eating or talking, so she slid into the booth across from the writer. "What's up, Steve?" she said.

He fiddled with his pen and then pushed it away. "I need to ask you something."

"Okay, ask."

He hemmed and hawed, arranged his pens and shifted his notebook to the other side of his lunch. He looked at the bowl of soup but didn't pick up his spoon.

Finally, Fay lost patience. "Spit it out, Steve. I can't sit here too long. Someone will want something in a minute."

"Okay, okay," he said. "Can I ask you something?"

She nodded and kept quiet, letting him work up to whatever he wanted to talk about.

"I've, uh, I've decided to admit to being Layne Wilcox."

She folded her hands on the table. "Okay. What's the

problem with that? You should get the credit for your own work."

He squirmed in his seat. "Yeah, but what if my readers won't accept that their favorite woman author is a guy named Steve?"

She rubbed her chin. "I see the problem. Have you talked to your agent about it?"

"I have, and he thinks no one will make a fuss after the initial surprise. I keep cranking out the books, and nothing will change when it says by Steve Nelson writing as Layne Wilcox or whatever they decide to put on the cover."

"Well, there's always going to be a few crybabies that complain that things aren't the same as before they knew you're a guy, but mostly I think you'll get more readers."

He cocked his head. "How do you figure that?"

"Just think of all the guys who like romances; they'll be relieved to know that a real man writes them."

"But I'm not a real man," Steve said.

"How do you figure that?"

"Well, I'm not some he-man who runs marathons or wrestles alligators."

Fay laughed. "Most men don't run marathons or wrestle alligators. Most men work at their jobs and do their hobbies, nothing fancy, just everyday guys. Like you."

"Do you really think so?"

She reached over and patted his hand. "I really think so."

Just then a voice from behind her said, "Miss?"

"Gotta go, Steve, but I think you should own your writing." She picked up her tray and turned away, saying, "What can I do for you?"

Telling Fay his pen name and letting her see what he was writing worked a rapid change in Steve. Within a couple of weeks he was sitting with the coffee codgers a time or two each week and had told them all what he wrote.

"My wife is your biggest fan," Elmer said. "She's got all the Layne Wilcox books lined up on her bookshelf. She didn't believe me when I told her that the real Layne Wilcox is a retired guy living in Stinson." He fumbled a piece of paper from his shirt pocket. "Uh, can I have your autograph for her?"

Steve smiled. "Sure," he said and signed the scrap of paper *'Best wishes, Layne Wilcox.'* "I'm talking with my publisher about coming out and owning my books. I'm tired of hiding behind that pen name. I'm starting a detective series too and plan to publish it under my real name, so once the first of those books is out and, hopefully, successful, I'll let the cat out of the bag, so to speak."

Raymond always had an opinion about everything, and as Steve's ex-boss he felt it was his duty to say what he thought. "Don't you think everybody will think you're a pansy for writing all that sappy love crap? My wife read those books too, and they're nothing a real man would want to read."

Steve shook his head. "I don't think so, Raymond. Layne gets lots of fan mail from men, and not pansies either, real men who like the exotic locales and the adventures the main characters get into. Besides, I don't care if people think I'm a pansy, just as long as they keep buying the books, I'm happy." He looked down the line of codgers. "But I'll still be Stevie the scribbler here."

Everybody laughed, except Raymond.

CHAPTER 25

Naomi's class load was weighing her down. She had Chemistry, Biology, Psychology, and English Comp. The English class was the only one where she felt like she knew anything at all. She joked to Brady, "At least I understand the language in that one. In Biology and Chemistry, I'd be lost without my lab partners."

Brady nudged her with his elbow. "You'll figure it out. Give it time; you just started."

They stood side by side at the prep table in the diner kitchen. Brady was finishing up the last of the day's soups, and Naomi was making a big pan of biscuits. She knew John made the biscuits during the week, after all she had taught him her recipe, but the regulars swore they could tell the difference. And hers were the best. That made her feel good and like she was being selfish going to school.

"You don't owe those ingrates anything," Fay said to her. "They always find something to complain about. John's biscuits are just fine. You owe it to yourself to go to school. Following your dreams is important, and Marcus needs to see you doing it, so he stays focused on his college dreams too." Fay swept out of the kitchen with a bus tub full of clean dishes to get the diner set up to open.

Naomi put the pan of biscuits into the oven and went to the swinging doors into the diner. "How's the dancing going? How's Norm?"

Fay kept stacking mugs on the shelf below the coffeemaker, but Naomi could see that she was blushing. "It's fine, he's fine, we're all fine."

Naomi crossed her arms. "I miss having supper with you a couple of nights a week. I'm always studying, and you're always going to dance class."

Fay looked at her. "I guess that's what happens when you get a life."

Naomi turned back into the kitchen. "Yeah, but I don't have to like it."

Fay worked the opening shift on a couple of Saturdays a month; the others she took off so that she and Norm could travel around the state to dance competitions. They'd placed third a few times, second a few times, and first one glorious time.

They had gained a following. Fay's knitting friends had come to a competition and enjoyed it so much that they followed them around from city to city. The three women sat in the stands with their knitting in their hands and called out Fay and Norm's number as they twirled by. Fay had tried to knit in between dances to calm her nerves, but it didn't work. Her hands shook too much, and she kept dropping stitches, so she went back to wringing her hands until Norm held one of them to calm her down.

"How can you still be so nervous, Fay? We've been in eight competitions and came first once. We're pretty good, and we have a good time. Relax."

Fay jerked her hand away. "You relax. I'm a nervous person, and no amount of your telling me to will help me relax."

Norm blinked at her, and his face went still. "All right. You be nervous, I won't stop you."

Fay reached out and touched his arm. "Don't be mad,

Norm. Breaking my shoe and falling feels like a huge deal. We're out of the foxtrot competition because of it, and I feel like I failed you."

His face softened, and he leaned down to touch his forehead to hers. "You didn't fail me; it was an accident. We've still got the waltz to go, and we're going to be awesome. Try on your new shoes."

She dried her eyes, careful not to smudge her eyeliner, and opened the box. "Oh, Norm, they're beautiful."

The pearl-colored shoes glowed in the box and would be amazing in the bright lights of the dance floor.

"I thought you might like them. Try them on."

She did, and they fit perfectly. "I feel like Cinderella." She looked up at him from under her eyelashes. "And you're my Prince Charming."

He leaned in and touched his lips to hers.

CHAPTER 26

Fay looked up and was happy to see Honey come through the door of the diner. "Hey, Honey, long time no see. How are you?"

Honey smiled and walked down between the booths and the counter to give Fay a hug. "I'm fine, Fay. Been doing a lot of changing."

"Yeah? Well, sit down and tell me all about it." Fay ushered her to a booth, got her a mug of coffee, and made the quick rounds of the other customers so she could stand and talk to Honey for a few minutes. She stood at the end of the booth and smiled. "What's up?"

Honey fiddled with her mug handle. "Well, first and most important, I've left Ham."

Fay whooped. Heads turned, and she clapped her hands over her mouth. "Sorry. Good for you." She reached out to touch Honey's shoulder. "How's that going?"

"Good. After we were in here and he slapped me, Naomi must have put the fear of God into him because he barely came near me after that." She sipped her coffee. "Things weren't going well at the mill. I think his temper, which he used to take out on me, started coming out at work. He was encouraged to take anger management class which he hated, and he finally retired."

"Be right back." Fay left to wait on customers. She cleared tables, carried a bus tub into the kitchen, and filled coffee mugs. Since it was the end of breakfast time, there were few new diners and only the codgers and Steve left. Soon she was back at Honey's booth. "So, Ham retired. Then what?"

"Well, he wanted to go back home to Tennessee, but I didn't want to go. I got my real estate license a couple of months ago and have built a clientele. I didn't want to start over. I told him either to stay here or to go without me. We had a big fight about it, but for once he didn't hit me. I guess either Naomi or anger management class changed him. Anyway, he packed up his things and drove away about a month ago."

"How does that feel?"

Honey smiled. "It feels like freedom. In all my life, I've never been on my own. I sold our big house and split the proceeds with Ham, then I bought a condo in that new development on Webster Avenue, just across from Zambaldi Beer. It's great to be in a smaller place and all by myself."

"Are you getting a divorce?"

"Yes, the papers are already signed. We have a court date, but Ham isn't contesting it, and I doubt he'll come back for it." Honey looked around at the pass-through. "Is Naomi here? I want to say hello and thank her again for what she did for me."

Fay shook her head. "No, Naomi only works weekend mornings now. She's in college studying to be a nurse."

"A nurse. What motivated her to do that? I thought she liked cooking here."

"She did, she does, but it was always her dream to be a nurse, and Brady talked her into applying to school. She got lots of scholarships and grants so she could go to college and not go back on welfare. She cooks here on Saturdays and Sundays just to spend time with Brady, I think."

Honey smiled. "Oh, really? She wants to spend time with Brady?"

"Yeah, they're kind of dating."

"How do you kind of date?" Honey said.

"Well, okay, they've been on a few dates, but they're both

BARBARA ANGERMEIER MALCOLM

so busy that the time she's here is sometimes the only time they see each other through the week."

"And you? What have you been up to?"

Fay lifted her arms in a dance pose. "Officer Bates, Norm, and I have been taking dance lessons and entering competitions. We've won prizes, ribbons, but we only came in first once. So far."

"What kind of dance lessons?"

"Ballroom dancing. I have long dresses with big swirly skirts and sequins or rhinestones or feathers and silver shoes especially for dancing. It's a lot of fun."

"I bet it is. You'll have to tell me when your next competition is and where so I can come and watch. It's okay for me to come and watch, isn't it?"

"Sure," said Fay, "three knitters who come here for lunch every week come to watch and knit and holler out our number. You can come too if you want."

"I'd love to see you and Officer Bates dance."

Fay pulled out a menu. "Can I get you something besides coffee?"

"Let me look at the menu."

"I'll be back." Fay said, and she went to check on the other diners.

Brady dinged the bell. As she leaned in to pick up the food, Brady said, "Is that the lady whose husband slapped her a while back?"

"Yes," said Fay, "but she's left him. Well, he retired and went back to Tennessee, leaving her here. So, I guess he left her. Same difference."

"How's she doing?"

"Sounds like she's doing fine. She's got her real estate license. Do you want to buy a house?"

Brady shook his head. "Hell, no. I have enough trouble keeping this place afloat without having a mortgage to pay and a house and yard to take care of."

Fay turned away and went to deliver the order.

The next week when Taffy came in for her shift, she remarked to Fay that Raymond had been in one evening with a lady. "Who was it?" Fay asked.

"I think it was one of the bridge ladies," said Taffy.

"Oh, wait until I see Raymond tomorrow morning," Fay said. "I'm going to tease him about it."

"Don't do that. You'll embarrass him."

Fay rubbed her hands together. "That's my plan."

On Saturday night, Fay and Norm left dance class in time to get to Better Than Mom's before it closed. They sat at the counter, and Taffy came over to take their orders.

"Well, if it isn't the twinkle-toes couple," she said. "What can I get you?"

"Pie," they said in unison.

Norm had his usual blueberry a la mode, and Fay decided on banana cream with extra whipped cream. As Fay looked down the diner, she saw Raymond at a table in back with a lady.

"Is that Raymond I see back there with a date?" she asked Taffy.

"Yep, they've been in here at least once a week for the last couple of weeks. They're kind of cute together."

Fay snorted. "I can't imagine Raymond being cute. He's an opinionated and bossy old fart. What can that lady see in him?"

Taffy shrugged. "I don't know, but she seems to really like

him." She set down the plates of pie. "Coffee?"

Fay shook her head, but Norm nodded, saying, "Decaf."

Fay nearly fell off her stool craning her neck to watch Raymond and his lady friend.

"Fay, for god's sake, pay attention to what you're doing. You almost lost your bite of pie."

She put down her fork and turned back to Norm. "Sorry, but I can't get over Raymond being here with a date. Who'd want to date him?"

Norm nodded at the back of the diner. "That lady evidently now pay attention to me."

Fay bumped him with her shoulder. "I've been paying attention to you all night," she said with a grin.

"You mean stepping on my toes all night."

The grin slid off her face. "What do you mean I've been stepping on your toes all night? I did it maybe once."

"Once? Ha, I think you were on my feet more than you were on your own."

"Oh, really?"

"Yes, really. You keep trying to lead and step on my feet at least once a dance."

"Well, if it's such a problem, why do you keep dancing with me?"

Norm smeared his fork through the blueberry sauce and melted ice cream on his plate. He looked up at Fay and said, "Maybe because I'm falling in love with you."

Fay's mouth dropped open. "Falling... Oh no you don't. You aren't going to get around me like that. First you insult me and then you tell me you love me. How am I supposed to deal with that? I'm not falling in love with a dancing cop in a small Wisconsin town. No, I have bigger plans for my life. You're just a rest stop on my trip to California. As soon as my car is fixed, I'm out of here." Tears filled her eyes, and she wiped them away with her napkin. "Don't say love just to get out of an argument."

Norm took her hand and held it tight when she tried to shake him away. "I'm not saying that I love you just to avoid an argument. I think I'm falling in love with you. I love dancing with you. I love spending time with you. I love kissing you."

"Yeah, and you're good at that too, so how can I stay mad at you for long? You're too charming for your own good. For my own good."

He turned her hand over and traced a finger over her palm. "And Fay? You've had your car back for three months and you're still here."

She snatched her hand away. "Well, I have to save up money for the next part of my trip, don't I? I've spent all my cash on car repairs, rent, and dance stuff. I need to start saving my money. Saving my tips."

Norm drained his coffee mug and set it gently back on the counter. "I'm sorry I made you angry by telling you I love you. If I could take it back, I would, but I can't. I love you, Fay."

CHAPTER 27

Marcus threw down his pen and pushed away from the table. He'd come to the diner right after school, had a meatloaf sandwich, and got down to his homework. Business Practices class was giving him a hard time. He wasn't used to the regimented thinking of the business world and chafed against parroting back the lessons from the textbook.

"Anything I can do to help?"

Marcus jumped when Raymond set his coffee mug down on the table next to his notebook. "What do you mean?" Marcus asked.

"Well, you know I used to run the mill, so I know a lot about business. Ask me anything, go on."

Marcus sighed and pulled the Business Math book toward himself.

"Here, this chapter is about projections. How can you predict what will happen in a year? It makes no sense."

Raymond took the book and leaned in to read. "Damned cheap printers making the print small to save ink," he said. "I can barely read it."

Marcus smiled, knowing that it was Raymond's old eyes that were the problem. Raymond leaned over until his nose was nearly touching the page. "I can't make head nor tail out of this. How can they teach you something that it takes years to learn from experience?" He flipped the pages. "Where are the questions?"

"At the end of the chapter."

"Show me."

Marcus took the textbook back and turned the page. The list of questions filled one page and spilled over onto the next.

"Read me one," Raymond said.

"Your company manufactures widgets used in the automobile industry. Your biggest supplier needs a projection of how many you'll make in the next fiscal year. How will you calculate that?"

"Well, what have you learned?"

Marcus stared at the page and then pulled his notebook over so that he could see his notes from class. "I think I need to know the projected number of widgets that the auto industry will need over the next year so that I can figure out how many I need to make. That way I'll be able to figure out my raw material needs. Right?"

Raymond nodded. "Good thinking, son. What's your name again?"

"I'm Marcus, Naomi's my mom."

"Right. You're Naomi's boy. How's your mama doing in school? Do you think she'll be taking any business courses? I could help her too."

Marcus shook his head. "No, she's studying nursing, so I don't think she'll be taking any business courses, but I'll tell her you offered your help."

Raymond and Marcus made their way through the questions. Marcus paged back in the chapter to find the answers, and Raymond told him to "just delegate. That's why you have employees."

Marcus said that he didn't think his teacher would give him credit for that answer. The teacher was more interested in what the book said than in Raymond's real-life experiences. "Besides, I won't start at the top of the ladder; I'll have to work my way up, so I'll need to know what to do when someone delegates to me."

"Good point."

"And anyway, I won't be needing this stuff for my professional football career, will I? I'll have an agent and probably a manager to take care of my money and contracts."

Raymond snorted. "If you're one in a hundred guys lucky enough to make it to the pros, you'll still need to know these things to make sure that you're not getting cheated by your manager and agent. It's too easy to put your trust in someone and have them hornswoggle you out of everything you earn."

Now it was Marcus' turn to snort. "Hornswoggle? What does that mean? I've never heard that word. You made that up, didn't you?"

"No, I didn't make that up. It means to cheat or deceive. It's a perfectly good word."

Marcus began packing up his books and notebooks and put them into his backpack. "Thanks for your help, Raymond. Homework's all done, and it's time to get to work." He stood up, slung his pack over one shoulder, and made his way through the swinging doors into the kitchen where he parked his backpack in the office and grabbed a clean apron to put on.

John couldn't have been prouder. Brady got so many requests for John's Tamale Pie that he made it a regular feature on the buffet, and there was rarely any left for Fay to take home for supper. His Texas Black Bean Soup was also in the three-soups-every-day rotation. It was a popular soup, and Steve always bought a quart to take home. Brady and John developed a rhythm that was almost as seamless as Brady and Naomi's had been. John's biscuits improved so that customers couldn't tell the difference between his biscuits and Naomi's.

When John and Rosa got married, Brady closed the diner at noon so that they could have their wedding luncheon at Better Than Mom's. John cooked all night before the wedding. He made enchiladas in big roasting pans, tamale pie in sheet pans, and he barbecued briskets on a grill that he brought from home.

"Rosa's mama and her sisters are making salads and collard greens and other sides that they'll bring," John told Brady. "I hope that's okay."

Brady nodded. "As long as it's for the private party, it'll be okay. No serving paying customers food not made in our kitchen."

"That won't be a problem, Mr. Brady," John said with a smile. "After the party, there won't be a scrap left. Our families and friends know how to eat."

John invited Brady, Naomi, Fay, Norm, Marcus, Taffy, and James, the whole staff of the diner plus the local cop. He also invited Raymond and the rest of the coffee codgers because, he said, "They're my best biscuit fans." Leo and Raymond could be counted on to have two biscuits with their coffee of a morning, and each of them got into the habit of taking half a dozen home at least once a week.

Brady, Fay, Taffy, and Naomi worked quickly to clear away the breakfast service and get the place ready for the wedding party. They slotted John's pans of food into the hot buffet and cleared the counter so that there was room for all the bowls of salads and sides that the guests contributed to the feast.

The newlyweds showed up at the diner at twelve-thirty, trailing confetti in their wake. John held Rosa's hand and looked like he'd never let go. He wore a dark suit with his best cowboy boots polished until they gleamed. He had on a white shirt with a string tie with a big chunk of turquoise on the slide, and his cowboy hat was brushed to perfection. Rosa was the epitome of a blushing bride. She wore a full-skirted white dress with lace sleeves and beads sewn on the bodice with a lace mantilla as a veil. She carried a bouquet of white roses and baby's breath.

Two of John's cousins carried in a washtub filled with ice and bottles of beer. Brady wasn't expecting that and worried because he didn't have a liquor license, but he figured as long as it was a private party it'd be okay.

The party went on all afternoon and into the evening. People ate nearly all of John's food and the dishes that the ladies of the party had brought. Fay finally got to taste John's enchiladas and understood why there was never any left. It was delicious. Naomi ate carefully, trying to pick out the different spices that were in each dish. She especially liked the hush puppies that Rosa's mother made. They were a mix of savory and spicy that Naomi couldn't get enough of. Who doesn't like fried dough? Naomi sat with Marie, Rosa's mother, and the two women talked cooking all afternoon.

"I put a tiny pinch of cayenne pepper in with the dry ingredients," Marie said. "It adds a little kick but not too much. You can put in corn kernels too if you want or bacon, but I like the plain ones with just minced onion and that little cayenne best."

Naomi nodded as Marie told her the recipe. She pulled out her phone and wrote it down so that she could make them at home. "I'm going to make us some one of these weekends when I don't have too much homework. They'd be good with my fried chicken or a beef roast. Or anything."

Marie nodded. "Sometimes I just make hush puppies when I'm not too hungry for supper. They're good all on their own."

"I've never had plain pinto beans either," Naomi said. "They're so good with just onions, garlic, and tomato. I'll be making those too." She finished adding that recipe to her phone.

"I think soon you will have more Texas on your menu," Marie said with a smile.

The wedding cake was a beautiful creation made by John's cousin's wife. She had a little sideline in custom cakes and made a lemon cake with buttercream frosting for John and Rosa's wedding. It had two tiers and was decorated with a trailing line of white roses. Rosa's sister cut the cake, and Fay handed out the plates.

"This is the best wedding I've ever been to," Fay said to Naomi as she put down pieces of cake in front of her and Marie. "Nobody's drunk and nobody's fighting. It's amazing."

"You've led an interesting life," Naomi said.

Fay was walking away but turned back and said, "I'll say."

Once the cake was cut and served, the party wound down. Brady had to persuade John that he, Marcus, and James could clear the small food remains and get the dishes washed. "Go on, go with Rosa; we'll take care of all of this."

"Are you sure, Mr. Brady? I can roll up my sleeves and help."

Brady shook his head. "No, the groom does not clean up after his own wedding. Go."

Nearly all the guests had left when Rosa slid her small hand over John's. "It's time to leave, husband," she said. "Husband, I like that word." She smiled up at him, looking like the happiest woman in the world. John picked up his hat, settled it on his head, and escorted his new bride from the diner.

The only people left in the place were Brady and his staff. Everyone pitched in and got the food and dishes cleaned up in a short time.

Fay said, "Remember what Raymond said when he left. He expects us all to be here in the morning ready to serve him coffee."

"I guess that means I make biscuits in the morning," Naomi said. "Maybe Raymond will tell the difference between mine and John's."

"Probably not," said Brady. "John has gotten really good at making biscuits these last few months."

Naomi swatted him on the shoulder. "That's not nice. You always said that my biscuits were the best. Now you say that John's are just as good? Maybe I'll be busy the next time you want to take a walk along the river."

"Oh no, don't do that. I barely get to see you as it is. Please don't be mad at me, Naomi; your biscuits are still the best. I just don't think that Raymond will be able to tell. That's what I meant." Brady looked stricken.

Naomi took pity on him. "I was kidding. I've had John's biscuits, and they're nearly as good as mine. Raymond will never be able to tell. I'll be over to make a batch of biscuits before church, and you can bake them for me while I'm gone. I'll be back after the service to help with the breakfast rush."

Brady smiled and picked up a bus tub of dirty plates and carried it back through the swinging doors into the kitchen where Fay and Norm were loading the dishwasher. "More?" Norm said. "How many people were here? It seems like we're doing dishes for an army."

"There had to be forty or fifty people," said Fay, "that many people make lots of dirty dishes."

Soon all the dishes were washed and put away. Naomi, Marcus, Taffy, and James went over the diner one more time with bottles of spray cleaner and fresh rags to make sure that all was ready for the next morning. Seven tired people met at the back door, ready to leave. "We'll be back in the morning," Fay called out to the darkened diner.

Everyone laughed and filed out. Brady locked the door behind them. "It was a good day," he said.

CHAPTER 28

Steve came in with a big smile on his face. Fay followed him down the length of the diner with the coffee pot ready to pour his first mug as soon as he sat down.

"What's with the smile? You look like you won the lottery," she said as she poured the hot brew.

Steve set his briefcase down on the seat next to him and grinned up at her. "My new book came out with 'by Steve Nelson writing as Layne Wilcox' and hardly anyone seemed to notice. Sales are right up there, and aside from a few emails asking what happened to Layne, it's going okay."

Fay grinned right back at him. "That's great news, Steve. I told you that people would be okay with knowing that their favorite woman author was really a man. Good for you."

"Have you read it yet?" he asked.

She shook her head. "Not yet. I'm still working on your detective story. It's a complicated tale, but I'm enjoying it. You sure have some surprising ideas."

"I've got you stumped, have I?"

"For now," she said, "but I'll figure it out before the end. I know I will."

Steve shook his head. "You might not. I was pretty clever. I've been working on that story for a long time. Since I was in college. I don't think many people will figure it out before the end. Who are your suspects?"

Fay backed away. "Oh, no you don't. I'm not going to lay out my suspicions and let you laugh at me. I'll just keep on reading and figure it out." She picked up the coffeepot and turned to walk away. "Flag me down when you're ready to order. Texas Black Bean Soup is on the menu today."

As she turned, Fay almost bumped into Raymond, who was holding a book. "Sorry, Raymond."

The older man held a book close to his chest so he wouldn't drop it. "You're excused, Fay. I just want a word with Steve."

Steve looked up with a wary look on his face. He had been the butt of Raymond's laughter when he had admitted that he wrote romance novels and wasn't sure he was willing to let Raymond burst his happiness today. "What can I do for you, Raymond?"

Raymond shuffled in place and finally laid the book down on the table with a thump. "This is a real good story. I was wondering if you'd sign it for me." His face turned pink as he spoke, and he wouldn't meet Steve's eyes.

Steve pulled a pen from his shirt pocket and turned the book over to the front, seeing his first detective novel. "I'd be happy to sign your book. Shall I inscribe it to you?"

Raymond jingled the change in his pocket. "You can if you want to. I can spell Tolliver for you if you need me to."

"That won't be necessary. I remember how to spell your name from all those years of memos." He scrawled 'To my old boss, Raymond Tolliver. Thanks for all your support. Steve Nelson,' on the title page, then closed the cover, and slid it across the table. "Here you go, Raymond. I'm glad you liked the story."

"Maralee gave it to me for my birthday. She knows I like detective stories. I read it in just two days. Really pulled me in." He rubbed his hand over the cover. "Will you be writing another one?"

Steve smiled. "I'm working on another one now." He patted the briefcase on the booth seat beside him. "It'll be a while before it's done and published but don't worry another story is coming."

"Well, that's good. Thanks." Raymond picked up the book and went back to his seat at the counter.

Fay and Norm were acquiring a following. Honey joined

the knitting trio of older ladies. Naomi showed up a time or two when she had time between homework and Brady. Even Raymond came with his lady friend, Maralee. Fay was always more nervous when Raymond was there.

"He's usually got something to say on Mondays about my dress or my performance. He's a distraction. I wish he wouldn't come," she said to Norm as they peered out at the audience before their first dance.

Norm put his hand on her shoulder and rubbed down her arm. "Don't let him get to you. He's just an unhappy old man who likes to get under your skin. Ignore him."

"I can't," she said, motioning to where the older man sat in the stands. "He's right there in the front where I can't help but see him when we get onto the floor. Then he shouts our number like he's bidding at a cattle auction. Drives me nuts."

"Dancers, fifteen minutes until the waltz competition." The voice on the public address system made Fay's shoulders tighten under Norm's hand.

"Oh man, I've got to go check my hair and makeup," Fay said. "I just know that my hair isn't going to hold up today."

Norm said, "You look beautiful." But he was talking to her back as she hurried to the dressing area to use another half-can of hair spray on her already sprayed curls.

Fay had bought her dance dresses online instead of at the local thrift store. Naomi was too busy with school and homework to help her embellish the formals she found at Goodwill and Salvation Army stores in Stinson, and the dresses made for dancing were better made. They held up better. If Fay had had her way, she would have bought a new dress for each competition, but her budget wouldn't stretch to that. She had the peach dress with the feathers around the hem that was her first competition dress, and she bought a pale aqua blue dress from eBay that had beads on the deep-V of the bodice and across the hips, and detachable feather cuffs. That one cost her almost a month's tips, but the first time she put it on she knew it was money well spent. Norm had a vest and bowtie made of the same color satin. They looked marvelous dancing together.

"Dancers, it's time for the waltz competition. Please take the floor."

Fay reached a hand up to make sure there were no stray hairs coming loose from her updo and then slid her arm through Norm's as he led her out onto the dance floor.

"You look wonderful," he said, leaning down to her ear. "Stop fidgeting."

They reached an open spot on the gleaming wood floor and faced each other, joined hands, and then moved into their first pose. The lights shone on the beads on Fay's dress, and she sparkled. The long feathers of her cuffs quivered in the air flowing around the room and from her nervous shaking.

"Smile," Norm said without moving his lips.

Fay licked her lips and stretched them into a smile. "I'm smiling but I'm so nervous."

Just then Raymond brayed, "You look beautiful, Fay."

Hearing her name knocked the smile off her face, and the music started. She was so off-balance that she started to move on the first note, but Norm held her still.

"Two, three, four," he said as he had to do nearly every time. He stepped forward into the waltz, and Fay moved backwards in perfect step.

"Three-seventy-eight!" Raymond's loud voice echoed through the room. He was the first to call out a number.

Norm and Fay were at the opposite end of the dance floor from where Raymond sat, and Fay barely heard him. They swayed and twirled, dipped and posed their way through the song and ended up right in front of their fans. Five female voices called out their number as the applause swelled.

They bowed to the judges and then to the crowd. Norm held Fay's hand as they left the floor. He lifted their joined hands and kissed Fay's fingertips. "You were magnificent. You didn't let Raymond distract you."

"I didn't hear him after that first shout right before the music started."

Norm pulled a tissue out of a box nearby and patted his forehead, then gently blotted Fay's face so as not to muss her makeup.

"Oh no, am I sweating?" Fay's hands reached up toward her face.

"You're glowing," Norm said. "I just dabbed your face to make sure your makeup stays fresh."

She took the tissue and pressed it under her lower lashes. "I can feel sweat right here."

The announcer called the couples who had made the cut back to the floor. "Three-seventy-eight!" was the first number that he called. Norm took Fay's hand and led her back onto the floor. He chose a spot far away from Raymond and Maralee, hoping that distance would dilute the force of Raymond's voice. There were five couples in the second round, so they had more room to show off their dancing. The music started, and the waltz began again.

Fay's feet felt like they had wings. She could feel Norm's strong hand on her back and the steadiness of his grip and felt free. She leaned into the music and let the notes and her new dress carry her along. The lights in the room and the gleam of the chandeliers made it feel like they were dancing in the starry sky. If anyone called out their number, she didn't hear it. Applause washed over them as the music ended and the dance was over. Now it was up to the judges to decide their fate.

Five couples clustered at the side of the room waiting for the judges to announce who had won.

"In third place, couple three-eighty-one!" A woman in a wine-red dress rushed onto the floor with her tuxedo-clad partner.

"In second place, couple three-seventy-seven!" The purple couple pushed past to accept their award.

Fay and Norm looked at each other, their shoulders beginning to sag in disappointment.

"And in first place, couple three-seventy-eight!" They had won first place. Fay grabbed Norm's hand and pulled him into the spotlight. She had a broad smile on her face, and there were pink spots high on her cheekbones. Norm flushed with pleasure as he lifted Fay's hand and twirled her around so that her aqua skirt swirled out. This time Fay heard the applause and heard their friends calling out their names and number.

It was a raucous crowd that got to Better Than Mom's that night in time for pie. Naomi was there in the back, just finishing her homework, and her head popped up when the loud voices and happy people came through the door. Fay spotted her friend and called, "We won!"

"What?" Naomi was on her feet and moving toward Fay.

"We won first place in the waltz," said Fay. She took Norm's hand and raised up the trophy he held. "See? We got a trophy and everything."

Everyone in the place clapped, and a few even stomped their feet. The customers who weren't regulars looked around in amazement as the eight people, two in fancy dress, commandeered a pair of tables, shoved them together, and sat down in the back of the diner. Naomi gathered up her books and papers, tucked them into her backpack, and joined the happy throng.

Taffy came toward them grinning. "Congratulations," she said. "It's the new dress that did the trick."

Steve got up from his usual booth to clap Norm on the back and kiss Fay on the cheek. "I knew you could do it," said Steve. "You've worked hard enough. It had to happen eventually. Great job!"

The pie tasted extra good that night and, wonder of wonders, Raymond picked up the tab.

CHAPTER 29

It was snowing. Really snowing with a strong north wind blowing the snow around. Schools were closed, and there weren't many customers at Better Than Mom's. Raymond straggled in at close to six-thirty, half an hour after his usual arrival time, but he was the only coffee codger there that morning. Steve came in right after Raymond and stood brushing snow off his shoulders in the entryway. He took off his knit hat and shook the snow off that.

"Good morning, Raymond," he said. "I'm surprised to see you here on a day like this."   Raymond lifted his coffee mug. "My coffee is even worse than Brady's swill. I had to come for self-preservation."

Steve said, "I came for the soup." The men shared a chuckle as Steve walked down the diner to his usual end booth. Fay came out of the kitchen, amazed to see them.

"What are you guys doing here? It's a blizzard outside." She picked up the coffeepot. "I wouldn't be here if I had had to drive. Walking over was treacherous enough." She filled Raymond's mug and went down to fill Steve's mug. "John didn't make it this morning. His tires are bald, and he couldn't get out of his driveway, so it's only me and Brady to deal with you."

She heard the back door shut with a bang and then Naomi's voice. "School's closed, so Marcus is still asleep, and I'm here to help," Naomi said. "Are there any customers foolish enough to be out in this?"

Fay poked her head through the swinging doors. "Raymond and Steve are here, but I'm guessing they'll be the only ones."

Just then, Norm came through the door.

Fay looked at him. "What are you doing here?"

Norm walked over to her and kissed her cheek. "I came to make sure that you made it to work okay. I'm glad to see you too."

Fay kissed him back. "I hope you're not out patrolling in this. It's a whiteout out there. I barely found my way on foot, and my apartment's not even a block away." She set a mug of coffee down in front of him. "Do you have time for some coffee and maybe some breakfast before you go back out?"

He picked up the mug and took a sip. "Ooh, hot. I've got time for coffee, but I have to get back out there. Keep Stinson safe, you know." The mic on his shoulder crackled, and he tipped his head to listen to what sounded like static to Fay. "10-4," he said, pushing the "talk" button then setting down his coffee. "Gotta go. Some fool is doing cheerios in the middle of the Mason and Military intersection."

Fay touched his hand. "Be careful, Norm, I don't want anything to happen to you."

He touched her cheek. "Thanks, love, I'll be careful. I always am." Norm went out into the blowing snow, settling his fur-lined hat on his head.

Fay watched him get into his squad car, turn on the blue and red light bar, and drive out of the lot heading for the big intersection a long block away. She shook her head and turned back to Raymond. "Do you want anything to eat this morning?"

Raymond craned to see into the kitchen through the pass-through. "Do you think Naomi's making biscuits? I could eat a couple of biscuits with some of that homemade strawberry jam you've got hidden under the counter."

Fay put down the coffeepot. "I'll go ask." She went through the swinging doors. Brady and Naomi were just finishing prepping the third soup of the day—chicken vegetable with noodles. "Any chance you're making biscuits today, Naomi? Raymond said he could eat some if you feel like making them."

Naomi looked at Brady. "I could make a small batch. I don't suppose that we'll have enough customers to warrant making a big batch."

Brady nodded. "A small batch would be okay, I guess. It's hard to say how many customers we'll get on a day like today. Could be a lot, could just be Raymond and Steve."

Naomi pulled the flour canister toward herself and got a big crockery bowl down off the shelf. "Can't make good biscuits in a stainless-steel bowl," she said. "Gotta have a good old bowl like this one." She got to work measuring and mixing. It didn't take her long to have a bowl of dough that she kneaded just once on the floured steel work surface before rolling it out into a rectangle. Naomi cut the dough into squares and placed them bottom side up on a baking sheet lined with parchment paper. She brushed the tops with a little milk and got them into the oven.

"Why do you turn them over?" Brady asked.

"My mama always did that. She said that it made the tops of the biscuits nice and flat. I guess that's a good thing." She shrugged. "I don't know. That's the way I do it."

Brady chuckled. "Well, don't change what you do. People rave about your biscuits. Even though you taught John your recipe and method, his still aren't quite as good as yours are."

"Thanks for saying that, Brady." She leaned over and kissed him.

One by one, more regulars staggered in, shaking off snow and complaining about the roads. Elmer Bump said, "There's a real mess down at the Military and Mason intersection. Some fool ran into a squad car and banged it up pretty bad."

Fay nearly dropped the coffeepot she was carrying. The smile slid off her face, and she turned pale. "A squad car? Was the driver hurt? Norm just went down there. Elmer, what did you see?"

Elmer shook his head. "I think somebody got hurt. There were two rescue squads there. The cop car got hit in the driver's door. That's all I could see. They were detouring us around the wrecked cars while the firemen were using the Jaws of Life and EMT's were waiting with a gurney."

Fay put the pot down on the counter. "I've gotta go see if Norm's okay." She rushed into the kitchen saying, "I think Norm's been hurt. There's a squad car been hit down at Military and Mason and that's where he was headed. I have to go." She pulled on her parka, wrapped a scarf around her face, and shoved her feet into her boots.

Brady stopped her at the back door. "You can't go out there when the weather's like this. You'll get lost before you get fifty feet. Besides, they'll have taken anyone injured to the hospital."

She put her hands up to shove Brady to the side. "I have to go. What if Norm's really hurt? What if he's dead? Let me go, Brady." She struggled to pull her arms from Brady's grip.

"Fay," he said, "call the police station. Someone there will be able to tell you if Norm's been hurt. By the time you make it down that long block on foot, they'll have left. Only the tow truck drivers and someone directing traffic will be there. You'll get cold and wet for nothing."

Mascara-stained tears coursed down her cheeks. "I need to know. I need to go."

Brady put his arm around her. "Come on, honey. Come into the office. I'll call the station to see what I can find out."

"Okay." She sniffed, dabbing at her tears with the end of her scarf.

He gently lowered Fay into the guest chair, went around the desk, and sat behind it. He dialed the non-emergency number and was amazed to get right through. "Hi, this is Brady Gallagher. We hear that a squad car was hit on Military and Mason just now. My waitress has been dating Norm Bates, and we're afraid that he's been injured. Can you tell me anything?"

He held the phone to his ear. "Yeah. Yeah. Uh-huh. Okay, thanks." He put the phone down.

Fay sat on the edge of the chair, gripping Brady's desk so hard that her nails made crescent shapes in the wood. "What did they say?"

"Well," he swallowed, "Norm was hit, and he was hurt. They don't know how bad it is. He's at St. Mary's. The lady said to call back later when they might know more."

She looked around. "How can I get there? My car won't make it in this storm."

Brady made up his mind. "I'll take you in my truck. It's got four-wheel drive. Give me a minute to talk to Naomi, and we can go."

Within ten minutes, Brady had asked Naomi to make meatloaf with mashed potatoes and green beans, which was what he was planning for the lunch special, gotten bundled up, and he and Fay were slowly making their way through the storm to the hospital nearby. There were still tow trucks and officers at the intersection where the accident happened, and Fay gasped when she saw the mangled driver's side of Norm's squad car.

"Oh, Brady," she whispered, "how could he have survived that?"

Keeping his eyes on what he could see of the road, he said, "Remember they had to cut the door, so it probably looks worse than it was. We're almost there." He eased around the last corner onto Shawano Avenue and pulled into the lot by the emergency entrance of the hospital. He found a parking place, and he and Fay made their way through the wind and driving snow to the entrance.

"Can I help you?" said the receptionist.

"How's Norm?" Fay blurted out. "I need to know how Norm is. You have to tell me."

"I'm sorry, ma'am, I can't divulge patient information unless you're his next of kin."

"He's my dancing partner. We're almost engaged. Please, can't you tell me how he is?"

The woman shook her head and went back to tapping on her keyboard. Just then, a pair of police officers came out of the doors to the treatment area.

Fay spotted them, recognized one, and hurried to intercept them. "Murphy, can you tell me how Norm is? I heard he got hit, and she won't tell me anything."

Murphy took Fay's arm and steered her to the waiting

area. "Fay, honey, Norm's pretty busted up. His leg's broken, and his arm's broken, and he's got broken ribs. They think he's got a concussion, and they're checking for internal injuries. Before you ask, he'll make it, but he'll be laid up for quite a while."

Fay shook her head. "I don't care if he's broken; he'll heal. I just want him to be alive."

"He's alive."

"Is he conscious? Can I go see him?"

Murphy shook his head. "No, he's not conscious, and I'm sure they won't let you go back to see him. Give them the rest of the day to get him patched up, and then when he's ready for visitors, I'll come get you and take you to see him. Okay?"

"Okay." She pulled tissues from a box on the table next to her chair, wiped her eyes, and blew her nose. "Thanks, Murphy. I guess that's the best I can hope for right now." She turned to Brady. "Let's get back to the diner. Naomi's going to need help."

When they went outside, the storm had stopped. It was still a little windy, but the snow had stopped falling, so the drive back to Better Than Mom's wasn't as treacherous.

"Thanks, Brady," said Fay. "I don't know what I'd have done if I hadn't gotten to find out how Norm is. Thanks for taking me to the hospital, even though I didn't get to see him. At least I found out that he's alive and will get better."

Brady glanced at her and smiled. "Anything for a friend."

They got back to the diner just in time. The snowplow had been working up and down Mason Street during the storm, so it was pretty passable. That let customers trickle in looking for something warm to eat and someplace cheerful to eat it in. They sold a lot of soup and meatloaf that day.

Fay was back to her sassy self, laughing and joking with the customers. Most of the time.

Three long days passed before Fay got to visit Norm in the hospital. He had surgery to repair his broken leg, and they kept him in the ICU for a couple of days until they determined that his concussion wasn't as bad as they'd feared. True to his word,

Murphy picked Fay up when she got off work and drove her down to St. Mary's. Fay stopped in the hall outside Norm's room and took a deep breath.

"It's okay, Fay," Murphy said. "He's waiting to see you."

She looked up at the policeman. "He remembers me? I was afraid that he'd forget me with his head injury."

Murphy shook his head. "No, the nurse tells me he's been asking for you ever since he regained consciousness. Today is the first day they're letting him have visitors. I told him earlier that I would bring you after work. He made me promise." Murphy reached past Fay and pushed open the door to the room. The shades were lowered, and a dim light shone at the head of the bed.

"Fay?"

She took her time getting to the bedside. She was afraid that she'd burst out crying when she saw him. "Yeah," she said, "it's me. How are you doing, Norm?"

He looked like a wreck. The whole left side of his face was swollen and bruised. He had cuts all over his face. His left leg and arm were in casts and elevated, and he had an IV in his right arm.

Norm gave her a lopsided smile. "I'm doing just great. Ready to go dancing as soon as I'm out of here."

She reached out and touched his right hand, the only part of him that didn't look like it hurt. "We should maybe wait until you're out of the casts before we go dancing."

"Nah," he said with a slight shake of his head, "I'll be ready before the casts are off. Maybe there's a wheelchair division, then we could start right away."

Tears filled Fay's eyes, but she blinked them away. "I'll check with the judges."

Norm turned his hand over to grasp Fay's hand. "I hear you told them we were engaged trying to get in to see me the day of the accident."

Fay blushed to the roots of her dyed hair. "I might have said that we were almost engaged. I was desperate to get to see you. I was willing to lie to make sure that you weren't dead."

Murphy quietly went out into the hall, pulling the door shut behind him.

Norm turned his head slightly toward her. "We could make it not a lie if you say yes."

Fay suddenly felt trapped. "I… I'm not sure I'm divorced from Butch. I never sent him my address in Stinson, so I'm probably still married."

Norm's fingers tightened on hers. "Why don't you check that out? I'm going to need some nursing when I get out of here, and if you're my fiancée, you could stay with me and help me rehab."

"Wouldn't it be better in a place with real nurses and physical therapists and stuff? I'm just a waitress; I'm no nurse."

He lifted her hand and kissed her fingers one at a time. "At first, I'll be in a rehab place, but once I can go home, I'll probably have visiting nurses and therapists. You could be my night nurse. What do you say? Will you think about it?"

"Yeah, yeah, I'll think about it." She pulled her hand away and leaned down to kiss his cheek. "I'll think about it really hard. I gotta go." She almost ran out of the room, hearing Norm say, "I love you, Fay" as she went through the door.

Murphy leaned in to say goodbye to Norm and then hurried to catch up to Fay at the elevator. "You okay?" he said.

Fay nodded. "Fine. I'm just fine. Why wouldn't I be?"

He turned away so she wouldn't see his smile. "No reason."

CHAPTER 30

Brady and Naomi had trouble finding time to spend together. Most nights Brady stayed at Better Than Mom's until closing or near enough, and Naomi was buried under her studies. It had taken a while, but she was much happier at school than she had been last semester. She had kept at it and eventually her brain absorbed the information rather than letting it bounce off. This semester she had more science classes, so she was constantly studying to keep up. She met another returning woman student in the nursing program who was a year ahead of her, so she had someone to turn to when things got to be too much or too confusing. Naomi kept working Saturday and Sunday mornings at the diner just so she had an excuse to see Brady.

"You know you can stop working weekends if you get behind in your studies," Brady said to her.

Naomi put her hands on her hips. "And if I do exactly when will I see you? When I come in to study at night, you're in the kitchen and I'm at a table in the back. We can't even see each other."

"I know, I know. Maybe I can schedule James to cook one night a week so that we can have a date. We could take a walk or something."

She shook her head. "I'm not a fan of walking in the bitter cold and snow up past my knees. We have to think of something else to do."

"A movie? And before you say no, we could rent a movie and watch it at my place. That way we can talk and not disturb other people. We could have pizza. I know how much you love pizza."

"Pizza would be good." She put her arms around Brady's neck. "Pizza and a movie sounds like a nice date. See if James can work one night next week. I miss spending time with you."

Brady slid his arms around Naomi's waist and kissed her. They stood in the kitchen kissing until they heard someone clear their throat. They jumped apart to see Fay grinning at them in the pass-through.

She clipped a piece of paper onto the carousel and said, "Sorry to intrude, but it's time to go back to work. Order up!"

Norm worked really hard to rehabilitate his injuries. It took ten weeks before he could put any weight on his leg, and then not too much or too often. Fay was glad he was in a rehab facility because she couldn't imagine being able to take care of him night and day the way he needed someone to.

True to her word, Fay contacted Butch to find out that she was indeed divorced, and had been since six months after she left him. The grounds Butch used for the divorce were desertion, which Fay thought was funny since she felt like he had deserted her for pool months before she left. She didn't tell Norm right away because she wasn't sure she wanted to get right back into a serious relationship. Norm said he loved her, but she wasn't sure that she loved him, not in an "until death do us part" way, anyway. She loved dancing with Norm, loved spending time with him, loved the way he treated her, which was better than any other man had ever treated her, but something in her held back from saying that she loved him and agreeing to wear his ring.

Fay wished Naomi wasn't so busy with school, homework, work, and Brady. She missed the times when Naomi would bring down a plate of supper and they'd sit and talk about life and their dreams. She missed walking through Kmart or Safeway with Naomi shopping or browsing the racks and laughing. Fay could talk to Naomi about anything. Naomi would understand her reluctance to tie herself to another man when she still felt like California was her eventual destination. Or was it?

For years, Fay's life had been messy and disrupted. Her parents were dead, she was an only child, and the rest of her family had abandoned her long ago. Running away from Norm would mean running away from all of her friends at Better Than Mom's. Fay didn't know if she had the strength.

The next time Fay visited Norm at the rehab center, he showed her how well he could walk with one crutch. "Having my left arm in a cast sure is slowing down my walking," he said. "I can't use two crutches, so I have to limp along with one. That's going to slow down our getting back to dancing."

The physical therapist helping him walk chuckled but said nothing.

"I miss dancing with you too," said Fay, "but I'm glad to see you on your feet instead of in that wheelchair."

"I still need the wheelchair most of the time, but it's getting to be less all the time." The therapist and the PT aide helped him back into the wheelchair, and the aide began wheeling him back to his room. Fay walked alongside. "Pretty soon I won't need it at all," Norm told her, "but my arm's not healing as fast as my leg. Every X-ray shows only a little recalcification. Not fast enough for me."

Fay held up the small cooler she carried. "Hey, I brought us some pie. I even have a little cup of vanilla ice cream for your blueberry slice. We'd better eat it before it's vanilla soup." She got busy getting the pie out of the cooler while the PT aide locked the wheels and said goodbye.

"I'm glad I didn't break my right arm," Norm said around a bite of pie and ice cream. "I'd never be able to eat this left-handed without getting it all over myself. Thanks, Fay, this is great."

"Anytime."

That word hung in the air between them. Suddenly it seemed to carry more weight than those seven letters should. Fay bolted the last few bites of her banana cream pie, slid her plate and fork into the cooler, and stood up. "I have to run," she said. "I'll pick up your plate and fork tomorrow."

"No need," Norm said. "I'm finished. Here." He pushed the empty plate and fork toward her across the bed table that was in front of his wheelchair. When Fay reached for the plate, he laid his hand over hers. "When are you going to stop running away, Fay?"

"I'm not running away; I have an appointment. To get my oil changed." She tugged her hand away and put his plate and fork into the cooler with hers.

"Fay."

Tears filled her eyes, and she dropped back into her chair. "Okay, I don't have an appointment. I'm scared, Norm."

"What are you scared of?"

She shook her head. "You. Us. I'm scared that all we have in common is dancing, and what if that's not enough? What if I fall in love with you, get engaged to you, marry you, and the next time you're hurt on the job you're dead?"

Norm moved the rolling table back over his bed, unlocked the wheels of his chair, and rolled himself until his feet touched hers. "Fay, I can't promise you I won't get hurt at work anymore. Even crossing guards are out on the street and can get hurt." He reached out and held her hand. "But I can promise you I'll be the best husband you've ever had or, if you don't want a husband, the best long-term boyfriend ever. I don't have to get married to love you. It'd make things like insurance and next-of-kin issues easier if we were married, but those are things we can deal with later. Right now, I just want to love you and have you come see me every day. I'd like you to move in with me when I get out of here, if you're willing."

She smiled at him. "You don't know what you're asking. I can't cook except to microwave frozen meals, and I come with four boxes of high-heeled shoes. Besides, like I said, I'm a waitress; I'm no nurse."

Norm shook his head. "I won't need a nurse, just someone to help me move around until my leg gets stronger and my stupid arm heals. I can cook, and until I'm able to, we can get takeout from Better Than Mom's."

"Are you nuts? Do you know how much that will cost us? You can teach me to cook." She stopped talking, realizing that she had just agreed to move in with him. "Exactly how far away from the diner do you live? I go in early, remember."

"I live barely a mile away. Why do you think I show up there so often?"

"I thought it was to see me."

He nodded. "That and the fact that it's my local diner, close to home and good food."

Fay crossed her arms over her chest. "So how come I never saw you in there before the vandalism?"

Norm had the grace to blush. "Okay, okay, I confess, I come in to see you—and because of the blueberry pie."

"I knew it was the pie," she said, and she leaned forward to rest her head on his shoulder.

He reached out with his right arm and scooped her onto his lap, holding her close to his chest. "I miss holding you. Sit here on my lap for a while."

She tried to raise up off his legs. "Am I going to hurt your leg? I'm not a lightweight, you know."

"You're as light as a feather," he said with a laugh. "Sit still and let me hold you."

She slipped her arms around him and hugged him close. "I miss holding you too."

Fay didn't move in with Norm as soon as he got home from rehab. She was still skittish about the whole idea of giving up her apartment and her freedom. Not that she had some other guy on the string, but she was comfortable in her place, Naomi was right down the hall if she needed her, and she could walk to work. A couple of times she loaded Norm into her car, stuffed his wheelchair in the back, and took him over to Better Than Mom's for supper. Everyone was glad to see him, clustering around to clap him on the back, and say that he was looking good.

"It would have been a lot worse if the roads hadn't been so slick," he said. "My squad car slid away from the impact, so all I got was a broken arm and leg and a few cracked ribs, which hurt worse than the rest put together. If the roads had been dry, I'd have been a goner."

Fay's stomach felt cold when she heard that. It never occurred to her that it could have been worse. She put her hand on Norm's shoulder and squeezed, just to make sure that he was real and mostly whole.

Naomi had been studying at one of the back tables and came over to see them. "Hi, Norm," she said. "Hey, Fay. How are things going with you two? I haven't seen you since the accident."

Norm reached up to pull Naomi down for a hug. "We've been busy. I'm trying to knit my bones back together, and Fay's just knitting." He chuckled. "How's nursing school? I could use a good nurse since I'm out of rehab."

Fay touched his arm. "I thought I was in line to be your nurse."

"My night nurse, yes," he said with a smile, "but I still need a day nurse every once in a while. Too bad that you're not doing practice nursing, Naomi, I'd put you to work."

Naomi shook her head. "Sorry, Norm, I'm just learning anatomy and physiology. We don't do practicals until next year. Besides, I'm in class all day every day, so I wouldn't have time to be your day nurse and still go to school."

"Too bad," he said. "I could have done with some of your good cooking. Fay's great with the microwave, but she's just learning to cook."

"She is?" Naomi looked at Fay. "What are you learning to cook?"

Fay straightened up with a proud look on her face. "I can make scrambled eggs, toast, and spaghetti. Meatballs are next. Norm's teaching me. He sits at the table and bosses me around. It's working pretty well. Maybe someday I'll graduate to biscuits."

"Maybe. Biscuits are easy to mix together and hard to make tender. I can't tell you how many batches I fed to the birds before I got it right," Naomi said. "I've got some easy skillet supper recipes I can share with you to get you started. I'll print them off and bring them down later."

Fay blushed. "I won't be home later; I'll be at Norm's. Can you bring them here on Sunday? I work Sunday morning."

"I can do that. It'll give me time to sort through my recipe file and pick out the good ones. Between Norm and me, we'll make a cook out of you yet."

Fay stayed over at Norm's a few nights a week for about a month before giving notice, packing up her belongings, and moving in with him. By then she had a repertoire of suppers and soups that she could make. Naomi had given her skillet recipes that used meat, canned soups, and frozen vegetables, with instant rice or mashed potatoes on the side that were easy for a beginning cook to make. Norm loved them, and Fay felt very accomplished. Every once in a while, she still brought home takeout from Better Than Mom's when something that they really liked was on the buffet. Brady rarely charged her for it, and Fay didn't try to pass it off as homemade.

Taffy didn't show up for work. Brady tried calling her, but all he got was her voicemail. "Call me, Taffy," he said after the beep, "I need to know when you'll be back." Luckily, John was still there and able to man the grill while Brady waited tables during the supper rush. They got through the evening, but it was a scramble.

"That's not like Taffy," Brady said to John. "She's always been reliable. I'll check my messages to see if she called." But there wasn't a message from her.

When James came in for his shift busing tables, Brady pressed him into service at the grill so that John could go home to Rosa, who was expecting their first baby any day. "I'll take over at your regular quitting time, so you don't get home too late to get to school on time tomorrow," Brady told him.

James nodded and pushed back through the swinging doors into the kitchen. "I'll take over the grill, John," said James. "You go on home; you've been here too long already."

"Okay, thanks. My feet are aching." John handed over the spatula and shook the basket of fries that he'd just dropped. "These are about done."

"Thanks, John, I've got them." James lifted the basket, checked the color of the fries, and eased it back into the hot oil.

Taffy didn't call that evening or leave a message overnight, and she didn't show up the next afternoon. Brady called Marcus. "Hey, Taffy isn't here again. Can you come in a little early and either man the grill or wait tables? John can't stay, and I need help."

"My homework's done. I can come over right away," Marcus said. "Give me five and I'll be there."

"Thanks, man, I really appreciate it."

That night Brady cooked, and Marcus waited tables.

Steve came in to write for the evening and to have some of John's Texas Black Bean Soup. "Where's Taffy?" he said when Marcus showed up to take his order.

"Not sure," said Marcus. "She hasn't been in the last couple nights, and she hasn't called."

Steve looked puzzled. "Hm, she didn't say anything to me about not feeling well or planning to be away the other night. I saw her two or three nights ago, and she seemed the same."

"Yeah, I was here the same night, and she didn't seem sick or anything. In fact, she hardly talked at all that night." Marcus wrote Steve's order. "I'll be right back with your soup."

He had taken one step away when Steve called him back. "Do you have any cornbread? I like it with John's bean soup."

"I'll check."

There was one square of cornbread left, which Marcus put on a plate with a couple of pats of butter and carried it to Steve's regular booth along with a big bowl of Texas Black Bean Soup. "Here you go. You're lucky; it's the last piece."

"Thanks." Steve put a napkin in his lap and leaned over the bowl to sniff the warm aroma. "Smells great. Can you fix up a quart for me to take home? I'll be here a while; I want to get some writing done, but I don't want the soup to run out."

Marcus wrote it down. "I'll get it ready as soon as I wait on that table that just sat down. I'll put it in the cooler, so don't forget to ask when you leave."

Steve just nodded; his mouth was full of soup.

A steady stream of diners kept Marcus hopping for the next hour. Finally, he had a moment to take Steve's empty plate and soup bowl off the table and ask him if he wanted dessert.

"Sorry, I've been too busy to get back here. Can I get you some dessert? A piece of pie?"

Steve shoved his notebook aside. "Yeah, I'll have a slice of lemon pie and a cup of decaf."

"Whipped cream on the pie?"

"Of course. Hey, I remember Taffy saying that she had a new boyfriend, and then he came in a few nights ago and sat glowering at her whenever she talked to a guy. I wonder if that has anything to do with her not showing up."

Marcus set the dirty dishes in the bus tub on the rack and said, "Let me get your pie and coffee first, and then I'll tell Brady what you said. Maybe he noticed the new boyfriend too."

Brady hadn't noticed the glowering boyfriend, but he remembered Taffy changed from happy and outgoing to quiet the last night she worked. "By the end of her shift, she hardly said a word. I wonder what's going on."

He was determined to find out what had happened to his waitress. The next morning after the breakfast rush, Brady left John in charge and drove to Taffy's address. She lived on the first floor of an apartment in an old house converted into four flats. He rang the bell, and when no one came, he pounded on the door. "Taffy, are you in there?"

The door across the hall opened, and a gray-haired lady poked her nose out. "She's in there, but he won't let her go out."

Brady jumped at the voice and turned to look at her.

"What?"

"She's in there, but that new boyfriend is making her stay there. I heard him hollering at her a few nights ago, saying that she had to stay home because she was too friendly."

"But she has to go to classes."

The lady shook her head. "He told her she had to drop out because there were too many men at the college and in her classes. I don't know why she's listening to him, but she's in there. I heard her crying."

Brady scratched his head. "Is he there now?"

"No, he's gone to work and locked her in her room."

"Jesus. I've gotta get her out of there. Do you have a ladder I can borrow?"

"There's one in the garage. Hurry; he comes home for lunch."

He clenched his fists. "Oh, I hope he comes home while I'm here. I'll set him straight on a few things."

Brady went out into the garage, hauled the ladder around to the side of the house, and set it by the bedroom window. He rapped on the glass. "Taffy? Taffy, it's Brady. Come to the window."

A small hand grasped the edge of the curtain and pulled it aside just enough for an eye to peek out. "Brady, what are you doing here?" Taffy said.

"Evidently, I'm saving you from your new boyfriend. Open the window, and I'll help you climb out."

Tears filled her eyes. "I can't. Anthony nailed the window shut so I can't open it."

"Then stand back so I can break the glass. You're getting out of there right now." He climbed down, picked up a brick from the edge of the flowerbed, and used it to smash the glass. He ran the brick around the edge of the frame to remove all the shards and held out his hand to Taffy. "Come on. I'll help you down."

She reached for Brady's hand and then shrank back. "I can't. He'll be home soon, and I need to be here."

"No, you don't. You don't need to be here at all. I'm taking you someplace safe." He held out his hand. "Come on. Let's go."

"Okay." Her voice was a whisper, but she grabbed Brady's hand and climbed out onto the ladder.

They had just gotten into Brady's pickup truck when Taffy gasped. A gold Subaru SUV had turned the corner and was coming toward them down the street. "It's Anthony," she said.

Brady put his hand on the back of her neck. "Duck down so he can't see you. I'll get us out of here." He put the truck in gear and drove away just as a tall, light-haired man got out of the SUV and started up the steps to the porch.

As he drove off, Taffy stayed lying on the front seat of the truck, shaking, and crying. Brady patted her shoulder.

"It's okay," he said. "It'll be okay. I'm taking you to the shelter where they know how to protect women like you. I'll make sure that Anthony never bothers you again."

Brady got Taffy delivered to the abused women's center and was back at Better Than Mom's an hour later when Anthony stormed in.

"Where's Taffy?" he said, craning his neck to see down the length of the building.

"She isn't here," Marcus said. "She hasn't been in for a few days. Sorry."

Anthony stepped closer to the young man. "What have you done with her? The neighbor said that a man came and took her away and the men here are the only men she knows."

Marcus didn't back down. "Look, pal," he said, but Brady interrupted.

"I'm the one who took her away," said Brady. "You can't lock someone up and make them quit their entire life. She's someplace safe now. Get out of my restaurant."

Anthony's face turned pale and then reddened. His hands clenched into fists, and he raised them toward Brady. "I ought to..."

Brady faced him down. "You ought to what? Pick on somebody your own size instead of bullying a little woman who doesn't fight back?" Brady started forward and Anthony backed away. Brady said, "I asked you to leave my diner, sir. I think you should go. Oh, and I helped Taffy swear out a restraining order on you so that if you come within a hundred feet of her or harass her on the phone, she can have you arrested. Now get out."

Anthony's face was set in a grimace. "I'll go, but you'll regret interfering in my life. You're welcome to the dirty little slut. I know that you're all banging her. I was trying to save her from you. Well, the joke's on her."

Brady and Marcus both stepped forward at that, fists at their sides but rising, and Anthony raised his hands and backed away. "I'm going," he said, "I'm going, and I won't be back."

"Good," said Marcus and Brady together.

Brady added, "Make sure you stay away from here and from Taffy."

Brady, Marcus, and James kept filling in for Taffy with help from Fay every once in a while, until Taffy got her confidence back. She moved into Fay's old apartment in the building behind the diner. Brady and Naomi took Taffy back to her apartment to get her belongings one afternoon when Anthony was still at work, and they could leave the diner to John and the boys for a couple of hours when business was slow.

Taffy was jumpy for the first few weeks after her ordeal with Anthony. She saw a therapist and joined a support group for abused women. Brady and the boys made sure that she was never alone in the diner; one of them was always within sight to reassure her she was safe and would continue to be safe. She was convinced that Anthony was driving by her new place and throwing stones at her window to get her attention. Norm called the station and had a patrol car swing by the apartment building a couple of times a night to chase him away if he was there. That had the added benefit of curtailing the drug business that flourished in the complex, cutting down on vandalism, and sending the prostitutes and pimps scrambling for another place to ply their trade.

CHAPTER 31

Brady went out the backdoor of the diner and was surprised to see a man hunched down next to the dumpster. "You can't stay there, buddy," he said to the bearded man.

"I know; I was waiting for you, and I got cold."

Brady looked at him. He was dressed in old BDUs, had a knitted cap pulled down to his eyebrows, and was wearing boots with one loose sole. "Why didn't you come in the front door?"

The man began pushing himself up to his feet, using the wall and the dumpster for support. "I didn't think you'd let me in. I don't look like the kind of person you'd welcome in your nice clean restaurant."

"Why are you waiting for me?"

"I'm hungry, and I need a job. I thought maybe you needed a dishwasher or had an extra meal you could spare."

"You a veteran or do you shop at the Army/Navy store?"

"Nah, I served. I was in the Army and served two tours. You serve?"

Brady nodded. "Navy. I was in twenty-three years. Cooked on ships all over the oceans." He pulled open the door. "Come on in. I've got some soup simmering. Would you like a bowl? What's your name?"

The man pulled off his hat as he walked through the door. "Vince. My name's Vince, Vince Weaver. A bowl of soup would be good." He held out his hand, and Brady took it.

"I'm Brady Gallagher. I'm the owner." Brady pulled a chair out of his office and ladled out a bowl of Beef Barley soup for Vince. "Here, sit down right here and eat this soup. Once you're finished, we can talk about the possibility of a job."

Vince's head bobbed, and he cradled the bowl in his big hand. "Thanks a lot. I really appreciate it." It didn't take long for Vince to eat the bowl of soup.

Brady handed him a slice of bread to sop up the last of the broth.

"Thank you," Vince said. "That was the best soup I've ever eaten."

Brady smiled at him over his shoulder from his place at the grill. "I'm glad you liked it. Now, I've been thinking. I could use a morning busser and dishwasher. You'd have to be clean and sober. I won't tolerate drugs or people working when they've been drinking. I saw too much of that in the Navy, and I won't have it on my watch."

Vince was nodding. "I've been going to AA meetings for eight months and haven't had a drop. The only drugs I take are the anti-depressants I get from the VA."

"That's good. You have a place to live?"

"Yeah, I live in the apartments right behind here. One of the neighbors told me about your diner and said you ran a good place to eat. I haven't had any spare money to come in to buy a meal; rent takes most of my disability check, and welfare pays for my food. I can't afford to put gas in my old car, so I'm hoping to find work where I can walk to get there."

Brady plated the food from the grill, rang the bell for order pickup, and turned to face Vince. "Let's give it a week's trial. I need you to be showered and to have your hair tied back. Wear a bandana or a backwards ball cap."

Vince smiled through his beard. "I'll clean up. I got some pants that I wear to AA and a plain t-shirt." He looked down at his feet. "These are my only shoes, though. Will they be alright?"

Brady looked down at his own feet and then at Vince's. "What size shoes do you wear?"

"I wear a twelve."

"Me too. I'll bring in a pair of sneakers for you to wear. They'll be more comfortable to work in than that pair of boots."

"Aw, you don't have to…"

Brady shook his head. "It's not charity; they're not new. I want you to be able to work from six in the morning until three in the afternoon, and those boots won't make it."

Vince put his empty bowl in the sink and went over to Brady, his hand outstretched. "Thanks, man, I won't let you down."

Fay came in through the swinging doors carrying a full bus tub. "Hey, Brady, the bridge ladies raved about the chicken salad sandwich. Did you change the recipe?" She noticed Vince standing next to Brady. "Oh, hi. Say, don't you live in the building just behind here?"

"Yeah, I do."

"I used to live there too. I'm Fay." She lifted the tub up onto the apron of the sink. "Man, these things get heavier every day."

Brady said, "Well, starting tomorrow you won't have to carry them. I just hired Vince here to be the morning busser and dishwasher."

Fay threw up her hands. "Hallelujah! I've been hoping you'd find somebody. Me and John will be glad to have him aboard." She threw him a salute. "See you in the morning, Vince."

The next morning, Vince was waiting by the back door when Brady pulled up in the pre-dawn dark. "Hey, Vince, good to see you. You're early. Let's get in out of the cold." Brady opened the door and flicked on the lights. Once he had the coffee brewing, he showed Vince around, where to find the bus tubs, where the clean dishes went, and gave him a quick rundown on operating the dishwasher. "Here's an apron and a pair of sneakers. Once we've got some dirty dishes, either John or I will show you how to run this beast."

Vince nodded. "That'll be good."

Brady picked up a bag of potatoes. "In the meantime, will you scrub these potatoes for me? I want to make Ike's Potato Soup today, and I'll need every spud. There's a brush with an orange handle in the crock on the back of the sink for scrubbing vegetables."

Vince laughed. "Good thing it's got an orange handle. Orange I can see. I'm red/green colorblind, but I can see orange and blue. Just let me change into these shoes."

"That's fine."

Vince went into the office, sat on the chair, took off his old boots, and put on the used sneakers that Brady had given him. "Oh man, these feel great."

Brady got busy chopping onions, and soon John joined him.

"Good morning, Brady. Good morning, Vince. I'm glad to see you today," said John. "The baby hasn't been sleeping well, so I'm a little tired these days. I'm happy for you to be hauling the dishes."

Vince was up to his elbows in wet potatoes. "You have a baby? Lucky you."

John puffed out his chest. "I have a son. William John is his name. He is six months old, and he's teething. Rosa is very tired; I'm tired too because I can't sleep when he cries."

Brady shook his head. "Makes me glad I never had kids. I need my sleep."

Vince looked up from scrubbing the last potato. "I always wanted kids but never found the right woman to have them with."

The back door swung open, and Fay came in. "Good morning, guys," she said. "It's kind of cold out there this morning. I bet we'll sell a lot of soup today." She hung her purse on a hook in Brady's office and hung her jacket over it. She checked her watch. "It's almost six o'clock. Soon Raymond will be battering down the door to get in. I'd better get the coffee started." And she went through the swinging doors into the diner, where they could hear her making the coffee and talking to herself about it. "Two high test and one decaf..." there was a clunk on the door, "and there's Raymond."

In less than an hour, Fay stuck her head through the swinging doors into the kitchen. "Vince, there's a full tub out here for you."

Vince had been cleaning vegetables for Brady and John to make soup with, so he wiped off his hands and went through to the diner. Fay showed him where the full bus tub was and said that John would teach him how to run the dishwasher; she was busy. The coffee codgers were interested to see a new face come through from the kitchen.

"Who's that?" Raymond said.

Fay was walking down the length of the counter filling coffee mugs. "That's our new dishwasher and morning busser, Vince. He seems like a good guy. Today is his first day, so be nice."

Raymond looked offended. "I'm always nice."

Fay stood making more coffee. Behind her, the coffee codgers were squabbling about something in the day's paper. Brady and John were helping Vince learn how to load and run the dishwasher.

She never really had a family, not like the ones she saw on television or read about in books, but at Better Than Mom's she had one. Brady was like a big brother, keeping them all fed, safe, and protected. John was the little brother who looked up to Fay and was her biggest fan. Vince was new, but Fay could already tell that he would fit right in. Raymond was the grumpy grandfather, quick with a criticism or a dig, but on your side when you needed him. Steve was the misfit uncle, writing his stories and keeping to himself most of the time. Naomi was like a favorite sister, willing to listen and always ready with support when you needed it. The rest of the coffee codgers, the knitting ladies, and the bridge ladies were like a big extended family of aunts, uncles, and cousins. They shared stories of their kids and grandkids, told jokes and laughed together, and cheered you on when you put yourself out there, like at the dancing competitions.

Fay couldn't imagine Better Than Mom's without them all. She was glad that she had decided to stay.

She turned away from her musings with a pot in each hand. "Alright, who needs more coffee?"

THE END

If you've enjoyed reading Better Than Mom's, please go to Amazon.com and leave a review. Thanks. I really appreciate it.

BOOKS BY THIS AUTHOR

The Seaview (The Seaview Series Book 1)

She knew it would be hard work, but what she didn't plan on was the electrically charged subcontractor and the way he made her feel.

Despite her son's vehement objections, Rose buys the ramshackle Caribbean beachfront bed and breakfast. She's confident that she can oversee the work in time for the start of tourist season. That is until the Health Inspector locks them out of the building.

Desperate to get the crew back to work she pleads with the plumber to get the key and finish at least one bathroom. The plumber has his own agenda. Rose's confidence is nearly destroyed by this major setback.

Can Rose and her crew finish the job before the first guest arrives?

The Seaview is the first book of The Seaview Series. If you like engaging islanders, breathtaking scenery above and below water, and a little romance this book is for you.

Open For Business (The Seaview Series Book 2)

It's opening day, and Rose eagerly awaits her first guest. Juggling excitement and nerves, she's determined to keep her new bed &

breakfast afloat despite bad weather and a lecherous plumber.

Now that Seaview is refurbished and reopened Rose's dream seems to be coming true, but the arrival of Hurricane Alphonso might end her dream before it can really begin. Her first guests are in residence and one of them acts like the hurricane with its wind, rain, and power outages is a personal affront.

Her attempts to fit into the island community are thwarted by nasty rumors spread by a local woman who resents Rose's romance with Ignatius "Iggy" Solomon. And a lecherous plumber just won't take "No!" for an answer.

In Open For Business, the second book of The Seaview Series escape to the Caribbean island of Anguilla. Enjoy Seaview with its changing cast of guests and the ever-faithful Iggy for delectable homemade breakfasts, beachside dancing, and rum punch as you dive into a tropical women's fiction story.

Spies Don't Retire (The Seaview Series Book 3)

Some secrets refuse to stay buried... even in paradise.

Rose is settling into being a newlywed and hosting guests at Seaview Bed & Breakfast on the Caribbean island of Anguilla. Whispers of spies on the island begin to circulate. Someone threatens to unmask them. Rose's peaceful retreat risks becoming a battleground.

At a lavish party, the hostess introduces a British couple to a Russian one, and the tension seethes. Recognition. Sizzling hostility. Delicious gossip makes the grapevine hum. Were the men spies on opposite sides? Or do the wives share a more dangerous past?

As rumors fly, Rose finds herself caught between keeping

Seaview's reputation intact and navigating the conflict between feuding friends. In the meantime, she's fighting to clear her name from the lingering lies of her nemesis.

Can Rose mend fences with the local women who distrust her? Will the two warring couples declare a truce—or set the island ablaze with old rivalries?

Spies Don't Retire, the third book in The Seaview Series, takes you back to the tropical shores of Anguilla where intrigue, scandal, and delectable island fare await. Escape to paradise.

Horizon

Gail Logan, a widow in her mid-fifties, has lived her life by what other people think. That has to change.

Signing up for a watercolor class and thrifting a new wardrobe with a young classmate makes a good start. Replanting her regimented flower garden is another idea, but at the garden center, Abel Baker dismisses her plan and tells her what to buy. Gail doesn't appreciate his interference.

Widower Abel turns up in Gail's path again and again, but she buried one bossy man, and she's not interested in another. Should she give Abel a chance?

Her sons and her best friend feel threatened by all of Gail's changes. Should she go back to her dull existence or keep moving forward?

Immerse yourself in Gail's journey for a fresh perspective on life in Horizon. Enjoy her adventures learning to paint with watercolor, making new friends, and changing her life to please herself in this mature love after loss women's fiction story.

Island Dreams

He found his dream job. She's reduced to cleaning vacation rental homes.

Ella Thomas and Dan Martinson are excited to leave their families and friends behind in Green Bay and move to the island of Bonaire in the Caribbean to pursue their dream of owning a dive shop.

Dan finds a job as a diving instructor immediately, but Ella can't get a work permit. The excitement and beauty of the coral reefs fill Dan's days. Ella's stuck cleaning up other people's messes for cash under the table.

They're dedicated to saving as much as they can so that when a dive shop becomes available, they can act fast. An unexpected opportunity threatens to drive a wedge between them.

A frustrated Ella comes up with a plan to maximize their savings by chasing that once-in-a-lifetime opportunity. Will Dan go along or stubbornly insist that they stick to their original plan?

Follow the ups and downs of life with Ella and Dan as they chase their Island Dreams.

Christmas At Seaview

Her daughter wants to get married. At Seaview. In four days.

Rose is excited about Christmas. Her children and their partners arrive on Christmas Eve at Rose's bed-and-breakfast on the island of Anguilla in the Caribbean. Two bombshell announcements on Christmas Day make her ecstatic. But her happiness turns into panic when her daughter makes a decision that turns the week upside down. Can Rose plan a wedding and take care of her paying guests during the most stressful week of the year?

The days tick away, and Rose is powerless to slow things down. Friday is coming fast. Will her guests feel ignored in all the wedding prep hubbub? Food, flowers, officiant. How will she get everything arranged before it's time to say, "I do?"

Pick up your copy of Christmas at Seaview, a novella that takes you along on Rose's wild ride through the week she never expected. Escape to the Caribbean this Christmas for a heartwarming story filled with joy, chaos, and family cheer.

ACKNOWLEDGEMENT

Heartfelt thanks to Judy Bridges and all the writers in the Women's Writing Retreat over the years who listened to endless pieces of this story and gave valuable advice and critiques. I couldn't have done it without each and every one of you.

ABOUT THE AUTHOR

Barbara Angermeier Malcolm

Barbara Angermeier Malcolm is an avid traveler and former retail SCUBA sales professional.

She has journeyed to countless islands with her family on diving vacations, collecting inspiration and stories along the way. A passionate storyteller, Barbara has been crafting tales for years.

When she's not writing, you'll find her sketching, painting with watercolors, knitting, cooking, or doting on her grandchildren. She is an active member of the Green Bay writing community and a proud member of the Green Bay Area Writers Guild and Wisconsin Writers Association.

www.ingramcontent.com/pod-product-compliance
Lightning Source LLC
Chambersburg PA
CBHW060625260626
47161CB00008B/2809